LIZZIE FLOWERS AND THE FAMILY FIRM

CAROL RIVERS

CR
Publications

Details of the Carol Rivers Newsletter can be found at the back of this book.

LIZZIE'S STORY SO FAR

Lizzie's story begins in 1919 after Lizzie Allen's mother's untimely death. Lizzie's disabled war veteran father Tom, has been left a broken and bitter man; her elder brother Vinnie, is a villain in the making and her two younger sisters are in danger of being taken into care. Lizzie is left to pick up the pieces of their lives, without even her sweetheart Danny Flowers to help her, as he sets sail for Australia to seek his fortune.

Determined to unite her family with the help of close friends and neighbours, yet unable to escape the poverty of the slums, heartbroken Lizzie is tricked into marriage by Danny's unscrupulous brother, Frank Flowers.

It is only with Frank's death, and her great success at running the Flowers greengrocer's, that gives Lizzie independence at last. With the support of the East End community and Danny returning from Australia, Lizzie's happiness seems complete. But as their wedding day dawns, Frank rises from the dead and Lizzie's life is once again thrown into turmoil.

1934: Having struggled through the years of the Depression and won her battle against the protectionists and thugs who have threatened the East End, Lizzie buys the lease of a disreputable dockland's pub called the Mill Wall. Even Danny warns her she's bitten off more than she can chew this time. The word on the street is that Lizzie Flowers and her family are finished - *but are they?*

Lizzie is not beaten yet. She calls in favours, refusing to be intimidated and determined to keep the Mill Wall clean. But even her friend and close ally, the canny south London Irishman, Murphy, is outwitted by the most cunning crime lord of them all. He's infamously known as *The Prince*, but is far from royalty. His currency is women and he will stop at nothing to conquer Lizzie's turf.

It's said that where there is muck there's money. But when Lizzie's success comes at a cost of losing all she has worked so hard for, a pact with *The Prince* may be the only way to go. We re-join Lizzie at one of her spectacular new enterprises, the prosperous Ripon Street Bakery. It's here that Lizzie's sick and desperate best friend Ethel Ryde, returns from exile to plead with Lizzie for help and protection for herself and her illegitimate baby ...

Now, read on!

PROLOGUE

Lewisham
South London

November 1934

ETHEL RYDE COWERED in fear at the sight of her enraged mother-in-law. Cora Ryde's tall, skeletal frame and contemptuous eyes were a sight to behold; a sight Ethel had always feared she would be faced with one day. The confrontation had been in the offing and it was only Ethel's strict avoidance of Cora that had so far kept a roof over their heads. Now the older woman's anger knew no bounds and it was terrifying.

'I've done my Christian duty and given shelter to you and your baby,' Cora insisted. 'But enough is enough. Your child was never destined to survive its sinful conception. It's time you considered my son's children, Rosie and Timothy. You must give your bastard over to the authorities.'

Ethel shook her head determinedly as she clutched her baby. Her mother-in-law's ultimatum was unthinkable. Wasn't it enough punishment that Cora had already evicted them from the home they had shared as a family when Richard was alive? 'Callum's done nothing wrong,' she defended. 'He needs his mother, just like Rosie and Timothy. If only you'd not turned us out of our house ... '

'*My* house!' Cora interrupted, freezing the protest on Ethel's lips. 'Did you really think I would allow you to stay?'

'Doesn't your Christian faith teach mercy?' Ethel pleaded as the salty tears pierced the corners of her eyes. 'Richard and me lived there all our married life.'

'You should have thought about that before you took a lover.' The red blush of fury showed under the deep grooves embedded in Cora's gaunt cheeks. 'I've held my tongue long enough, but the truth will out. To think what you've put your children through. A humiliation beyond words. My Richard was a God-fearing man and devoted son. He was a faithful husband to you, decent and upright. Thank the good Lord he never knew of your shame.'

Ethel felt herself falling against the wall, the words striking at her heart like a poisoned dart. Cora had reminded her daily of her adultery and it was heartbreaking to Ethel.

'I've tried to make amends,' Ethel pleaded as she held her eight-month-old baby to her chest. 'There's not a day gone by when I haven't mourned Richard. Or the fact I went with another man. If I could turn back the clock - '

'How dare you!' Cora interrupted, stabbing an accusing finger in Ethel's face. 'You're not fit to speak my son's name.'

'But I've done everything you asked,' Ethel wailed. 'I've hidden Callum from the world and not ventured out. Not till he needed the doctor - '

'Whereupon you refused his advice!' Cora looked as though she had just been scalded by hot water. 'The boy would have been taken away there and then without further fuss.'

'But I'm his mother,' Ethel protested. 'He's my baby! How could I give him away?'

Cora lifted her chin and sneered. 'Then there's no more to be said on the matter.'

Suddenly there was movement at the top of the winding staircase. The big Victorian house echoed Ethel's teenage daughter's soft sobs. Rosie's tear-stained cheeks were hidden under her thick blonde hair. At sixteen, Rosie was already a beauty. Ethel's stomach cramped at the thought of how she had betrayed her family. Beside Rosie stood seventeen-year-old Timothy, her brother. Tall and lanky, his fair hair was swept over the crown of his head just as his father Richard had worn his.

Ethel marvelled at the sight of her handsome son. She gazed into eyes that were the same shade of china blue as her own and yearned to beg his forgiveness.

But the two young adults stood solemnly, as if separated from their mother by an invisible wall. Ethel looked pleadingly at them, desperate for understanding. 'Please give me another chance. I'll do everything your grandmother asks. I'll not set a foot outside again until I can find a place for us all to live.'

Rosie stared at her mother with sympathy and even a little concern as if considering Ethel's heartfelt plea. A small flame of hope flickered in Ethel's heart only to be dashed as Cora positioned herself squarely at the foot of the stairs. Folding her long arms across her chest, she held her head high.

'Rosie, Timothy,' she intoned in a long-suffering voice, 'you know how much I've tried to help your mother in her hour of need. But now my health is suffering. Despite offering her a solution to her disgrace she refuses to listen. It's time for you to make your choice. There is a home for you here as long as you want it. But if you leave today then I shall wash my hands of the whole sordid affair.' She took out her handkerchief and dabbed at her nose.

Ethel was trembling violently as she stood by the open door; a chill winter breeze gusted in from the street, causing the baby to cough.

Surely Rosie and Timothy will join me, Ethel thought incredulously. Wasn't it obvious that Cora was trying to drive a wedge between them?

Ethel's wait was long and agonising. The seconds laboured into minutes until Ethel could stand it no longer.

'Rosie, Timothy, we're a family,' she beseeched for the last time. 'I know I did wrong, but I love you and need you with me.'

Earnestly she stared into her son's eyes, willing him to come down the stairs and stand at her side. For wasn't the love between a mother and her children unbreakable? But Timothy only stared back, his expression cold and devoid of sympathy. Ethel knew then that the son she had reared and comforted in the face of Richard's selfish neglect, was about to disown her.

'Timothy!' Ethel screamed as he turned his back and walked away.

'Mum?' Rosie's voice was soft, her eyes brimming with tears. 'Timmy is heartbroken. I am too. Can't you see that?'

'Yes, yes, of course I can,' Ethel agreed desperately, 'and I vow to make it up to you every day of your lives. In time you'll understand. You'll even grow to love your little brother. I know you will.'

'Don't ask me and Timmy for more than we can give,' Rosie said emptily, reminding Ethel of the confused adolescent she had once been after the war had taken her brothers' lives. She had tried to compensate her parents for their agony but in doing so, had lost her own identity. Now she was making the same demands on her own daughter and Ethel hated herself for it.

'We'll go back to Langley Street,' Ethel promised, almost hysterical with panic. 'We'll start afresh at Nan's. A new life for us all. You can get the job you said you wanted. I won't stop you.'

'Go back to the island?' Rosie repeated as if insulted. 'To us all being squashed in one room; you and the baby, me and Timmy, with Nan on at us every minute she gets a chance? No, Mum. I couldn't stand it. Nor could Timmy. Nan and Granddad mean well, but it'd drive us mad being cooped up in their small house. And anyway, you know I've got a good job in Lewisham at the Co-Op. I've made friends. I've actually got a life together at long last. This isn't about you any more. Or even me and Timmy. It's Callum who needs you now.'

Cora Ryde smiled supportively. Slowly she unravelled herself from the widow's weeds she had worn since her son had met his fate under the wheels of a motor car the previous year. An event that in Cora's mind was linked inextricably to her daughter-in-law's promiscuity. 'If you please,' she muttered, gesturing to the wet and shiny pavement outside. Her eyes never left Ethel's, unmoved by the baby's wheezing.

Ethel lifted her leaden feet and stumbled through the open door, glancing back one last time in the hope her children would follow.

But the door closed quietly and firmly. A dozen or so raindrops danced on the highly polished brass knocker as though confirming that Cora Ryde had once and for all separated Ethel from her own kith and kin.

PART I

CHAPTER 1

NOT TWO MONTHS TO go until Christmas and we're already in profit, Lizzie reflected as she watched the customers bustle in and out of her new bakery. The shelves were stuffed full of sweet-smelling bagels, pies, pastries, sandwiches, tarts, cheesecakes and delicacies of all shapes and sizes. The seasonal speciality of home-cooked mince pies were selling as fast as Madge Hobson, her cook, could bake them. All in all, business was booming.

Though not the modest greengrocers she had planned with Ethel over a year ago, the bakery was just as encouraging. London's specialist outlets like The Aerated Bread Company's A.B.C tea shops and Lyons Corner Houses were making a reputation for themselves. Small cafés and bakeries like hers were also prospering.

Lizzie thoughtfully studied her manageress, Jenny Maguire. Wearing her white cap and apron, the petite young woman was busily serving customers, then stacking the shelves as they sold out. Madge could be heard clattering the trays of hot breads as she waited for the arrival of Elsie Booth, her kitchen assistant.

Jenny looked so well that Lizzie could hardly believe she was the same battered and bruised young woman of six months ago. Both Jenny and Madge now lived free of charge in the upper rooms; all three of her staff had survived incredible hardship. Jenny, abused first by her father and then her husband. Madge, terrorised by a drunkard son. Even poor little Elsie had been thrown in prison for stealing in order to put food on the table.

Lizzie politely bade goodbye to the customers, then made her way to the counter that was decorated with bunches of holly bought early this morning at the market.

'Hurry it up, Madge,' Jenny hollered through to the kitchen. She banged a floury fist on the hatch door. 'I want as many mince pies out here as you can muster.'

The hatch doors flew open. A round, matronly face appeared. 'Well you can tell the hungry buggers to wait, I ain't a bloody miracle-worker. I've got rotten indigestion and one of me turns coming on.'

'It's all them mince pies you scoff on the quiet,' laughed Jenny with a wink at Lizzie.

'I don't want no cheek, you young hussy,' yelled Madge as with fat, doughy fingers she dusted down her apron that covered her ample chest. Catching sight of Lizzie, she gasped, 'Oh, it's you, Lizzie love! Sorry for me French, gel.'

'Don't mind me, Madge,' Lizzie dismissed. 'How can I help?'

'What, and get all your nice clobber ruined?' Madge gestured to Lizzie's neat figure, elegantly clothed in a ruby red woollen suit. The rich colour contrasted strikingly with the hue of her lustrous green eyes and thick ebony hair pinned up behind her head. 'I was just letting off steam,' continued Madge getting redder and redder in the face. 'There's only room for one cook in this kitchen, at least till Elsie turns up.'

'Then you'll be able to sit down and drink your gin in peace,' Jenny teased with a straight face.

'Chance'd be a fine thing,' Madge hurled back. 'I sweat meself silly over these stoves. Don't slum it like you, Jenny Maguire, waltzing about with yer airs and graces!' The hatch doors slammed closed again.

'Madge has a short fuse in the mornings,' Jenny chuckled. 'Claims she can't get going until she's had her third cup of tea. But I wouldn't have it any other way, considering what my life was once like.'

Lizzie's heart had almost broken when she'd first heard Jenny's story. At twenty-two years of age Jenny had been beaten and abused all her childhood. Fists and boots were her father's religion. He had followed his baser nature as though violence was his bible. Her ill-fated marriage to another waster had fared no better. That was, until she'd struggled into Lizzie's greengrocery shop on the corner of Ebondale Street and collapsed. She'd miscarried her baby but Jenny had survived and now she managed the bakery as if she had been born to the trade.

Lizzie took a small leather pouch from her bag and placed it on the counter. 'There's enough change here for today,' she explained as Jenny took hold of the money bag and tipped the coins noisily into the till. 'But if the past few weeks are anything to go by, I think we'll soon double our takings.'

'I've taken orders from the markets an' all,' Jenny said proudly. 'We're reeling them in, traders and public alike.'

'Have we enough staff?'

'Elsie's a fine little worker,' Jenny replied thoughtfully. 'But she ain't a good timekeeper. She has to get here from Lavender Court over Bow. One of them seedy tenements off the high street. It's a filthy place, but all she can afford with that sick husband of hers.'

'Perhaps we'll engage another woman in the new year?'

'We could try down the women's 'ostel,' Jenny suggested eagerly. 'I kipped there once when my old man was pie-eyed. Some of the poor cows I met were worse off than me. If they stayed off the drink, they would clean up a treat - ' Jenny stopped speaking and peered out onto the street. 'What's that brother of yours up to? Got his head stuck under the bonnet of yer car as if he knows what he's doing.'

Lizzie laughed. 'Bert's out to impress a certain young lady.'

Jenny stared at her innocently. 'What, me?'

'You know he's sweet on you, Jenny.' Lizzie raised an eyebrow at the giant of a man tinkering about in the Wolseley's engine.

'I'm surprised he ain't spoken for,' Jenny replied coyly.

'Bert's wed to the shop,' Lizzie admitted. 'Give him a cauliflower or a spud to discuss and he'd talk the hind legs off a donkey. But girls? He don't know where to put himself!'

'I'll remember that,' Jenny answered with a blush. 'Talking of blokes, is your old man behaving himself?'

'I don't expect miracles, Jen,' Lizzie replied on a half-hearted sigh as she thought of her estranged husband. 'But I'm giving Frank a chance. He's still family after all.'

'Yer never thought of giving him the boot?'

'Many times,' Lizzie admitted. 'But I've discovered that Frank is safer where I can see him. The Mill Wall is a rough and ready dockers' pub and managing it won't be a pushover. But if he turns trade around, he'll have earned his keep and my respect into the bargain.'

'Well, I hope he don't let you down,' Jenny retorted, 'What with setting up this bakery and taking on a pub like the Mill Wall, you've got your hands full. But remember, you're young yet. You gotta enjoy a bit of life as well. Find a nice sweetheart to cuddle up to.'

I did have a nice sweetheart, Lizzie thought sadly, one I wouldn't have traded for all the world. But Danny Flowers was also a man with a mind of his own. A fact that had been brought home to her all too painfully when he'd left the island last year and moved to a luxurious new showroom at Euston. Neither could she dispute the fact that Danny had asked her to leave with him.

But the Isle of Dogs was her home. She had been born in Langley Street twenty-nine years ago and had learned her trade in the shop on the corner of Ebondale Street. For better or worse, it was East End blood that flowed through her veins. She'd fought the racketeers and the protectionists; she'd defended her turf – and won. To give it up now was too much of an ask. Even for Danny.

Lizzie shivered a little as she remembered the barrow boy she'd fallen in love with. Tousled blond hair, tall and broad-shouldered, with eyes as blue as a summer's sky. Danny Flowers was her man. Despite the decade he'd spent in Australia, he was the one for her.

And to Lizzie, their falling out had been heartbreaking.

CHAPTER 2

NOW IN HIS THIRTY-THIRD YEAR, Danny Flowers stood tall and upright at the door of his upmarket car showrooms in London's West End. As he surveyed the endless streams of traffic, he ran a hand over the scar on his forehead just visible beneath his well-groomed fair hair. The slash of raised skin reminded him that he was now free! Free from the villains who had previously threatened his livelihood.

Fleetingly, he thought of his old dockland garage and of his best mate and first class mechanic, Cal Bronga. Danny could still see Cal in his minds's eye, his wild black hair accentuating the rare smile that would splinter across his rugged face as he wrestled with the mechanics of some oil-leaking critter. But after Leonard Savage had burned down their livelihood last year - their dream had ended.

Heartbroken after the end of his affair with Ethel Ryde, Cal had returned to Australia. There had been nothing left for Danny in the East End and so he'd sold up. A smile touched Danny's lips as he thought of the twist of fate that had brought him such good fortune - for no one had been more surprised than him when the land had netted him a near fortune!

An elegant double-fronted city property had caught his eye and he'd turned the place into a classy car sales, fully expecting Lizzie to join him. But with his good luck had come bitter disappointment. For Lizzie had refused his offer ...

But why was he thinking of Lizzie now? Why was Lizzie on his mind, when only this morning he had enjoyed April's warm embrace? Shaking his head as if to rid himself of the confusion, his gaze returned to the interior of his showroom and the tastefully furnished office where his salesman, Hugo Price, was in conversation with a customer. Hugo's faultless taste in fashion and astute head for figures was a perfect addition to the business. His head was bent over a large polished desk. On its surface lay an open diary and beside it a newly-installed telephone.

There was a good deal of cigar smoke and laughter as they drank from tumblers of decanted whisky. Up for discussion was the purchase of the three-litre, six-cylinder Lagonda currently on display. All shimmering chrome and flawless paintwork, the motor was a work of art in itself.

It was at times like this, Danny was still unable to believe he had achieved his ambition. Prosperity was once a mere dream. Who would have thought that his life could turn out in such a way?

'I say, old chap,' greeted a voice beside him. 'I've watched your progress in Euston and you seem to be doing just fine.'

Danny smiled, roused from his thoughts by a tall, black-haired man wearing a dark beard. He had an unusual lilt to his voice, but quite pleasant to listen to. 'Thank you,' Danny replied. 'Are you interested in cars?'

'Horses more like, my friend. But I could be tempted.'

'I like horses too,' Danny agreed. 'My father kept them for

his business many years ago. To pull carts.' Danny regretted his admission, remembering April's advice, that with their new clientele he should adopt a different approach.

'What was he in?' asked the stranger.

'Retail,' said Danny vaguely. 'And you?'

'Breeding,' came the easy reply. 'I'd wager a good mare is a better investment than that!' He nodded to the Lagonda.

'Perhaps I can change your mind?' Danny gestured to the new Riley on his left. 'Like a run out?'

The bearded gent laughed. 'Why not? I have time to spare. Tell me, how much do you take in a day?'

As Danny walked to the Riley he shrugged. 'That would be telling.'

'Yes,' his customer agreed. 'I suppose it would. But comparing notes might not do any harm from one garage proprietor to a stable owner.'

Danny opened the passenger door of the car. 'Stables, eh?'

'Quite,' said the man as he bowed his dark head and slipped inside.

'May I be so bold as to enquire after your accent? It's not one I recognise.'

The handsome features hardened somewhat. 'My ancestors come from a very small island in the Mediterranean, south of Sicily. And you? Are you a Londoner by birth?'

Danny nodded. 'And proud of it.'

'So you should be, my friend,' came the flattering response.

Danny had noted the impeccable cloth of the stranger's suit, though slightly stained on the trouser bottoms. His brogues, too, had been polished but a tell-tale trace of mud lay about the heel. No doubt from his stables, Danny thought curiously. 'You must let me try to convince you of a new way to travel,' he offered. 'Do you drive?'

The stranger looked up at him through the lowered

window with piercing black eyes and a charming smile. 'Oh, yes, indeed I do, Mr Flowers. A very hard bargain!'

They both laughed at the quip. But as Danny prepared to take his customer for a spin the thought occurred to him that he had not given the man his name. The nameplate above the glass doors showed only, 'The Euston Showrooms'.

But he did not have time to consider this for long. He fetched the keys from the office and they soon fell into discussion over the pros and cons of travelling by mechanical wheels.

CHAPTER 3

'CRIKEY, WHAT'S GOING ON?' Jenny exclaimed, bringing Lizzie sharply back to the present as she peered through the bakery window. 'Someone's in trouble out there!'

Lizzie narrowed her eyes and saw Bert on his knees, supporting a limp figure. Leaving Jenny to serve her customers, she hurried out into the rain.

'It's Ethel!' Bert gasped when she joined him. Staring down at the pitiful figure that her brother was cradling, Lizzie hardly recognized her old friend, Ethel Ryde. Soaked through to the skin, her fair hair was plastered to the sides of her rain-streaked face. Her faded blue eyes were bruised by heavy shadows. This was not the healthy, happy girl she had once known.

'Ethel, Ethel, it's me, Lizzie,' she whispered, taking Ethel's wet, cold hand.

'H ... help me,' Ethel stammered, sliding her fingers from Lizzie's grasp. She gently pushed the wet rags from the bundle she was carrying. 'This is my baby ... '

'Oh, Ethel, ' Lizzie breathed, unable to believe this poor little wretch was Ethel's child. 'What's happened to you?'

'Cora wanted me to give him up. But I couldn't. I ... I've been walking, thinking what to do. Somehow I found myself here. '

'Hush,' Lizzie soothed gently. 'You're safe now. You and your baby. No one is going to take him from you.'

'Promise me?'

'Of course I promise.'

'What am I to do, Lizzie?'

'Stop fretting, my love,' Lizzie said softly. 'Bert will help you to the car and drive us all back to Ebondale Street.'

A faint but grateful smile touched Ethel's quivering lips. Slowly she closed her eyes. 'Blimey, she's passed out!' Bert said in alarm.

'Carry her to the car, Bert. I'll take the baby.' Lizzie slid her hands under the weightless bundle and hugged the child to her. 'The poor little mite is soaked to the skin. I'll find something warm in the shop to wrap him with.'

Leaving Bert to attend to Ethel, Lizzie made her way back to the bakery.

'Oh Gawd!' Madge hollered as she bustled out of the kitchen to join Jenny. 'What have you got there?' Her eyes went wide when she saw the baby and she quickly made the sign of the cross. 'Jesus, Mary and Joseph, a poor soaked bairn!'

'Looks like a parcel of wet rags,' Jenny gasped, a hand flying to her mouth.

'How did the poor wench out there get in such a state?' Madge demanded, glancing through the window.

'Heaven knows,' Lizzie responded. 'Ethel's my best mate, but I've not seen her in over a year. I didn't even know her baby son was born.'

'There's no time to lose,' said Madge, pushing a greying lock of hair under her cook's hat. 'Jenny, while I get me breath back, find a spare towel to dry him with!'

A rough-looking cloth was snatched from the counter and Madge nodded approvingly, swiping her sweating forehead with her wrist. 'We use the oven towel for the hot trays and it's a bit floury, but it'll do the job nicely. But let's have them wet rags off him first,' said Madge, taking the little boy and allowing Lizzie to discard the wet clothing.

'Oh, Gawd blimey!' Jenny shrieked. 'Listen to that chest of his. I wouldn't put it past him getting pneumonia!'

'You know his mother, then?' Madge asked breathlessly as she helped Lizzie to make the baby more comfortable.

'We lived next door to each other in Langley Street,' Lizzie explained. 'Ethel got married and went to live in Blackheath with her husband Richard. But he died last year.'

'So, she's a widow already?' Jenny asked, her eyes wide.

Madge waved her away. 'That's none of your business, ducks. Now get along and serve your customers and I'll see Lizzie off.' Madge handed the swaddled infant back to Lizzie. 'You must get his chest looked at, my dear. I don't like the sound of that wheeze, not one bit.'

Lizzie held the baby against her. 'I'll send Bert for the doctor as soon as we're home.' She drew her finger tenderly over the baby's smooth, toffee-coloured skin. He was as light as a feather and she suspected that like Ethel, he was undernourished.

'Off you go, then,' Madge said, smiling broadly and flashing her one gold tooth of which she was very proud. 'You've done your good deed for the day, bless you. I'll say a rosary tonight for that poor girl and her child.'

With Madge's blessing Lizzie left the shop and hurried to the car where Bert was fussing over Ethel.

'I covered her with me old coat,' he said, looking worried. 'But she's out cold.'

Lizzie wondered what could have happened during the past twelve months at Cora Ryde's house? Ethel had cut all ties after her husband Richard's death. Not even her parents, Lil and Doug Sharpe, had managed to get a foot past Cora.

Lizzie gently rocked the little boy snuggled in her arms. He looked up at her with his big, dark eyes fringed by thick black lashes. Lizzie's heart melted.

Patting his back to ease his cough, she felt his tiny body shudder. 'Will the car go any faster?' she asked Bert anxiously as he cursed the rain-soaked windscreen.

'Hold on to your horses,' he shouted. 'We're about to find out.'

With a forceful surge of energy, Lizzie felt the powerful vehicle roar them away towards Ebondale Street, taking them deeper into the heart of the East End. Back to her turf, where Ethel and her baby would be safe, no matter what crisis had befallen them.

CHAPTER 4

IT WAS over an hour later when Lizzie gently tucked the bed covers around Ethel. A faint flush of colour had crept into her pale cheeks. Her wet clothes were drying in the kitchen on the airing line over the stove and had been replaced by one of Lizzie's cotton nightdresses.

Once so healthy and bonny, Ethel looked starved. How had she managed to make the journey across the river from Lewisham?

'Lizzie?' Ethel's voice was faint as she opened her eyes.

'I'm here, Ethel.'

'Where's Callum?'

'That's a lovely name. It suits him.' Lizzie thought of Cal Bronga, the Australian whom Ethel had fallen in love with during her ill-fated marriage. She eased the baby into Ethel's arms. 'He's got a rotten cough though. I'm going to send for the doctor.'

'No!' Ethel hugged Callum against her. 'You mustn't! They'll take him away.'

Lizzie shook her head, perplexed. 'Who will?'

Ethel's voice broke into tiny sobs. 'That's why I left. That's why I couldn't stay at Cora's. Even though I had to leave Rosie and Timothy.' She moved her head violently, her eyes protruding from their sockets. 'You don't know the half. Cora told the doctor to take Callum from me. He almost did. Oh God, Lizzie, I can't bear to think of it!'

'Hush,' Lizzie consoled, pressing her back on the pillows. 'Try to rest now.'

Ethel shuddered, looked wildly around her, catching hold of Lizzie's arm. 'No doctor, Lizzie, please!'

Lizzie gave a half-hearted nod and slowly Ethel's head sank into the pillow. Her eyes closed and she lay there, exhausted from her efforts.

Lizzie lifted Callum into her arms. 'You must be very hungry, my little sweetheart,' she whispered kissing him softly on his silky black cap of hair. Nestled between the thick layers of Bert's cut-down combinations, he gazed at her with trusting eyes.

Lizzie stood rocking him as her thoughts returned to the time when she had done the very same with Polly. Her sister's child had been born with great difficulty. Babs was not a natural mother. Perhaps it was no surprise that she'd turned against her child. But Lizzie had loved her niece from the moment she had set eyes on her. And now she held this little boy in her arms, wondering what was best to do. Just as she had wondered with Polly.

Callum coughed and Lizzie left Ethel to rest. She made her way along the passage of the upper rooms above the shop to the kitchen where Bert was eating at the big wooden table.

'What's the score?' he asked in concern as he jumped to his feet.

'Ethel's resting,' she explained. 'But in her condition, she had no milk to feed him. And worse, she refuses to have a doctor.'

Bert's jaw fell open. 'The kid needs help! So does she, poor cow.'

'She thinks the doctor will take Callum away.'

'Gawd love us, he wouldn't do that.'

'Cora's doctor had a good try,' Lizzie said as she took a seat. 'Now put the kettle on Bert and bring me the Friar's Balsam. We'll get it steaming while I give Callum his milk from Polly's bottle.'

Bert, who had enjoyed Lizzie's home remedies for the best part of his thirty-two years, as large as he was, sprang like a five-year-old to the larder where the reviving elixir was kept.

Later, as he sat beside her enjoying the wholesome camphor that now filled the kitchen, he watched the baby suck hungrily at the bottle. Already Callum seemed revived. Bert marvelled at the resourcefulness of his childless sister.

She had mothered the entire Allen family after their parents' early deaths. And, it was only through Lizzie's care that Polly had survived. Now Lizzie was once again in the business of child rearing.

He watched in admiration as she tended to the boy, bathing his face, patting his back, wiping the mucus from his nose. A mother if ever there was one, Bert thought to himself and not for the first time. She should have wed Danny Flowers and not his bastard brother, Frank. It was the unkindest trick of fate that Bert had ever witnessed.

'You reckon the balsam's working?' Bert asked doubtfully. 'Bit niffy, ain't it? Me eyes are watering something rotten.'

Amidst the healing vapour filling the kitchen, Lizzie continued to rock the baby. 'If he's not improved by tonight, I'll give you five bob to fetch the doctor. He can visit while Ethel's asleep and she won't know he's been.' Lizzie glanced up, her eyes fixed determinedly on her brother. 'But first go down to the shop and tell Elmo I want those spuds brought in from the storeroom. Have them priced in pounds before the day is out. Fowler can sweep through and empty the pig bins. And Bert?'

'Yes, gel?'

'Drive over to Langley Street. Break the news to Lil and Doug. Ethel's their daughter, after all. And Callum their grandson. Though what they'll say when they see the pair of them in this state, is anyone's guess.'

'Salt of the earth are the Sharpes,' Bert observed dryly as he paused by the door. 'They'll pull out all the stops for their girl.'

'I hope you're right,' Lizzie answered, wondering if Lil, her friend of many years and next-door neighbour from days long gone by, would forgive the ousting that Ethel had given her parents in preference to Cora Ryde.

But that had been almost a year ago. Time for Lil to sink her pride and show the better side of her nature.

CHAPTER 5

SITTING ANXIOUSLY in the rear of the luxurious Wolseley, Lil Sharpe reflected on the new crisis at Ebondale Street. She was irritated that Bert had remained tight-lipped, providing no details, other than to say that Lizzie had summoned them, with the hint that she and Doug had no choice in the matter.

Not only had she left her washing on the line under a heavy sky swollen with rain and occasional bursts of sun, but she had backache second to none, from lifting pails of sodden clothing from her broken boiler.

Doug had warned her it was on the blink, but today of all days! Now it seemed they were faced with yet another drama at the Flowers, though what more could go wrong after last year, twelve months of hell and not to put a finer point on it – high water. And, if all the Flowers family were to be believed, the very same foul water that had filled Leonard Savage's hostelry well, sending that bugger to Hades.

The thought of the greasy-looking racketeer with his army of murdering muscle still made Lil's skin crawl. She had not one single regret that he had suffered such an excruciating end. Not only had he expected to capitalize on

Lizzie's business but he'd also demolished Danny Flowers's workshop and garage in the process. Her hope was that Savage had rotted slowly and agonisingly in his watery tomb. But even such torment would not bring back Richard Ryde, her son-in-law. Although a mother's boy and with no balls at all to satisfy his wife, Richard did not deserve to die by Savage's hand. To perish with your bicycle clips round your ankles, well, it was a humiliation of the first order. Though they had never seen eye to eye, Richard was, nevertheless, the father of her grandchildren, Rosie and Timmy. If anyone needed a severe slap it was his mother Cora Ryde. She had smothered her son in order to keep him. At least, that was what Lil believed and she was entitled to her opinion.

She glanced surreptitiously at Doug sitting next to her. What was he thinking? She admired and respected the man she was married to; Doug would always be the young boy she'd first met as a girl. As lifetime sweethearts, for better or worse, they'd had their fair share of tragedy. Their beloved teenage sons, Greg and Neil had sacrificed their lives in the conflict and it was a wound to her and Doug that would never heal. But it was Kate Allen, Lizzie's mother, to whom she owed her recovery. If it hadn't been for her next door neighbour's friendship, she would surely have perished in that stormy sea of grief. And so, whatever the problem was today, Lil knew that she would back Lizzie to the hilt, no matter what.

'You alright, ducks?' Doug asked as he felt her gaze.

She smiled at the average-looking man sitting beside her in the comfortable rear of the car. Though Doug was in his sixties, his amiable face had weathered very well. Unlike her, he was free from those ravaging furrows of time; if it wasn't for the blessed Max Factor, she'd be in a fine state! Doug simply shaved and threw a handful of water across his face. He wasn't perturbed by his paunch or the fact that the last button of his smart waistcoats were left undone. At least she didn't have that bother; she was as thin as a rake, no doubt down to the fags and port wine that she relied on to settle her nerves. And as long as she had the wherewithal to purchase it, the bottle of henna in the cupboard was essential for her crowning glory.

'I'm alright, cocker,' she assured her husband, raising her voice so that Bert who was driving, could hear every vowel. 'But I hope this ain't a storm in a teacup. I need to get back to me cooking. Why, it's December already and I'm not even started on me Christmas cakes yet.'

'I'll have you returned in no time at all, Lil,' Bert promised over his shoulder. 'Nearly there now.'

'I should hope so too,' Lil said grudgingly. She was not only house-proud but a stickler for routine. 'There ain't many people I'd down tools for. And more to the point, why all this secrecy? It ain't that flamin' ex-husband of hers, Frank Flowers, is it?' she demanded without giving the driver a chance to reply. 'What's the score on that blockhead? Still acting the grand man at Lizzie's pub? Like the Jonah he is, I wouldn't be surprised if those voices he says he hears in his head have given him directions all the way to hell and back.'

'No, it ain't Frank,' Bert clarified in his deep voice. 'Lizzie says he's keeping his head down and making a go of being a landlord. Reckons he's even given up wearing his pinstripes and two-tones now, trying to look like he ain't a villain.'

'Then he's onto a losing wicket,' Lil smirked, touching the end of her long nose. She sniffed disdainfully. 'Frank's a born loser if ever I met one. To this day, I can't work out why Lizzie married the geezer. It was – and still is – his brother she loves.'

'Now, now,' Doug said firmly and patted her knee. 'All in the past now.'

'Well if it's in the past,' Lil challenged, 'why don't Danny do something about the present? Everyone knows him and Lizzie were made for each other.'

But Doug reminded her of the obvious. 'She's still married to Frank – legally.'

'Why don't your sister get a divorce?' Lil addressed this comment to Bert, who merely gave a non-committal shrug of his broad shoulders.

Lil had to smile; people might think Bert was all muscle and no brain but they would be wrong to underestimate him. He adored his sister and had stuck by her through thick and thin. Good riddance though, to Kate's youngest son, Vinnie, a petty crook with a vicious streak and Babs, a common tart who couldn't give a damn about Polly, her daughter. The youngest Allen though, Lil had all the time in the world for. Flo Allen still lived next door in the Allen's family home with her husband Syd Miller and their mischief of a son, little Nelson. They were good neighbours and Lil prided herself on their close friendship.

'Here we are,' said Bert as he stopped the car outside the greengrocery. 'I'll help yer out, Lil.'

'I ain't a bloody cripple, ducks.' Lil pushed the heavy door open, eager to get inside and get this storm in a teacup over and done with.

CHAPTER 6

'OH, my God, it ain't my Ethel, is it?' Lil shrieked the moment she walked into Lizzie's bedroom and saw her daughter lying in Lizzie's bed. 'What's happened to my girl? And, is that what I think it is?'

Lil's agonized plea twisted Lizzie's heartstrings and she reached out to support her old friend. Lil was rigid with shock and Lizzie knew it would be a long time before anyone could calm her.

'Bert, put the kettle on.' Lizzie gave her brother the nod, which meant he was to make himself scarce and he duly complied.

She ushered Lil and Doug to the wooden kitchen chairs she had placed beside the bed. It was clear that Lil was trying to make up her mind how to react. Her piercing dark eyes were flitting between her daughter who had not yet made a sound and Polly's crib in which Callum was asleep.

'There's a lot to tell, Lil,' Lizzie began as she positioned herself by Ethel. 'I know it's been a while since we've all been together. From what I can gather from Ethel, she never intended to distance herself from you, or me come to that.'

'You could have bloody fooled me!' Lil spluttered, staring accusingly at her daughter.

'If you give Ethel a chance, she'll explain why she was forced to do what she did.'

Lil took a breath but once again was prevented from speaking by Doug, who with tears in his eyes, walked forward and bent over Ethel. Placing his lips gently on her cheek, he murmured huskily, 'Hello my old china. How are you doing?'

A very faint smile touched Ethel's lips, the briefest glow appearing in her faded blue eyes as she stared up at her father. 'Hello, Dad. I'm sorry...I'm so sorry.' The tears slid down her cheeks accompanied by sobs that were body-racking. While Doug squeezed Ethel's hand attempting to control his own emotions, Lizzie lifted the baby from the crib.

'Here Lil, take your grandson.'

'My God, my God,' was all Lil could breathe as Lizzie placed the child in her arms. 'Our grandson ...?'

'His name's Callum, Mum,' Ethel whispered as Lizzie helped her to sit up.

'So, you were up the duff!' Lil cleared her throat with an effort. 'I wasn't wrong. But I didn't know it would be – that you'd have - '

'Lil!' Doug prevented his wife from continuing as he released Ethel's fingers and pulled out one of the chairs. 'Sit down and let Ethel speak.'

Lizzie watched his feelings play out on his face as he gazed down at his grandson. Less easy to read than Lil, he stared at the little boy, his forehead furrowing as Callum coughed in Lil's arms.

To Lizzie's relief, Lil soon had the infant over her shoulder. 'One thing I can tell you,' Lil grumbled as she patted his back, 'he's got a bloody rotten chest. Have you had the doctor?'

'It's a long story, Mum.'

'I bet it bloody is,' Lil replied bluntly. 'Well, me and your father ain't going nowhere so if you have the stamina, we'd like to hear it.'

Lizzie looked at Ethel and smiled. 'I'll go and see how Bert's doing with the tea, then.'

'You do that, love. And no hurry,' Lil encouraged as she held her grandson out in front of her. 'Well, there ain't no mistake where this little fella sprang from, is there? He certainly ain't got Richard's fair looks and he don't have no bicycle clips round his ankles.'

The comment was Lil down to a 'T' and brought a rueful smile to Lizzie's lips as she left the bedroom.

CHAPTER 7

It was late in the day when Lil and Doug joined Lizzie in the kitchen. Downstairs the shop was closing and Lizzie could hear the voices of the departing customers.

She glanced at Lil who was now looking more her old self. Certainly a good deal better than Doug who sat at the big kitchen table, staring at the cup of cold tea in front of him. Lizzie's heart went out to the man who adored his daughter. He had been in deep distress at the story Ethel had told them.

'The heartless old mare!' Lil expounded, as she sipped her second port wine from the bottle Lizzie reserved for emergencies. 'To think she forbade our own daughter from seeing us! And Rosie and Timothy, too. If only we'd known! I would have had Ethel and the kids out of there before you could say Jack Robinson. I think we should go over to Lewisham and bring them back to Langley Street where they belong.'

'You heard what Ethel said,' Doug reproved. 'Rosie and Timothy are settled with Cora. We've got to face facts.'

'What a load of rubbish!' Lil declared angrily. 'She's keeping them there – like she kept our girl – a prisoner.'

Lizzie looked at Doug and knew that he had understood all his daughter had said. But Lil still refused to believe that her grandchildren had done nothing to prevent the ousting of their mother and stepbrother. It was this fact that had caught in Lil's craw. The unwelcome news that Rosie and Timothy preferred to live with Cora than return with their mother, had made her blood boil.

She was so furious, Lizzie realized, that she had completely let Ethel off the hook for sleeping with Cal Bronga. Lil had always suspected the affair, but now, in Lil's book, what was done was done. It was an anathema to her that her two grandchildren had disowned their own family, her and Doug included.

Lizzie saw that Lil had readily embraced the new addition; Callum was her grandson and had the Sharpe blood running in his veins. From the moment she had set eyes on him after the initial shock, he was included as part and parcel of her world. What she couldn't accept was the fact that Rosie and Timothy had turned into strangers under the influence of Cora Ryde. And Lil's fury at this knew no bounds.

'Now, now love,' Doug tried to placate his distraught wife. 'Let's go over the facts nice and calm like.'

'What facts might they be?' demanded Lil, still fuming.

'It seems Cora rubbed salt into the wound daily, causing our daughter to believe she was responsible for Richard's death. So she took her revenge by selling the Blackheath house that was never Richard's all along. The fact that it left Ethel and the kids destitute meant they would be forced to turn to her. A big house and all, in a nice area - how could we compete?' Doug shook his head solemnly. 'Unbelievable but true.'

'Richard lied to Ethel all their married life,' Lil croaked. 'He didn't own the house they were living in. There was no mortgage to pay, no debt. It belonged to Cora all the time. He kept our Ethel short for no reason. She never bought herself anything new and the kids always wore secondhand. It wasn't until she got a job at Rickards that she managed to give them proper school uniforms.'

'Perhaps it was his way of controlling their lives,' Doug reasoned. 'He was a stickler for things being just so.'

'You can say that again,' chimed in Lil. 'I'm not speaking ill of the dead when I say he was a funny customer. He never spent time with the kids. He was always on at Ethel over money. And he certainly didn't like her coming to our place. She was always on edge to get home.'

'That's true, but what I have trouble believing most,' Doug continued, 'is that Cora would try to get Callum taken away. Is that right do you think, Lizzie? I mean, in this day and age, that's outrageous.'

Lizzie nodded in full agreement. 'It was a choice she gave Ethel to make in front of Rosie and Timothy.'

'Christ, that's evil!' Lil stared open-mouthed at her husband. 'But Ethel only had to come to us! She knows we would have made room for them all and be happy to do so!'

Lizzie had no intention of explaining to Lil that Rosie had refused point blank to return to Langley Street. She wouldn't understand that Lewisham, being the classy area it was, held a strong appeal for her grandchildren; houses boasting at least three bedrooms, some as many as five like Cora's, completely detached from their neighbours. All had leafy rear gardens and there wasn't a backyard, closet or broken shed between them. The two teenagers had their own rooms and as much freedom as they wanted. It was clear to Lizzie that Cora was using this to win over Timothy and Rosie. It was a crafty but clever move.

'Well, I don't intend to let my grandchildren be influenced by a scheming old witch and her lolly,' Lil declared firmly.

'Lil, Ethel is thirty-five, love, not thirteen,' reasoned Doug. 'She's a woman for heaven's sake. She don't want us to interfere.'

'You can stuff that!' Lil exclaimed. 'Someone has to put Cora bloody Ryde in her place. My nature is to strike back at anyone who hurts me or mine. Gawd knows what she's planting into Timothy and Rosie's heads.' Lil slung the port down her throat and stared morosely at her empty glass.

'Have you considered that a confrontation would play into Cora's hands?' Doug said after a moment's thought. 'Rosie and Timothy have a bit of nous for the nicer things in life. You know how Timothy takes after his dad; everything proper and in its place. While Rosie's got this job in Lewisham. The girl must have made friends and by all accounts is doing well. What have we got to offer as an alternative?'

Lil's breath caught in her throat, her eyes a little glassy from the alcohol. 'Christ Doug, you make us sound like bloody paupers! Our grandkids ain't snobs, if that's what you're driving at.'

'I'm not saying they are,' Doug retaliated. 'But Rosie and Timothy are being treated like royalty. They are also still grieving for their dad and angry at Ethel. Now, anything adverse you do or say in front of them will play to Cora's strengths. She will look the innocent once again.'

'So, what do you suggest we do, brain-of-Britain?' Lil's black, pencilled eyebrows shot up fiercely.

'My feeling is we need to get our timing right. Be patient, wait on the sidelines. Because there's sure to be an eruption one day. They're gonna miss their mum after the shine wears off. And, we'll be there for them when they need us.'

'But they don't need us now. Is that what you're telling me?' Lil was close to tears once again. 'After all the years I've looked after them, changed their nappies and wiped the snot from their noses, you're saying we ain't good enough?'

Doug put his arm around his wife and drew her close. Lizzie felt the tears spring to her own eyes. Like Lil, she was devastated to think that Rosie and Timothy were not here now, supporting Ethel no matter what she had done.

Lil blew her nose on Doug's proffered handkerchief. She nervously touched her hair. 'I just feel so ruddy powerless,' she confessed. 'Our hands are tied. Having survived over half a century on this earth, that's a feeling I'm unaccustomed to.'

'You'd fight to the death to protect your family, we all know that,' said Lizzie soothingly. 'But I have to agree with Doug and Ethel on this one.'

The room was quiet once again, with only the noises of the shop drifting up from below.

'My poor bleeding Ethel,' Lil sniffed. 'She had so much to give to the world once. Now look at the poor bitch. Saddled with a fatherless kid and an old woman in looks. Where did life start to go wrong for her? Was it me? Did I push her into marrying Richard? Was it my fault things have turned out the way they have?'

'Course not, love,' Doug replied firmly. 'After we lost Neil and Greg, perhaps we loved her too much. Worried too much. We thought marriage to a boy she'd grown up with and who we knew well, was safest all round. But maybe we didn't give Ethel a chance to try to find her feet in the world.'

Lizzie admired Doug's reasoning and it seemed to have a calming effect on Lil, too.

'It's your new grandson who needs you now,' Lizzie pointed out. 'He's sick, but if I call the doctor, I'm afraid of upsetting Ethel all the more. As you know, she's terrified the authorities will take Callum away from her.'

'Over my dead body,' said Lil, perking up.

'They can't do that,' Doug muttered indignantly. 'Not

without good reason. Ethel might have made a mistake in her marriage but that don't mean she's a bad mother. Now, either we've got to call the doctor in without her knowing or think of something pretty quick to get that little boy back to good health.'

Lil grabbed hold of Lizzie's arm. 'You said you've given Callum a dose of the Friar's Balsam. Is it helping?'

'I think so.'

'That's good. Now, there's an old trick that me and your mum used for you kids,' Lil reflected. 'Whenever you had a cold we'd give you a couple of drops of raw onion juice added to a teaspoon of cod liver oil.'

Lizzie smiled. 'Now you mention it, I remember. It tasted vile, but Ma swore by it."

'And there's another thing we can do …' Lil slipped into her natural nurturing role, reeling off the remedies that they might attempt before calling in the doctor.

Whether or not they would work, was anyone's guess, but Lizzie was happy to try. Lil was in her element. And that was good news all round; especially for Ethel.

CHAPTER 8

POLLY WAS SITTING on the edge of Ethel's bed as she held Callum, running her fingers through his abundance of silky black hair. This performance was a morning ritual now as Ethel prepared his breakfast in the kitchen. For the past two weeks Polly had been inseparable from Callum and Lizzie knew their bond was deepening. Polly was up early every morning before school to nurse him and when she came home, she gave him small amounts of mashed food for his tea. Polly's love and attention knew no bounds and the little boy had responded.

From under her mass of tumbling auburn curls, Polly looked up at Lizzie with wide, turquoise-blue eyes. 'Callum's nearly better, Auntie Lizzie. Can he live with us?'

Lizzie sat beside her niece and smiled. 'Lil and Doug want their grandson home.'

Polly sighed. 'I love babies.'

Lizzie watched as Callum clutched Polly's finger and blew bubbles. His huge dark eyes were fixed on the little girl who adored him.

'Was I as small as him once?' Polly asked curiously.

'You were - and very beautiful.'

'Then why did my mum go away? Auntie Ethel wouldn't leave Callum, would she?'

Lizzie slipped her arm around her ward's shoulders. Polly was growing fast. In December she would be eight but revealing the truth of her mother's rejection was more than Lizzie could ever bring herself to do. If only Babs had tried harder to care for Polly who had turned out to be the spitting image of Babs. Like her mother, Polly had masses of copper-coloured curls bouncing over her shoulders. Even the freckles sprinkled over the neat little nose, reminded Lizzie of Babs. But Polly had inherited her father's blue eyes and when they looked at her, Lizzie could see the man that Frank might have been, had he stuck to the straight and narrow. Polly had always known him as her 'Uncle Frank', thankfully unaware of the fact that Frank and Babs's wild affair many years ago had resulted in her conception.

'Your mum left you in our care,' Lizzie answered, careful to choose the right words. 'That is, me and your Auntie Flo and Uncle Bert. She knew we would look out for you while she was away.'

'Will she ever come back?'

'I hope so,' Lizzie replied as she had many times before, though now the question was coming more frequently. 'But sometimes people have to follow their dreams.'

'Wasn't I in me mum's dreams then, like Callum's in Auntie Ethel's?'

Lizzie hesitated, for Polly was no fool. 'You were, my love. But your mum had her own path to follow.'

Polly looked curiously at Lizzie, a small frown on her forehead. 'Uncle Danny came back from Australia to see you, didn't he?'

Lizzie smiled. 'And he brought Tom with him, too.'

' 'Cos Tom didn't have no parents, so Uncle Danny

adopted him.' Obligingly, Polly completed the story she had heard many times before. 'He calls Uncle Danny his dad, so why do I call you Auntie Lizzie?'

'It doesn't really matter what we call each other,' Lizzie tried to explain. 'It's what you feel that counts.'

'I know,' Polly agreed in her grown-up fashion. 'Mrs Price says that even if Uncle Frank was a commie once and tried to blow up our shop, he's probably not a commie now. And even if Auntie Flo and Uncle Syd and baby Nelson are called Millers, it doesn't mean to say Nelson is gonna turn out bad like all the other Millers.'

'Mrs Price said that?' Lizzie questioned.

'She says some of the Miller kids went to our school. They burned down the caretaker's cottage. Mind, it was a very old cottage and the caretaker got a nice house instead.'

'Mrs Price seems to know a lot.'

'She's a bit of a gasbag.'

Lizzie giggled. 'Who taught you that word?'

'Uncle Frank.' Polly went pink. 'When I told him Mrs Price said he was a commie, he said she was half right, 'cos in winter he wears coms under his trousers.'

This set them both laughing and Lizzie affectionately brushed a lock of hair from Polly's eyes. 'Did Uncle Frank explain what a communist is?'

'No, he just said he ain't one.'

'That's true.'

'Uncle Frank makes me laugh. But I miss Uncle Danny and Tom. They used to come by a lot.' Polly blushed deeper as she held Callum close to her chest, looking mischievously up at Lizzie. 'Do you want to know a secret?'

'Well, it won't be a secret if you tell me.'

'Don't matter. I've got lots of others.'

Lizzie laughed.

'Tom and me was in the playground at school. He said the

lady that looks after him and Uncle Danny, said to call her Aunt April.'

'That's very nice of her.'

'She's really bossy.'

'Oh, dear.'

'Tom reckons if you was to ask Uncle Danny to get married, he'd leave Mrs Williams and come to live with us.'

'What am I missing?' Ethel asked as she came into the room and gently took Callum from Polly's arms.

'News on the grapevine,' Lizzie answered discreetly.

'What's a grapevine?' Polly threaded her thumbs through the braces of her dungarees. With a frown on her forehead, she rocked back and forth in her lace-up boots.

'Branches where grapes grow,' Lizzie explained, quickly glancing at Ethel.

'Do we sell grapes in the shop?' was the next enquiry.

'You'd better ask Uncle Bert.'

Polly skipped to the door. 'Is Granda coming over?'

'He'll be here any minute to look after the shop while I go to the pub.'

'Good. I like helping Granda. He gives me a tanner to sell the mouldy stuff off cheap.'

Lizzie smothered a grin. Polly looked forward to the pocket money she earned on Saturdays. Her grandfather, Bill Flowers, father to Danny and Frank, wasn't the energetic young coster he used to be, but he still kept an interest in the business.

'Bye Callum, bye Auntie Ethel.' Polly ran from the room. Her tiny footsteps echoed on the wooden stairs leading down to the shop.

When all was quiet, Lizzie and Ethel exchanged glances.

'So, what's all this about grapevines?' Ethel asked curiously.

'I gather Danny's landlady has told Tom to call her Aunt

April. It hasn't gone down well.'

'Don't Tom like her?' asked Ethel as she sat on the nursing chair.

'Polly say he thinks she's bossy.'

'Well, Tom is growing fast, too. Perhaps he needs a firm hand.' Ethel glanced down at her son. 'I never had much trouble with Rosie and Timothy. But I have a feeling this one might be a rascal.'

Lizzie's thoughts went to Vinnie, her older brother, who had become a tearaway at Tom's age. A boy needed a father, no one knew that better than her. Before the war, the Allens had been a close-knit family; Bert, Vinnie, Babs, and Flo – the Allen tribe as they were known on the Isle of Dogs. Mucking about on the river, mud-larking and jumping the barges were part and parcel of their everyday life. Pa had been strong and healthy then. He'd ruled his five children with a rod of iron yet he had always been fair. But after the war he'd returned a half-man from the trenches of Flanders. Without his legs he had grown bitter and angry with life and all those around him. Their mother, Kate, must have known that he was slowly dying from gangrene. Valiantly, she had tried to hold the family together, just as Lizzie had tried after her death. But without parents to guide them, the Allens, like many bereaved families in the country, had broken apart.

'Did Polly ask about Babs?' enquired Ethel, bringing Lizzie back to the moment.

'I told her the usual.'

'That Babs went off to follow her dreams?'

'What else can I say?'

'How about the truth? That her mother slept with your husband and after screaming blue murder while having his baby, she promptly disappeared and left you to care for Pol,' was Ethel's unsympathetic reply.

'Ethel, that's very harsh.'

'My point is, Polly needs to know about Frank's part in all this. At the moment, he has a halo around his head. And it's you who has helped to put it there.'

Lizzie sighed deeply. There was little to say in Frank's defence. But he had sworn to reform, which of course, no one believed for a second. Polly adored him and for good reason. Frank could be charming and agreeable when he tried and in a sort of bewildering way he was doing his best to win Polly's affection.

'Sorry,' Ethel apologised as Lizzie lapsed into silence. 'Babs is your sister after all. And Frank your husband, albeit a rotten one. Perhaps it's my own guilt that's talking.'

'Guilt over Callum?'

'And Richard, too.'

'You weren't responsible for Richard's death. Ethel. It was an accident. Richard was in the wrong place at the wrong time. No one can blame you for that.'

Ethel's voice was husky when she replied. 'My kids must blame me or else they'd be here right now. Rosie told me straight. It was like she was saying goodbye, as if it was the end when I left Cora's.'

Lizzie knew Ethel was going through torture and it was heartbreaking to witness. 'Rosie is just a normal teenager,' Lizzie tried to console. 'When you are sixteen, you don't know what you want or how to get it. You develop a new body and step into another world.'

Ethel nodded. 'That's why I want her with me.'

'Callum's thriving, Ethel. Thank God for that. Rosie will come 'round in her own good time. Callum's going to need all your love now.'

Ethel smiled sadly. 'Loving him is so easy. In my eyes he's beautiful, perfect even. But I know it's going to be very hard for him when he realizes he's a different colour to other kids round here.'

'Then why not write to Cal?'

A spark of life came into Ethel's empty eyes, but the light soon went out. 'What would I write? What could I say to change the past? He left me, remember?'

'No, he left England because he had nothing to stay for. You'd cold-shouldered him Ethel.'

'He didn't try very hard to change my mind.'

'He would be here today if he knew about Callum,' Lizzie protested.

Ethel squeezed her eyes shut. 'Out of duty or sympathy perhaps. But our affair was wrong. So wrong. How could we ever be happy after what we did?' She lifted Callum to her shoulder and stood up. 'I'll put him down for his nap. You'd better get off to the pub.'

Lizzie watched her friend lay the baby in the cot and pull over the covers. She wanted to assure her there was nothing to fear. But whenever the subject of Cal came up, Ethel refused to listen.

Lizzie walked to the door. 'Your mum and dad will be dropping by later.'

Ethel suddenly shook herself and looked up. 'I know I'm a bloody liability to you. I'm sorry.'

'That's a daft thing to say.'

'I'll go to Mum's soon.'

'Do you feel ready to leave?'

'Rosie and Timothy might call on Mum. She is their other gran after all.'

Lizzie dredged up a smile. 'Yes, there's always that chance.'

As she left the bedroom, Lizzie's heart was heavy. Rosie and Timothy's return to Langley Street was unlikely. But Ethel held on to hope.

Just as I do for Danny, Lizzie reflected wistfully.

CHAPTER 9

'TOM, WEAR THESE TONIGHT,' said April Williams, indicating the long grey trousers folded neatly over her arm. 'And when we eat dinner at Mrs Murdoch's be sure to use your napkin. We don't want a clean tie spoiled, do we?'

Eleven-year-old Tom Flowers took a step back, as if the trousers might bite him. He hated it when Aunt April made him wear such formal clothes and he looked to his father for support.

'Dad, I like me short trousers best.'

'Do as Aunt April says, Tom.'

'But they're too big. And they scratch my knees.'

'Tom,' Aunt April said patiently, 'they are the right size. It's just that you've grown accustomed to sloppy clothes. A proper school like St Augustine's requires a good uniform.'

Tom wrinkled his nose in disgust at the suggestion. 'Them straw hats are for sissies. I like me cap and shorts.'

'You're not a child,' Aunt April insisted. 'At St Augustine's, long trousers are regulation wear for boys of your age.'

'Dad!' Tom implored his father who sat in the fireside

chair reading a newspaper. 'I don't want to go to St Augustine's.'

Danny glanced up and smiled reassuringly. 'It's a good school, son.'

'But all my friends are at Ebondale Street.'

'You'll make new ones, don't worry.'

'Not like Polly I won't,' Tom argued. 'She's me best mate.'

'Now, my dear,' soothed Aunt April, pressing the trousers firmly into his hands, 'don't cheek your father. He's only doing what's best for you.'

Tom had to pinch himself sometimes to see if his life was real. His dad had changed and in ways that Tom couldn't understand. But he knew Aunt April had a lot to do with it.

He studied his father's new image; a dark suit that had been measured, cut, and hand-stitched at a tailor's with great care and expense. A black tie folded into the shape of a bow under his chin. Cufflinks that glittered on his shirt sleeves.

Tom had thought this quite funny at first. He'd only ever seen his father wearing overalls or working clothes. But now he had a new garage in Euston - *showrooms*, he was supposed to call it. And Aunt April seemed not to be their landlady now, but another sort of person altogether. She had even persuaded his dad that it was time to send him to another school. That evening they were going to visit a big house in London. Aunt April's friend, Mrs Murdoch lived there. She had a son who was a boarder at St Augustine's. Ralph wore long trousers and a boater, so Tom had been informed. Tom was beginning to wonder if life would ever be normal again.

He looked at Aunt April and saw the gravity of her expression. Her features were no longer kind and caring but tight and pinched. Curiously they matched up to the woolly, scratchy trousers he refused to wear. Once she had never minded that him and his dad had come home all oily and greasy from the workshop. She'd washed their clothes and talked to them about football. But now she favoured rugby and cricket. Tom vowed to himself that he would rather join the Navy than ever be sent to a boarding school.

He forced down the urge to run as fast as he could out of the house. Back to the dilapidated garage and workshop at Chalk Wharf where his dad had once worked with Cal. In summer he'd scoot down to the River Thames and watch the tide run fast down the estuary. With mud-caked legs, he'd collected slivers of wood and shiny black nuggets of coal and if he was lucky, a halfpenny encrusted with tar.

Later he'd climb down the ladder to the workshop where Cal would be working. They'd study his finds, getting their hands so black and dirty that Cal would paint streaks on their faces with his fingers. They'd pretend to be in the outback and chase the swamp monster. Half croc, half dog, the bunyip would rise from the billabong and snap you up. 'So, if ever you catch him down on them mudflats,' Cal would warn, 'run like the Yowi!'

Tom shivered with excitement at the memories; sun-burned days helping his dad and Cal in the garage, star-filled nights around the camp fire. But that was before the garage got burned down. Before his father and Cal almost perished at the bottom of Leonard Savage's well. Before Aunt April turned into the bunyip.

'Tom, are you listening?' Aunt April's brow was caught in an impatient frown. She held out the long, woolly trousers. To his deep dismay, a stiff white collar now accompanied them.

'Tom, do as your Aunt April says,' his dad urged from over the top of his newspaper.

'I've polished your nice new leather shoes, too,' Aunt April said with a smile.

He looked pleadingly at his father but there was no help forthcoming.

In under an hour the transformation was complete. Tom stood stiffly to attention with his father at the bottom of the staircase, waiting for Aunt April to appear in her very best camel coat, fox fur collar and leather gloves.

Tom stifled a groan. The tight-fitting collar scraped his chin. The trousers grated on his knees. The new shoes were tight across his toes.

Auntie Lizzie let Polly wear what she liked. And Auntie Lizzie didn't correct him for not sitting up straight or not using a napkin. Uncle Bert ate his chicken with his fingers and slopped bread around his breakfast plate. He made great drain-like noises when he drank his tea, just to make them giggle.

Tom manfully held back his tears. His dad didn't seem to notice they were trapped in this parcelled-up life. It reminded Tom of the time he and Polly had gone to market and watched the demonstration of a pair of laced corsets. To their amusement the trader had wrapped them around himself and pulled the laces so tight they'd stuck and he'd gone beetroot red in his face.

Exactly how Tom felt now.

CHAPTER 10

WEARING HER TRADEMARK WORKING GEAR, Lizzie was seated behind the driving wheel of the Wolseley. A subdued red wrap-over jacket and ankle length skirt hid the top of her laced leather boots. Her jaunty red beret was kept in place by her black hair pinned up in her customary style. One glossy wing fell gently across her forehead and softened her overall appearance. She drove the car with confidence, thanks to Danny who had helped her to cut her teeth on motorised vehicles many years before. She wasn't afraid of the new world and its challenges and was confident of negotiating the maze of East End backstreets.

She glanced briefly at Bert who sat beside her, unusually quiet. Like her passengers in the rear, he had been silent since they left the shop. Elmo and Fowler, too, wore their working clothes; reinforced metal toe-caps and heavy trench coats wide enough to hide the voluminous pouches sewn into their interiors to house their weapons of choice.

If nothing else, she was a realist. Elmo and Fowler had a job to do. The hefty men weren't going to maintain their reputation – or her business – by swatting the many contenders to her turf with a feather duster.

Bert shifted restlessly and drummed his powerful fingers on his outstretched knees. Lizzie knew her brother might look a battle-scarred bruiser, but was in fact, a gentle and caring man. Though since he had found himself, together with Danny and Frank, bound and gagged in Leonard Savage's Chancel Lane hostelry last year, a shotgun poised at his temple, his character had hardened somewhat. For the East End was not the place it used to be and Bert was homesick for the past.

'Don't like leaving Bill in the shop on his own,' Bert fretted.

'This won't take long,' Lizzie replied though with more conviction than she felt.

'Frank should've sorted this aggro,' Bert complained. 'That's what we pay him for.'

'We'll see what the score is when we get there, but you're right. He should have had a man, if not two, on the door.'

Lizzie knew she he had to impress on Frank that he was being given no slack. She expected him to take care of business in every respect. With her help - and as manager of the Mill Wall - she saw no reason why he couldn't turn the business into a legitimate earner. And to be fair, Lizzie thought generously, he had grown closer to Polly over the past year. And it was this relationship that mattered most to her.

Avoiding the horse-drawn traffic, the trams and lorries making their way to and from the docks, Lizzie breathed in the scents of docklands through the open window. The air was thick with the river's breath; the brine and the tar and the rain washed from the filthy roads into the gutters to join the capital's sewage.

The tang of street trading was comfortingly familiar; the muffin and bagel sellers, the toffee apple and shellfish traders, the rag-and-bone men and their stinking carts, the knife and scissor grinders casting sparks above their treadles, grinning toothlessly at the spinning metal.

Dragging herself back from her thoughts, she frowned at Bert. 'Tell me again what Whippet said.'

'The kid told me Frank had trouble in the snug,' Bert repeated. 'Some pimp after his due. Had a knife on his woman by all accounts.'

'Just a loner, then?'

Bert shrugged. 'I didn't get more out of the lad. The little runt had the mouth to demand a tanner before he spilled the beans.'

'I hope you coughed up,' Lizzie replied with a rueful smile as she turned the car into a Poplar side street. 'He's a handy little sort.'

'You're a soft touch, gel,' Bert said gruffly. 'But you wanna have a word. He's getting bolshie.'

Lizzie had grown fond of the fourteen-year-old street kid everyone called Whippet. Homeless and starving, he'd tried stealing the fruit from the shop. One day, Bert had grabbed him by the collar. The boy had kicked and punched at the air, his shoeless feet dangling above the ground. To cool him off Bert had dumped him in the yard trough where the icy water had soon put a stop to his cursing.

Lizzie smiled at the memory. Whippet had been running for her, a half year now. Before this, he had been a villain in the making. If truth be told, he reminded her of her older brother Vinnie, now serving time. But she saw the good in this lad as she had once done in Vinnie.

Bert peered out of the window. 'Why are we parking round here, gel? It's just the bins and cellar doors of the pub.'

Lizzie glanced at the darkened yard filled with rubbish. It was here the draymen, dressed in their leathers, pulled up their wagons and lowered the full barrels of brewery beer into the open cellar doors and roped up the empty casks.

Towering over this area was her tavern, the Mill Wall. The public house was all Victorian brickwork; filthy and crumbling ornate stone, its tall windows and chipped ledges fouled by the pigeons and rat droppings. Lizzie was fully aware of its notorious reputation for the pub had seen many years of dockland drinking. But she had secured the lease on terms that were dangerously liberal, for there were few applicants to take on such a challenging prospect.

'Lift the traps, Elmo,' she said in a quiet voice. 'Take Fowler and go by way of the cellars up to the bars.'

'And you, missus?' Elmo asked warily in his rough cockney dialect. His long red hair was hidden under the collar of his coat and his close-set eyes darted quickly in their sockets, alert for any movement.

Lizzie smiled at his concern. 'Don't fret over me. Go along now and watch out for yourselves.'

Fowler grunted uncertainly and like Elmo, stared suspiciously into the shadows of the gloomy yard. His unshaven jaw showed a silver growth of bristle and his hairless head and blunted features made him look fearsome. 'Don't like the smell of this,' he added with a snarl.

But without more ado the two men followed her orders and climbed out of the car. Quietly making their way to the cellar, they heaved up the traps and slithered into the rooms below.

'Fowler's right,' Bert muttered beside her. 'This don't feel kosher. Could be we're in for a surprise.'

'P'raps,' Lizzie agreed, opening the car door. 'But as we both know, Bert, there's only one way to find out.'

FRANK FLOWERS WAS NOT a brave man and he freely admitted his faults to anyone who would listen to him.

The problem was, he was suffering. His health was a travesty since his sojourn in the looney bin. On his release, he'd seen fit to put the mockers on Lizzie and Danny's wedding day, which if he was honest, was another misguided move. He should have stayed dead. He should have done Lizzie a favour and disappeared to Australia. Or to Uncle Sam across the pond. Or anywhere really, where he wasn't known for the bastard criminal – that in effect – he wasn't!

It was his voices that had dominated his life and, until the day they'd strapped him in a straitjacket and thrown the electric switch to his brain, the voices had governed him big time. He'd stolen his brother's woman, then messed up his marriage, banging anything in a skirt from day one. And finally – well perhaps not finally, but almost finally – done the deed with Lizzie's sister, Babs.

Frank took a deep breath, attempting to stiffen his injured spine. Since his trouncing by the Millers, his back had never been right. But he did at least have the pills to counteract the pain both physical and mental. Pop one or three, and he could act rationally. Though the fact he should wind up as the manager of a tavern when he'd taken the oath to stay dry, was a joke to him and the world at large. But what else was he going to do with his Godforsaken life? He still held a flame for the woman who loved his brother. Though everyone around him seemed to have forgotten, Lizzie was still his wife on paper. And, it was because he'd never lost hope that they'd be reunited that he'd followed her into the jaws of hell at Chancel Lane. He'd never been as arse-scared before nor, he hoped, would ever be again. But he'd not let her down and for the first time in his life, he'd known what it was to be legitimately proud of himself.

The firm tap on his shoulder made him jump as a meaty hand clamped over his mouth.

In the gloom of the cold passage leading into the bars, he froze. It wasn't until he heard a familiar whisper in his ear that he breathed a sigh of relief.

'Up the front and defending yer turf I see,' Elmo taunted. 'Those medals on your chest, Frank, are weighing you down, mate. I thought you was a hunchback.'

Fowler grinned but said nothing. Frank had a grudging respect for Fowler who kept himself to himself. But Elmo was a surly bugger with a razor-sharp tongue which always made Frank nervous.

'Is Lizzie here?' Frank managed to ask as he rearranged his crumpled shirt and adjusted his armbands.

Fowler nodded. 'She's coming in the front. Is the knifer still in the snug?'

'Three others are with him,' Frank added hurriedly. 'A couple more women, too.'

'Whippet said there was only one geezer and his tart.'

Frank blinked his blue eyes and pushed back his neatly combed blond hair oiled lavishly to produce a shine. 'There was when I gave Whippet the message. But after the kid left, the others turned up.'

'Where's all your muscle?' Elmo demanded, glancing around. 'You should have one geezer at least, if not two, on the door.'

'I did. They buggered off the minute they saw the knife.'

'Well, congratulations. You made a good choice there,' replied Elmo with a grimace.

'I can't help it if they do a midnight flit.'

'You're paid to help it,' came the accusing answer. 'Lizzie gave you the wherewithal to hire backup. Are you on the jollop again?'

Frank took umbrage to this. He'd packed in the booze since he started this job. More than once it had occurred to him he was living the life of a vestal virgin. He was about to voice his opinion when a ruckus started in the saloon bar. The two towering men pushed past him and standing shoulder to shoulder, they peered over the swing doors.

Frank patted his empty pockets nervously. He had nothing more than his baccy tin to defend himself with. But after the calamity with his dad's service revolver last year, when he'd shot a man by accident and Danny and Bert had been left to dispose of the corpse, he wasn't about to repeat the mistake.

Frank heard another sound; the sharp crack of splintering of wood. This was followed by the shattering of broken glass. To his further dismay came the high-pitched shrieks of Lenny the barman.

Frank stretched his neck to look over Fowler's shoulder. He saw the small, elf-like figure of Lenny encircled by three ugly brutes. Much to their amusement, they were shoving him around the floor. Lenny looked terrified. His cries of distress were witnessed by the customers who stared at the proceedings like the gormless idiots they were. Several of the chairs and stools had been broken and tables knocked over. Shards of glass glinted in the puddles of beer staining the sawdust.

Frank began to feel the old pit-of-the-stomach nausea. These were not just ordinary tarts' pimps. These men were troublemakers. It was clear to see they had an agenda and as such, were on a mission. Frank looked at Elmo and Fowler, who stood motionless, their eyes fixed ahead.

'Why don't you do something?' he whispered hoarsely. 'They're tearing up me furniture.'

'Tell you what,' Elmo growled without turning to face him, 'we'll follow your lead, Frank. You go out there first and lay down the law. Them ugly mugs don't look as though they could knock off an old dear's 'andbag. We'll have your back, don't worry.'

Frank swallowed and shrank away at Elmo's taunt. He was appalled at the idea of confronting trouble. When Elmo turned his red head and smirked contemptuously in his direction, Frank knew Elmo knew it too. The big ox never lost an opportunity to ridicule him. Frank's fingers curled into fists. What kind of world was it when blokes supposed to be on your side turned out to be the enemy?

Suddenly, and to Frank's further alarm, there was yet more shouting. Lenny's screams indicated the distress he was in. Once more, Frank strained to see what was happening.

To his horror, the front door of the pub had opened. Lizzie stood alone, her spine as stiff as the proverbial broom. With an agonising slow pace, she moved towards the three roughnecks.

Frank gulped as Lenny, with an eye the colour of an over-ripe banana tried to make an escape. But one of the men grabbed his collar. 'Where d'you think you're going, Hercules?' he demanded, clouting Lenny round the chops again.

Frank swallowed in distaste for that could have been him. Would have been him if he hadn't done a bunk the moment he sniffed trouble. But worse was to come he realized, as Lizzie walked up to the ugly geezer and stared him directly in the eye.

'Let Lenny go,' she said, as the barman shivered and shook pathetically.

'You what?' demanded the bruiser.

'Let my barman go,' Lizzie repeated in that tone of hers that Frank had come to respect. But she wasn't dealing with the likes of him here. She was well out of her league. Biggest mistake of all, she'd come without Bert.

'Hark at it!' scoffed the big ape, 'You must be jokin' yer silly bitch!'

'No joke,' returned Lizzie coldly. 'Do as I say, then clear out.'

Frank closed his eyes in despair. There was only Elmo and Fowler against three of the opposition. Where was Bert when he was needed? Back serving spuds in the shop no doubt!

Frank glanced to his far right and his stomach lurched as he saw the joker with the knife. Add him to the equation and the odds were well against Lizzie.

Frank shuddered at the threat of violence and the need for his participation. He had been doing all right as a porter at the hospital. He'd minded his own business and had created his own little stream of income with knock-offs from the drug store. Now he stood in the front line of battle, or at least, Elmo and Fowler did.

Becoming a pub landlord, he decided, was another punt altogether.

CHAPTER 12

LIZZIE GUESSED the man was only in his late twenties, but his general fetid appearance added another decade to his age. The stink coming off him was enough to make the eyes water and the other two men fared no better. Three sets of greedy, red-veined eyes stared in her direction. She returned their lusty smiles as she waited for the inevitable.

'So, it's an apology you're after?' The man closest to her sneered. He turned to his companions who duly laughed. 'Come here and I'll give you the best apology you ever had in yer life.' He pushed aside his coat and grasped at his groin.

Lizzie stared at him in amusement. 'My sympathies,' she answered boldly, 'with so little to boast of you will no doubt grow into a very lonely old man.'

A soft ripple of amusement filled the room. Her assailant blushed red in humiliation. With a roar of anger he kicked over a chair and banged his fist on a table. The occupants sat perfectly still, their eyes turning to Lizzie.

'You cow!' he bellowed advancing towards her. 'You need teaching a lesson.'

Lizzie stepped to one side as he made his leap, though he was more agile than she thought. He caught hold of her arm in a forceful grip.

Raising her free hand to her beret, she slid out the hidden hat pin. Swiftly she drove the sharp point into the soft skin between thumb and forefinger. Elmo and Fowler appeared in an instant and Bert joined them from the street where he been waiting to enter. Lizzie stepped back, allowing them to deal with the other men as Lenny fled through the saloon doors.

Then, without warning, a figure appeared from the snug. The man was tall and lean; a flash of steel glittered in his hand. A handful of women followed him and flung themselves into the fight, biting and kicking.

The stranger made his way towards her, cleverly avoiding attack. Before Lizzie could take a breath, the knife was pressed to her throat. The man's powerful body enfolded her; his eyes – as sharp as splinters of ice – were narrowed to slits behind a mask that covered the upper part of his face. A perfumed aroma drifted from his spiky dark hair. The scarf around his neck was made of silk and his coat was like no other she'd ever seen. The cloth was a smooth purple, with a dramatic half-cape that fell like wings from his shoulders. Brass buttons shone from the epaulets giving a military touch. All this she took note of as, unable to move in his grip, he forced her to meet his gaze.

'Who are you?' Lizzie demanded, struggling to be free.

'I am all things to those who step into my world,' he whispered in a faint accent. 'And you, Lizzie Flowers, have arrived without invitation.'

Lizzie caught her breath on a gasp. 'The Mill Wall is my tavern.'

He laughed softly. 'You may believe it is, but you are

mistaken. Think again before you turn out my women. The odds are in Salvo Vella's favour, not yours.'

She closed her eyes as she felt the point of the knife prick her skin. Was he going to kill her? But for what reason? And why had he said the Mill Wall was his?

When she opened her eyes, he was gone.

CHAPTER 13

LIZZIE SAT IN THE SNUG, now deserted, trying to gather herself. Her meeting with the foreigner had shaken her. The knife at her throat need only have moved an inch ...

Who was this man wearing a mask? And why had he threatened her? *His* women, he said. *His* world. She looked around her now, blanching at the unwholesome aromas left by the previous occupants. Strong tobacco, rank body odour and cheap perfume hung in the air and clung to the shabby upholstery. Every curtain was limp and faded. The brass rings on which they were hung, were tarnished with rust. The candles had melted into the wooden tables and been replaced without cleaning. She was ashamed of what she saw, for this was her turf, despite what the stranger had said.

'We've thrown out the geezers and their tarts,' Bert announced as he joined her, swatting the flies with his cap from the filthy wooden table. 'But I was too late to catch the sort with a knife. Did he hurt you?'

Lizzie put her hand to her throat. The pin-prick of blood was drying. 'No, it's nothing.'

'He moved like a bloody streak of lightening. Looked like

a comic turn from the Queens. One of them actors that dress up like dandies.'

'He was no dandy, Bert. He called himself Salvo Vella.'

'Never heard of him,' Bert scoffed. 'Sounds like a foreigner.'

'He had an accent, it's true, but I couldn't make it out.' Lizzie swallowed, still shocked and trembling from the threatening encounter.

'His flamin' whores was all over us,' Bert continued to complain. 'Nails out like cats and kicking us in the balls. I couldn't get to you in time.'

'I think that was his plan.'

Bert stared at her in surprise. 'You mean we was set up? By a load of females?'

'He knew my name, Bert. They were his women. He warned me to think again before I chucked them out.'

Bert clenched his big fists. 'Bloody sauce!'

Lizzie shook her head slowly. 'For some reason he thought the Mill Wall was his.'

'So that's his game, is it? Trading in the snug as if he owns the place and we are expected to put up with it. Well, he won't be bringing his knocking shop round here. Where's bloody Frank? I reckon he must know the bloke. Do you reckon Frank's blotto and taking a back-hander?'

'No,' Lizzie said at once. 'Frank might have his faults, but he's on the wagon.'

'It wouldn't take him long to fall off.'

Lizzie thoughtfully pleated her fingers together on the table. 'It was as if the women had deliberately caused a ruckus, in order to bring us here. When you and Elmo and Fowler were busy with the troublemakers, Vella came straight to me. He had a message to deliver and made sure I understood it.'

Bert moved closer and in a soft voice murmured, 'So you believe this is a serious case of aggro? Not a one off?'

Lizzie nodded slowly. 'The mask, the cape and brass buttons, now I think about them, he was dead set on making an impression. He meant business, I'm sure.'

Bert swiped his hand across the bloody scratches the women had left on his jaw. 'Let's wait to hear what Frank says.'

'What about Lenny? Did they rough him up?'

'He's scared witless but is willing to overlook the slap he took for a bonus.'

'See that he gets one.' Lizzie was beginning to feel a little better. Though it seemed clear to her now that today's meeting with Salvo Vella had been no accident.

Bert rose to his feet and lumbered off. She couldn't forget those piercing eyes and the melodrama that the man with the knife had created. It was as if every move he had made had been planned in advance. She felt as though the women and the roughnecks were all part of a colourful but lethal group of performers, the head of which was Salvo Vella.

She was still deep in thought by the time Bert returned. Beside him was the dapper-looking figure of her estranged husband, Frank Flowers. Gone was the look of the Chicago hoodlum wearing garish pin stripes and two-tone brogues. In their place was an expensive-looking waistcoat and pristine white shirt. At thirty-six, he was now the man-about-town, with all the trimmings. Fair hair styled close to his head and with a finely combed centre parting. She knew his apologetic features were arranged carefully for her benefit.

'Where have you been, Frank?' she asked shortly.

'In the khazi. You know what me stomach's like.'

Lizzie took a deep breath. 'It would have helped if you'd made it your business to get rid of those women before trouble started. Why did you let them in? This snug is supposed to be for the benefit of customers who want to sit and drink quietly. '

Frank's wide blue eyes and slightly open mouth indicated his surprise. 'Gawd only knows who they were. I've seen one or two of them before, wanting a bit of how's-yer-father, but never so many at once.'

'Did you tell them to leave on other occasions?'

'Course I did. But I ain't got eyes in the back of my head. The cows may have stole in when I'm not around.'

Lizzie frowned in dismay. 'Are you at the bookie's again?'

Frank looked affronted. 'I ain't seen a pony's backside in six months. I meant I'm only not here when I take Polly out.'

'But you only drive her up West and back again, Frank. It don't take all day.'

'True, but I take care not to rush our outings. You know how much she means to me.'

'Frank, don't use Polly as an excuse,' Lizzie berated. 'I'm glad you spend time with her, but you've also got a business to run. I've provided you with the wherewithal to engage muscle, so where are they?'

Frank lifted his shoulders in a shrug. 'Good men aren't easy to find.'

'Neither it seems are cleaners.' Lizzie indicated the grime-ridden surfaces and cobweb-strewn corners of the public house. And behind the bar, the brass pumps looked tarnished against the faded and peeling emerald green paint of the walls. 'Strip out this snug, Frank,' she said on a heavy sigh. 'Scrub the tables till they shine. I want to see my face in their polished surfaces when I visit next. Bring in more spittoons so the old boys can cough their lungs up without ruining my floors. And, most importantly of all, at the first hint of trade being done in this snug, have the chancers thrown out. Hang a sign outside; "The management of the Mill Wall now runs a clean house. No illicit trade." Or words to that effect.'

Frank was nodding his agreement, glancing anxiously at Bert who was stood behind his sister with arms folded across his barrel chest. 'Next time you call, you won't recognise the place,' Frank assured her.

'I'm leaving Elmo and Fowler to help you, so there will be no excuse to be slapdash.'

'I won't let you down again. I'll keep a lookout for those buggers. Next time they won't be so lucky.'

'Have you heard the name Salvo Vella?' she asked.

He looked blank. 'No. Who is he?'

'A man in a mask who thinks he has the right to work his women here. He carries a knife and wears outlandish clothes for effect – like you.'

'A smooth sort, then?' Frank said respectfully as he pulled back his shoulders.

If Lizzie hadn't been so annoyed, she would have found this remark amusing. But Frank was Frank. He could be relied upon to trip over his vanity so frequently that he didn't spot an insult when he heard one.

CHAPTER 14

BERT WAS MUTTERING under his breath as he drove them back to Ebondale Street. 'Leaving our best blokes to nursemaid Frank don't sit well in me stomach.'

Lizzie nodded her agreement. She sighed as her brother turned on the powerful headlights of the car to illuminate the dark and foggy streets ahead.

'After today we'll be prepared. I'll send Whippet to Deptford tomorrow to find Murphy.'

'He'll charge an arm and leg to hire his soldiers!'

'He has his price, Bert. But in view of the circumstances, I am prepared to pay it.'

Doubtless Murphy would take pleasure in reminding her that he had warned against taking on the pub. But she had insisted; the brewery deal was too tempting to turn down. The Mill Wall was ailing, a rough house going to seed. But she had argued that with the right management the upper floors could be let out as lodgings, the stables made fit for horses. Nevertheless, Murphy had strongly opposed the idea. Like Flo, he mistrusted Frank.

"Left to you, Lizzie Flowers, I have no doubt you would

put the tavern on its feet in under a month. But install the lily-livered wastrel you are supposing will harvest you this goldmine – ha! Frank Flowers will bring you more fecking problems than riches."

As the evening closed around them, Lizzie felt the bite of winter approaching. No matter what others thought or said, she was determined to make a success of her new enterprise. Once she had mastered the trade, nothing else would seem as hard again. Though Frank was a liability in some people's eyes, he was also Polly's father.

And in her book, that was what counted.

CHAPTER 15

IT WASN'T until early in December that Whippet arrived breathless at the shop. Lizzie always thought his baby soft skin made him look no more than ten. His curly fair hair escaped from under his cloth cap and dangled over his big blue eyes. It was a cold, crisp winter morning with a seasonal flavour but the boy was sweating in the navy-blue jacket and working trousers that Lizzie had supplied him with.

She was gratified to see that he had, at least, taken the trouble to wash the grime from his face. At fourteen, Whippet was blessed with nine lives, Lizzie often thought. He was small for his age and greyhound-quick, hence his name. The homeless boy was noted for his fast running in the opposite direction to the law. He lived rough by his own choosing and somehow escaped detection.

Lizzie knew full well that it was only his recent employ into her services that kept him out of trouble. She'd provided him with a barrow for the market and filled it with fruit and veg, enough to encourage his business acumen. But it was clear to one and all that he loved his running the best.

'I found your man over Deptford,' he boasted. 'Bit of

bovver he's had, with the contenders for his turf. But he's up for a meet.'

'How soon?' Lizzie enquired as she paid him the agreed two shillings.

'Murphy ain't the type to keep a diary,' Whippet retorted cheekily. He examined the silver closely. 'Strikes me he'll let you know when he's ready.'

'What kind of answer is that?' Bert demanded as he lugged a sack of potatoes from the storeroom to deposit them in a cloud of dust at the boy's feet. 'You was supposed to make proper arrangements.'

'If you ain't satisfied mister, you can run over the river yerself,' Whippet retorted. 'Though the lump you're carrying round yer waist would put you at a clear disadvantage.'

'Oy, none of your lip, smart Alec!' Bert exclaimed fiercely. 'You'd have something to crow about if your size matched the drivel that comes out of your gob.'

Lizzie stepped between her brother and the messenger. 'Be quiet, the pair of you. Whippet, I want you to run to Langley Street.'

'Blimey, you're working me to the bone, missus,' Whippet complained as he slipped the coins into his trouser pocket. 'Who am I looking for this time? Another dodgy geezer?'

'No, a friend of mine by the name of Lil Sharpe. She lives in Langley Street next door to my sister Flo, who you took a message to last week.'

'The one with a little kid and a mug on it like Fatty Arbuckle?'

Lizzie grinned for it was true; her sister's first child Nelson Stanley, had been a ten-pounder at birth last year and had trebled in size since. His face was as round as the moon and his rosy cheeks grew pinker by the day.

Though Lizzie adored her nephew, she knew she had been remiss in not visiting her sister lately, so she had sent an apology by way of Whippet. If the truth be known, she was hoping that distance would make the heart grow fonder. Her brother-in-law Sydney Miller had cold-shouldered her after a small disagreement. They had known each other for many years and had never had a cross word until he'd fallen into his notorious family's clutches. He'd previously been a fish porter but Lizzie knew that Syd had been lured away from his honest but lowly job. And it wasn't until the day of Nelson's birth that a fragile peace had been restored. Since then, Lizzie had visited Flo mostly when Syd was at work in the scrapyard belonging to his brothers.

'Make sure you give this note to Lil,' she impressed on Whippet, and passed him a scrap of paper. 'I'll be driving Ethel home tomorrow and will call in to see my sister then.'

Whippet stuck the note in his pocket along with the silver and looked greedily at a box of shiny red apples. 'S'pose I could 'tend to it immediately, though I ain't had me dinner yet and am in danger of fainting away.'

'Help yourself,' Lizzie offered. 'And on the way back from Langley Street, call at the bakery. Tell Jenny I sent you for a pie.'

The messenger smiled gratefully at Lizzie. He deliberately made a face at Bert before snatching an apple and bolting.

'The cheeky little sod,' Bert complained, lifting his huge fist at the departing figure. 'I'll give him a lump round me waist!'

'He's just a kid,' Lizzie replied with a shrug. 'Remember he's likely to go one way or the other, just like our Vinnie did.'

Bert mumbled under his breath, then looked Lizzie in the eye. 'Do you reckon that Vin doing time, has sorted him out?'

'I'd like to hope so, Bert.'

'Don't even know which jug he's in,' sighed Bert. 'He got three years in '32 for GBH. With good behaviour he could be out soon. But turning on us, his own family, still sticks in me craw.'

Lizzie didn't like to think of the path that Vinnie had chosen in life. But perhaps being in prison had reformed him? It upset her to think of her brother's determination to become a criminal. Pa would turn in his grave if he knew that.

'When are we going to have the pleasure of Jenny's company?' Lizzie asked, eager to change the subject.

Bert, who rarely showed any emotion, blushed to the roots of his hair. 'Dunno what you mean.'

'Jenny's a lovely girl.'

'I've got enough on my plate without all that nonsense,' Bert dismissed, tipping a generous portion of spuds into the big brass weighing scales.

'There's always time for a little romancing.'

Lizzie only heard a grunt in reply. Her matchmaking efforts always fell on deaf ears where her brother was concerned. But she was certain that Bert was attracted to Jenny. Lately he found any excuse to visit the bakery!

CHAPTER 16

APRIL WILLIAMS DIDN'T CONSIDER herself house-proud, but she liked to see everything in its right place. Which was why she had refused Tom's request for a Christmas tree. The expense was unnecessary. She worked hard to keep a clean and orderly home; it was in her nature. And why add to her chores, with a moulting tree that would only be discarded after the holiday?

At thirty-six years of age, April had observed lifelong rules. Cleanliness was next to Godliness – as her Chapel father had drummed into her. She had taken that same understanding into her first marriage to the late George Williams and intended to continue the same throughout her second to Daniel Flowers.

George had enjoyed an outdoor life at the weekends, but he'd always had a pair of slippers waiting for him by the front door. Living in her parents' Poplar house after they had both died, had brought April respectability. She had married sensibly to a clerk to the borough; an older man who had been both churchgoing and hardworking. In his youth, a game of football had been his one passion, though later, in his middle years, as the illness had claimed him and his lungs ceased to function, he'd spent most of his free time as a spectator.

Tucking the ends of her light brown hair into the neat bun on her neck, she glanced into the oval-bevelled mirror. Her slender face and deep-set eyes were nothing out of the ordinary. But made the most of what she had. She kept a slim figure, wore sensible shoes and enjoyed keeping the garden up to scratch. They were lucky to have even the small patch of garden with a square yard of grass, as most of the terraced houses had backyards. Her father had installed a privy by the high back gate. It was quite private. But there was a lot left to be desired. The rats were becoming a problem in Poplar. So, too, were the neighbours on one side; a newly moved-in rowdy family, often using course language, which was no good for Tom to hear.

She looked at the mantel clock, decorated with a single sprig of holly. Tom would soon be arriving home. She had many reservations about the Ebondale Street School. It was overcrowded and promised to be even more so as time went on. East End families bred like rabbits.

Leaving here will not be at all disappointing, April thought, as she saw in her mind's eye, the Euston villa that she and Daniel had viewed last week. While not detached, it was one of a short row of eight, with black iron railings, tall windows, white front steps and each with a garden at least three times the size of this one. There were good schools in the neighbourhood and the tube station close by. The city was at hand for shopping. And, Daniel's showroom just a ten-minute walk away.

April smiled to herself. Yes, with a few tweaks here and there, she could make a fine marriage with Daniel Flowers. It was not surprising he still had a few rough edges. Living on that uncouth continent on the other side of the world for a decade had left its marks. So too, had his dubious acquaintance with Lizzie Flowers. April vowed to make certain, as soon as the ring was on her finger, that both she and Daniel would be distanced from this unpleasant flaw.

And of course there was Tom!

Her intention was to send Tom to a school for boarders. He was a strong-willed child, but she had won his trust. At times, it was difficult to ignore the references he insisted on making to his past; to his costermonger Auntie Lizzie and her troubled, adopted child Polly. To that wretched shop on Ebondale Street that seemed the hub of so much disorder. But once he was separated from his peers and established at a new school, he would soon straighten out.

Just then, she heard the noise of an engine outside. April's heart beat a little faster as she went to greet Daniel. He was certainly no replica of her fine and upstanding George. But there was potential there. And opening the door wide, April smiled her welcome at the man she intended to make her own. Intimacy would not last forever, she assured herself. After a few years, when Daniel realized it was unlikely that she would conceive, they would sleep separately.

Bearing children had never been an attraction to her. George had contented himself with a grown son with his late first wife. In many respects, April felt she had enjoyed the perfect arrangement. Until of course, George had invested unwisely and lost all their money …

'Welcome home,' April murmured sweetly, 'I've missed you.'

Which was, for April, both truth and lie. For as a widow, she had long since enjoyed her own company.

All the same, she had not forgotten how to reel in a man.

CHAPTER 17

LIL SIGHED with satisfaction as she inspected her kitchen. It was a week to Christmas and the smell of Sunlight soap from the clothes she had washed and pegged on the line was still in the air, adding pleasantly to the aroma of plum pudding steaming in the pan on the stove. Doug had lit a fire in the hearth to take the chill off the place. And, Ethel's room upstairs was now furnished with a wooden crib. Doug had also installed a battered but sturdy chest of drawers from the market and painted it a nice blue colour. The shade matched the woollen pram suits, ribbon-trimmed bonnets and bootees that Lil had knitted for the baby.

The house was cleared of clutter and shone like a new pin. Even so, Lil felt nervous. Were there any last-minute improvements she could make?

The Christmas decorations had been made by Rosie and Timothy when they were knee-high. It pleased her to see them around the house. She'd left some of their drawings of Father Christmas and his reindeers beside Ethel's bed. They were no more than chalked straight lines and circles in red and green, but Lil treasured them. She hoped Ethel would find comfort in them, too.

Wedged around the mirrors and picture frames were sprigs of shiny, prickly holly. In a silver frame below there was a photograph of Rosie and Timothy when they were four and five, with Ethel beside them looking like the beautiful girl she had once been.

Lil had placed this picture strategically in the centre of the mantelpiece; she wanted plenty of reminders of her grandchildren about her and for Ethel to see as well. She would not give them up to Cora without a fight, despite what the rest of the world might think!

Lil savoured the moments before Ethel arrived. Today was a big event in her calendar. Her daughter and third grandchild were coming home. They were set free at last from that Hades in Lewisham! And not a minute too soon in her opinion. For it was Cora Ryde who was solely responsible for Ethel's depressed state of mind. Someone should remind Rosie and Timothy what a fine mother they had in Ethel.

Richard had not been a natural father. He was still a boy after fifteen years of marriage. She wasn't about to speak ill of the dead but her son-in-law had been what her mother would have called, a namby-pamby. Even the Blackheath house that Richard had boasted was his own had turned out to be his mother's. He had kept his family impoverished; on the breadline. Though Ethel had never complained, Lil knew that if it wasn't for her daughter's job at the local haberdashers, the kids would have gone short in every respect. Richard had hoarded his money, while her Ethel had worked like a navvy for years. She'd not enjoyed one word of praise from her husband. In fact, he'd resented her independence. He hated most things that made up Ethel's small world. Top of his list were his in-laws. Lil had sussed this out from the start of the marriage but she had swallowed on it for the sake of her grandchildren.

Grinding out the stub of her cigarette, she slipped the brown-stained saucer out of sight. Then she opened the kitchen window, wafting the smoke away with her hands. She steadied her nerves by taking a last look in the rectangular mirror above the sink. Licking the tip of her little finger, she smoothed it carefully over her black-pencilled eyebrows. Her make-up was decent enough, but the crows' feet around her eyes were beginning to annoy her. They were sly little perishers and turned overnight from laughter lines into ditches. Adding one more coat of lipstick, she smiled at her reflection.

Today marked a second chance for her family. The opportunity was even more precious after loosing the boys. Her two dead sons were unreachable; even their remains lay buried on foreign soil. But she still had Ethel and Callum. She had loved the little boy from the off. He was a gift from heaven in her view. It was unfortunate that it had taken the breaking of Ethel's marriage vows to bring his existence about. But you couldn't have everything. And right this minute she had enough – except Rosie and Timothy, of course. In time they would see the error of their ways. And she and Doug would be ready to welcome them with open arms.

Resolving not to waste a moment's more thought on Cora plum-in-the-mouth Ryde, she hurried to answer the knock at the front door.

'Well now, you two are a sight for sore eyes,' Lil gushed as she narrowed her dark eyes at her daughter and the baby in her arms. It was a struggle at first to keep the smile on her face. For Ethel looked – what were the words she was looking for? Defeated. Detached. Not of this world. And it scared Lil half to death. She had imagined that, at the prospect of returning to Langley Street, Ethel would miraculously spring to life.

But her daughter's once beautiful blonde hair was lank, without even the slightest wave. When Ethel was a kid, Lil had twisted it around her finger to make it curl. Like the little kids from the Ovaltineys advertisements.

And what had Ethel done to her figure? Talk about bag of bones! Had Lizzie not been feeding her? Well, of course she had, Lil answered herself immediately. Next to her own high standards, Lizzie's cooking came a close second. Was Ethel ill?

Lil smothered a wave of fear. If her daughter turned sideways, she'd be invisible!

'Come in, come in,' Lil invited eagerly. 'Leave that bag there, Lizzie. Doug will fetch it upstairs when he comes back with the newspaper. Now sit yourselves in the front room by the fire. Kettle's on the boil.'

Lil knew she was rabbiting but her nerves made her do it. All she wanted was to throw her arms around Ethel and hug the life out of her. She couldn't wait to hold her grandson. But Lizzie had warned her that Ethel would need patience and Lil had taken the hint. Though it was all she could do not to snatch the little boy to her breast.

'Something smells good,' Lizzie said brightly. Too brightly for Lil's liking, but she appreciated the effort.

'Thanks, love. We've got plum pudding for dinner as it's near to Christmas. It's the cinnamon you can smell. Used to be Ethel's favourite.'

She watched her daughter's unresponsive face and for the first time since Ethel had returned from Lewisham, Lil was beset not by anger but by a deep concern for her daughter's sanity. Lil had put the detachment down to having a baby. Lack of sleep could play havoc on the nerves. But now she could see there was more to the problem than that.

She gently touched Ethel's shoulder. But Ethel felt so rigid that Lil snatched her hand back. 'Lovely to have you home, ducks,' she said emotionally, trying to hide the catch in her voice. 'I've sorted out your room. Dad got hold of a lovely cot for Callum. Don't take up much space at all. We went up to Cox Street market and chose some decent nappies, a few woolly tops and some nice rompers. All a bit big but he'll soon grow into them. I know Lizzie let you borrow Polly's things, but there's plenty of choice in the chest of drawers upstairs.'

Once again Lil looked into her daughter's vacant eyes. The feeling of dread returned. There was nothing in Ethel's expression that she recognized. As if her girl, her beloved Ethel, had shrunk away from reach, leaving an outer shell.

'Shall I make a cuppa?' Lizzie asked as the kettle whistled in the kitchen.

Lil would normally have replied in the affirmative, but today she had to escape. She needed to pull herself together. Stop the shakes from taking over. She would have a quick fag and regroup, then return with the tea and a smile plastered on her face.

'No that's all right, love, I'll do it. Go in the front room with Ethel and have a chat.'

Tears were in her eyes as she hurried to the kitchen. That wasn't her Ethel that just walked in the door and the prospect terrified her. If only Doug would come in. He could always achieve miracles where Ethel was involved.

And Lil desperately needed a miracle now.

CHAPTER 18

WHILE HER SON, Nelson Stanley Miller, was taking a nap upstairs, Flo Miller was waiting anxiously to greet her sister. She hadn't seen Lizzie for the best part of three months and had been robbed of the opportunity to show off Nelson. Their brother Bert had dropped by with armfuls of fruit and veg. But when push came to shove, it was Lizzie she needed to see in person.

What would she think of Nelson? He was growing fast. A lovely little toddler with a cap of shining brown hair, as straight as a dye. The dark eyelashes over his huge brown eyes were the replicas of hers but he had Syd's build; stocky and powerful. Though he had plenty of puppy fat, he was agile and loved to be chased around the house. He was the light of their lives, of her in-laws, too.

She had been wary of the Miller's involvement at first because of their notorious reputation. Even Syd had kept his distance while they were courting. But since Nelson's birth, they had turned out trumps.

In view of their generous spirit and Syd's new job at the Miller's scrapyard, Flo had revised her opinion of the

Hoxton-bred family. It was true; the men had spent a good deal of time on their holidays. But she now believed Syd when he said their hearts were in the right place.

Syd's mother was known as the Missus and considered the head of the household. Syd's father, when not sleeping off the drink, spent most of his time at the tracks, drinking, smoking and generally enjoying an alcohol-fuelled haze. He reckoned he was quite an authority on racing anything with four moving legs. But he lost more money on his delusional fancies than he won. His family deliberately encouraged his mistaken belief in order to keep him out of their way.

The Missus loved her family with a passion. But Nelson was picking up bad habits, frequently using, 'arse', 'tits-up' and 'fanny' for starters. Not that anyone could understand his baby talk, but Flo knew that this was only the beginning.

Now as she looked from the kitchen window to the wooden half-fence in the backyard that Syd had erected complete with a gate leading to Lil's, Flo was proud of her husband's handiwork. The new timber was a vast improvement on the days when she had lived here as a child in this very house. She remembered clambering across the piles of trodden-down splintered wood that was the only barrier to Lil's yard.

That was the way of the East End in those days. Families grew up with nothing and expected nothing in return. It was share and share alike in Langley Street. No one had more than the other and the Sharpes and the Allens were no exception. As the oldest Allen girl, Lizzie had tried to support the family after their parents' deaths. And Flo loved her sister deeply for her efforts. But the rift had come when Babs and Vinnie had rebelled. And of course, when Frank the nutter had arrived on the scene. Or rather now, the reformed nutter – though Flo had reservations on that score. For all his supposed reversals, he was still not a man to be trusted, nor ever would be.

Not like her Syd who was salt of the earth. They were friends as well as mates. Syd had assured her that he would keep to the straight and narrow no matter what the temptation. And she believed him. The scrapyard had done well for them and his brothers had kept their promise to shield their young brother from trouble. There was money in scrap. It was a dirty trade but lucrative. What worried Flo most was the scandalous gossip about the Miller family.

Flo sighed deeply as she reflected on the current state of the Miller's domestic affairs. The Missus had assured her, that even if Syd had his collar felt, doing time often made a man of a boy. Well, that was of no comfort at all to Flo. Thereby she had warned the Missus that should her husband ever be put in harm's way, she would end their association forthwith. The Missus had swallowed on that, pointing out that her son, who had once been a lowly fish porter, had brought more to the table in six months than he had in the previous six years.

This fact was not to be argued with, Flo had decided. The Miller boys saw to it that their wives and children were always looked after. The Missus never went short as Flo had observed firsthand, since Nelson Stanley was often the beneficiary.

Thanks to the family, they now had a nice home. It was redecorated throughout in colours of her choice and furnished to her taste. Syd drove a motor car that was the envy of the street. All her clothes were either shop bought or made by herself on a brand-new Singer sewing machine from quality cloth. Nelson had the best in baby wear; not a stitch was secondhand. She had risen above the poverty of her childhood, thanks to the Millers.

Flo's heart leapt as she heard Lil's strident voice echoing

from next door. She peeped through the kitchen window. Lizzie was making her way through the yard gate. Her glossy black hair was pinned to the top of her head. Her simple, tailored suit sculpted her neat figure perfectly, giving her an air of authority.

Flo braced herself for the meeting; she always felt she had to defend her corner where Syd and the Millers were concerned.

Which was why, Flo reflected anxiously, she would have preferred to enjoy this rare occasion together without having to deliver some news that would not be easy for Lizzie to hear.

CHAPTER 19

'HELLO STRANGER. To what do I owe this honour?'

At the sound of her sister's welcome, Lizzie held out her arms. She drew Flo into a warm embrace, remembering as always, the days of their childhood. Despite the family squabbles, Flo was her baby sister and always would be.

To Lizzie she still looked like a young girl of fourteen. Flo wore her straight fringe and short, dark hair in a Dutch bob made famous by the exotic film star of the 1920's, Louise Brookes. As a teenager Flo had been determined to pursue both Syd Miller and her love of the cinema. She had won Syd's heart immediately and kept her sweetheart on the straight and narrow. Now a little more rounded after Nelson's birth, Flo's appearance had changed very little. Lizzie always marvelled at the fact that Flo still lived under the same roof that had been home to the Allens for as long as she could remember.

Lizzie smiled as Flo nodded to the kitchen table. 'Did Lil tell you I was calling today?'

Flo nodded, pulling out the chairs from under the table. 'So Ethel has come home after all?'

'Well, you could say that I suppose.'

'Poor cow,' Flo sympathised as they made themselves comfortable. 'But she's got her little boy. I can't wait to see him. Nelson's going to have a playmate at last. There's not many kids round here of his age. They're mostly all at school.'

Lizzie looked across to the stove. 'Do I get a cup of tea?'

'I would have thought you'd had enough in Lil's with all the gassing you two do.'

Lizzie laughed. 'As a matter of fact, you're right. I was wondering how many more cups I could drink. Lil was so anxious she was making tea every five minutes.'

'She's a bag of nerves,' Flo agreed. 'Every time she came back from your place after seeing Ethel, she was either on cloud nine or so down in the dumps that she polished off more port wine than monks in a monastery.' Flo chucked at her own joke. 'I don't know how Doug has coped. He loves both the women in his life and yet Lil and Ethel have always been opposites. The poor bloke has always had to referee. If his two boys had survived the war, it would have been different. The women would have sided against the men.'

'If Neil and Greg had lived,' Lizzie agreed wistfully, 'Lil would be a different person. After they went she was so scared of losing Ethel, she never let her out of her sight. Our mum was the one who helped Doug pull Lil through her depression. That's what made them such good mates.'

'Yes, but Ethel got the backlash,' Flo replied with a sniff. 'I always reckoned she married Richard to escape. He was her route to the big wide world.'

'And look how that turned out.'

'If Lil hadn't kept her on such a short leash - '

'But who can blame Lil?' Lizzie puzzled. 'The war took her two boys and it very nearly took her.'

They sat quietly reflecting for a few minutes. Lizzie looked admiringly around the kitchen. 'You've done this place up really nice, Flo.' She ran her hands over the varnished wooden table that had replaced its worm-eaten predecessor.

'I couldn't throw away Ma's old table,' Flo said, following her gaze. 'I use it for me sewing in the front room. Every time I sit there I think of how she'd sit sewing until the early hours, trying to make a few bob. With Pa the way he was, no legs and all, she must've wondered where the next penny was coming from.'

'She hated me pushing Pa to market,' Lizzie agreed. 'It was like asking for charity in her eyes.'

'She was proud, was Ma.'

Lizzie thought of the many hours she'd spent helping her mother in this kitchen; Kate Allen had always provided a daily hot meal, though God alone knew how she did it on the pittance their father brought in. Confined to a wheelchair, their father's only means of earning a living was selling souvenirs and in Kate's eyes that was begging. They had lived each day from hand to mouth and no one had suffered the humiliation more than their mother.

'If you're wondering where Ma's old rocking chair has gone, it's in the nursery.' Flo's voice broke slightly. 'So I had Syd put it by the crib.'

'Just where it should be,' Lizzie murmured. 'You can sit in it and tell him stories, just like I did with you. Remember them nights when you wouldn't sleep?'

Flo's face softened. 'They was the good old days, Lizzie.'

'There are some better ones to come,' Lizzie said with genuine feeling. 'Nelson will grow up without the prospect of war.'

'Don't know about that,' Flo said doubtfully. 'There are some scare stories circulating. That Nazi Adolf Hitler, announced himself as the head of Germany. Churchill warns we could be attacked.'

'That's just rumour.'

'It says so in the newspapers.'

'Don't read them for all the bad things they say. We've got enough trouble in the here and now without worrying about what's to happen in the future. Now, when can I see my nephew? I want to give him a hug.'

'He'll be awake soon,' Flo said with a smirk. 'I told him his Auntie Lizzie was coming – at last.'

'I'm sorry it's been so long.' Lizzie leaned forward to take her sister's small hand. 'I've no excuses, love. But with the bakery and the pub - '

'They're as good excuses as any I suppose.' Flo lifted her chin and shrugged. 'We're all busy these days, myself included.'

'I think of you and Nelson and Syd every day. You're my family, my nearest and dearest. But the shop don't run itself. And the bakery is only just finding its feet. As for the Mill Wall - '

'As for your pub,' Flo interrupted cuttingly, 'I suppose you know what you're doing, trying to turn a pig's ear in a silk purse. But I wouldn't mind betting that good-for-nothing husband of yours has already lumped you with trouble.'

Lizzie's expression hardened but she kept silent, aware that Flo was eager to express her irritation.

'Why for God's sake, don't you get rid of him, Lizzie? He's a bloody pariah. He'll drag you and the Mill Wall down with him. Frank will never change even if he swears his own life on it. Which I'm sure he's done many times over.'

Lizzie sighed softly, withdrawing her hand. 'It ain't a question of winning or losing. You know why he's in my life, Flo.'

'Because of Polly,' Flo stated flatly as if she had heard the excuse many times over. 'Well, for what it's worth, I believe you've persuaded yourself that Polly needs him. But she's got you and that's enough.'

'If Pol was to remain a child, I would agree with you,' Lizzie replied carefully. 'But she's growing up fast. Soon she will have to know the truth. Do I tell her that Frank, the uncle she has grown to love, is her father? Or do I say that Frank is the madman who once blew up me shop and did the dirty on me with her mother?'

'Our Babs had a choice,' Flo protested. 'She could have refused Frank. Instead she opened her legs for him.'

'And you recommend I tell Polly that?' Lizzie said in an astonished tone. 'When I've spent all these years encouraging her to believe in the goodness of her family.'

'I respect you for that, I do,' insisted Flo. 'But when it comes to families, you are quick enough to condemn my Syd and the Millers. Even though they've not put a foot wrong in my case.'

'Why should they?' Lizzie questioned. 'You are a beautiful and honest addition to their ranks, together with a grandson for the Missus. And I haven't condemned Syd, not at all. We've had our differences in the past, but they are outweighed by the happiness he's brought you.'

'I hope you remember that.'

'Why shouldn't I?'

'Because of Frank bloody Flowers always getting 'round you, that's why!' exclaimed Flo passionately.

Lizzie closed her eyes briefly. 'Listen Flo, Frank took a beating from Syd's brothers, Walter and Clifford. It was two against one and the odds were weighted against Frank. I don't doubt he deserved the hiding, but it was what they did afterwards that upset me. Walter stole Frank's watch, a family heirloom. I saw him wearing it.'

'Syd didn't know, I swear.'

'Which was why I asked Syd to stay out of my domestic upheavals.'

'You know what Syd is,' Flo defended. 'He's protective. Don't forget I have been witness to Frank's character since I was a kid. I had to watch my big sister being hoodwinked, swindled and abused. He stole you from Danny and made you his wife under false pretences. He tried to get me an' all, but I sussed him out from the very beginning when I had scarlet fever and was put in the isolation hospital. He was round you like a swarm of bees after honey. But I could see he was up to no good. I prayed you'd never fall for his lies. I told God I'd rather die of the fever than see you wed to Frank.'

'In which case, I'm glad God didn't listen,' Lizzie tried to joke.

'And you're still defending him to this day,' Flo continued, her pale cheeks glowing red as she spoke. 'I don't blame Danny one bit for going with another woman.'

Lizzie stared at her sister. 'What did you say?'

Flo's face fell. She looked down and twisted her fingers.

'Come on, Flo. Out with it.'

'Me and my big mouth. My feelings always get the better of me when I think of Frank.'

'I want to know about Danny, not Frank. What do you mean, another woman?'

Flo looked up from under her long, dark lashes. 'It's April Williams.'

'Danny's landlady? What about her?'

Flo paused, waiting for her meaning to sink in. 'I saw Danny in his car down by Island Gardens. He stopped and we sat on a bench for a while. Me with the pram. Him all done up in a bloomin' great coat that must have cost a fortune.'

'What did you talk about?'

'He wanted to know how things were.'

'What things?'

'You, of course.'

'What did you tell him?'

'The truth. I said I hadn't seen you in three months. And that if he wanted to know more he should go to the shop and ask you, personal like.' Flo straightened her shoulders indignantly. 'Course, I had to say about the pub and Frank. That in my humble opinion hell would freeze over before you dumped him.'

'Flo, how could you!'

'It's true, ain't it? Added to which, Frank sees Polly on a regular basis now. And that means he sees you. If you really wanted to be rid of him, you'd have given him the old heave-ho long ago.'

Lizzie tried to hide her annoyance. She knew that Flo would have said exactly this to Danny, embellished with more of her own opinion.

'I asked him if he liked flogging posh cars,' Flo went on. 'I have to say, Danny looks the part - '

'Flo, what's this all got to do with April Williams?' Lizzie interrupted.

Her sister let out a long sigh. 'He kept dropping her name into the conversation. April this. April that.'

'Was that all?'

'Why don't you tell him you're divorcing Frank?'

Lizzie stared at her sister. 'Because I'm not.'

Flo shook her head in frustration. 'Well you should. After Chancel Lane and what Savage did to you and Danny, he deserves to be part of your life. He's a good man, Lizzie.'

'I know that, Flo.'

'I'm just saying, if you're not careful, you'll lose him. Danny said they were moving from Terrace Street in Poplar to Euston.'

'What, *all* of them?'

Flo nodded. 'Course, she'd expect a ring on her finger first.'

'Is that what Danny told you?'

Flo rolled her eyes. 'Not in so many words. But it was a bloody big hint.'

Lizzie fell silent as she thought of the cross words that she and Danny had shared at their last meeting. It was not April Williams they had argued over, or Frank, but her refusal to leave the island. Now it seemed, if Flo wasn't exaggerating, there had been another reason for Danny to make changes.

She could still hear his voice; 'I want a peaceful life, Lizzie,' he'd told her. 'Savage almost destroyed us.'

'But he's dead,' she'd argued confidently. 'We did it, Danny. You and me together. We fought for what was ours. And won.'

He'd looked sadly at her with his lovely blue eyes. 'Come with me, Lizzie. We deserve a new start.'

'Maybe,' she'd answered quietly. 'But Ebondale Street is my home. Your dad loved the shop. He worked hard to make it the success it is. There's never a day goes by that I'm not grateful for the good living its provided me with.'

'Then stay if you must,' he'd replied with such conviction her heart had sunk to her boots. 'But it's the end of the road for me. I'm asking you one last time. If it's a yes, we'll find a nice gaff together in the city. Live the life that's due to us. Bugger Frank and you still being married. That don't count. What's a piece of paper, after all? We'll be a real family and Tom and Pol will grow up decent, not chancers or street kids living on their wits like we did.'

But Danny had seen the refusal in her eyes. Though in her heart she had always believed that somehow, they would come together again.

'Nelson's crying,' Flo said and Lizzie came out of her thoughts.

She held her sister's hand once more. They might have their differences but Lizzie knew that, as the eldest, she had to be the one to make up.

She hid her hurt over Danny and swallowed, hugging her sister close.

CHAPTER 20

DANNY DROVE the car through the imposing iron gates and along the driveway that led to St Augustine's Boarding School for Boys. Either side, the mowed lawns were like velvet, bordered by neat copses of trees and playing fields. He was impressed. The huge red-brick building set in acres of countryside looked more like a stately home than a school. In spite of his reluctance to agree to a visit, his eyes were riveted to the scene.

Two hours driving had brought them north of London. For this appointment with the school Head, he had brought the Singer Sports Tourer. The rare day out was a treat for April and he liked to see her excitement. Of late, Tom had been difficult. Although his son's nature was a happy one, he had become withdrawn and often a little rude. Though Danny had no complaint with the teachers at Ebondale Street, April had suggested St Augustine's. After all, Danny reflected, he now had the money to give Tom a sound education.

'It's beautiful here, don't you think?' said April who sat

beside him. 'Just look at the architecture. Edith was right. It's a very fine school indeed.'

Danny pulled on the brake and nodded. 'Yes, it is.'

'Mr Herbert will meet us in the reception hall.'

Danny climbed out of the car and walked with April up the wide steps that led up to the entrance. The heavy oak doors were decorated with a coat of arms, and once inside, an official-looking person in a grey suit greeted them.

'Mr Flowers, Mrs Williams?'

'Yes,' said April shyly from under the brim of her hat. 'You must be the headmaster, Mr Herbert?'

'Indeed. How was your journey?'

'Very good,' said Danny pleasantly.

'Right, onwards and upwards,' said Mr Herbert, leading the way through wood-panelled corridors to the cloistered passages. 'First, a round trip. Then a little refreshment. The school was built in the early 1800s to accommodate two hundred children, but now we have three hundred on the register – and growing!'

Danny fell behind, listening with one ear, as they were shown through the many rooms; formidable-looking classrooms with polished desks and just as polished boys. Then, smaller rooms, the science laboratory, storerooms full of powdered inks, pencils, pens, nibs and books. Next, a common room at the end of a stone-flagged hallway, a dining room filled with tables and benches and the music room, complete with piano and organ. Marching on for what seemed an eternity, they ascended a wide staircase, passing the lines of pupils as they scattered down the stairs, and on to the dormitories, where Danny paused for a moment, imagining his boy in one of the many austere grey-blanketed beds, as neat and tidy as if their mothers had made them.

Then back again, this time to tread over the lawns to visit

Matron and Nurse to view the sick and injured. Danny smiled at the young patients, with their striped pyjamas and pale faces. He indulged Matron by complimenting the wholesome atmosphere. But that was not what was really in his heart. How would Tom ever cope in such a place? They had never been parted and Danny had never thought he would be considering such an option. But was April right? Did a boy need this kind of education that only wealth and affluence could offer?

He gazed through the tall windows to the fields, to the boys on the playing fields beyond. Tom would be given a head start in life. He would benefit in the long run. And yet …

'Come along,' said Mr Herbert, tapping his arm. 'Just the gymnasium now.' He turned, raising his eyebrows to April. 'I hope so far, you've enjoyed what you've seen?'

April took a little gasp of breath. 'Everything,' she said, 'is just perfect.'

They returned to the ground floor and Danny braced himself. He could smell the ancient mustiness, the polish and the scrubbed wooden floors over which the uniformed boys were hurrying.

He pictured Tom amongst them, wearing his long grey trousers and boater. He tried to imagine his son growing into the routine of this prestigious boarding school. But the picture escaped him.

'Oh, Danny, what do you think?' April squeezed her hands tightly together as, two hours later, Danny sped them along the drive and the through the big iron gate. 'Tom would love it here, don't you agree?'

'A big change though, for the lad.' Danny concentrated on the road. He wanted to think, not talk, but April was overjoyed.

'Each morning and evening, the boys sing hymns and psalms,' said April in raptures. 'And did you see those beautiful classrooms? So many teachers and staff. Even maids and housekeepers! Edith told me to expect a surprise, but really, what more could we want for Tom?'

Danny was aware that April did not need an answer. She sat with a dreamy smile on her face. 'Such beautifully tended lawns and fields where the boys play rugby and hockey. And did you hear what Mr Herbert said about Sunday breakfast? Not just cereals but bacon! I should never have dreamt it was possible.'

'I suppose - ' began Danny hesitantly.

'Hot and cold showers,' continued April excitedly. 'A pretty walk through the village to church – plenty of things to see and do. Seven weeks holiday in summer, three weeks at Easter and Christmas - time for Tom to come home and be with us. Oh Daniel, I do hope you see the sense of it.'

'Tom's never been away from home before,' he protested. 'After his mother and father died in Aussie, I promised him we'd never be parted. They were good friends of mine you see, and I owe them.'

'What better way to keep your promise?' April replied. 'An education that will give him the key to many doors in society. I'm sure his parents would approve.'

Danny smiled as April clasped his arm eagerly. Her face turned up to him and he nodded. 'Perhaps you're right. I'll give it all some thought.'

'Oh, do, please do. Edith says they have never looked back since sending Ralph there.'

Danny's smile faded. He hadn't thought much of the pompous twelve-year-old who had scowled his way through dinner at the Murdoch's. He'd felt Tom's dismay and Danny's heart had clenched. He wanted to do what was right for his son. There was the question of marriage, too.

A matter he must soon resolve.

CHAPTER 21

IT WAS A COLD, crisp day in December when Lizzie drove from the East End to Gerrard Street in Soho. Her meeting with Murphy was arranged on neutral territory. They were both to arrive unaccompanied.

Bert had objected fiercely to this news, citing all manner of danger. Her brother meant well, she knew, but he had been like her shadow after the confrontation with Vella. She only had to turn and there he was. His huge body loomed over her, narrowing his eyes at the six square feet either side of her, as if the space contained an invisible enemy.

Today she needed no distractions. Bert's presence would only hinder; it had taken a great deal of Lizzie's resolve to refuse her brother's well-intentioned but unnecessary company. If there was one person she knew she could trust, it was Murphy.

Parking the Wolseley close by and pressing her fox fur collar up to her chin to keep out the cold, Lizzie made her way through the bustling streets of Soho. She had dressed accordingly; a small, smart beige hat under which she had pinned her hair, lowering the brim across her forehead and wearing a discreet set of pearls around her neck. Her steps were slow but assured as she made her way to the market and the Blue Posts public house where she expected to find Murphy.

The street darkened as she walked under the canopy of awnings and canvas that stretched across its narrow perimeters. Shopkeepers displayed their wares on the pavements, interspersed with the wares of the market traders. Busy crowds milled beneath, making a dense sea of bobbing heads, cloth caps, trilby hats, scarves and permanently waved hairstyles. The working women loitered, flaunting their painted faces, red-stained lips and encouraging smiles. The new bakeries – fancily called patisseries – abounded. Delicious smells followed her as she paused at the stalls. Customers elbowed each other, inspecting the cheap fabrics; row upon row of skirts, suits, jackets, trousers, blouses as far as the eye could see.

Across from the market stood the Blue Posts, a three-storey tavern gracing the busy street. As she entered, the punters were lined up at the bar, drinking in a well-behaved manner. City gents and tradesmen alike enjoying the warm hospitality. The interior had an old-world glow. There was not a dirty glass in sight.

She felt a light touch on her arm. 'Lizzie?'

There stood Murphy and her stomach clenched. For it was Leonard Savage – unfairly – whom she recalled whenever she set eyes on the Irishman. That night at the Chancel Lane hostelry when, had it not been for the man standing by her now, she would almost certainly have taken her last breath.

'Ah sure, Lizzie, 'tis good to see you,' he said with a broad smile, his Irish accent as beguiling as ever.

He took her gloved hand, drawing her close, to press a kiss to her cheek. She shivered. What was it that so disturbed her about this man, she wondered? For Murphy was not overbearing or intimidating, though he walked with an assured stride. He was lean and straight-backed with short-cropped brown hair and the leather waistcoat he wore was his trademark. His gaze was steady and confident; a confidence that she knew was perfectly justified.

'Likewise, Murphy,' she replied warmly.

'Come along, I've saved us a table.' He escorted her to the rear of the busy room where it was quieter. The semi-circle of polished walnut chairs and tables were set against the gold and green wallpaper that gave the place a comfortable elegance. Murphy asked her what she would like to drink and she ordered her customary port, her eyes following his agile figure as he joined the other punters at the bar.

Her first thought was that Murphy had chosen their meeting place wisely. The pleasant buzz of voices was kept to a minimum without rowdy interruption. Every table's surface was freshly wiped, enhancing the reflection of the polished wood under the tall windows.

Briefly she thought of the Mill Wall, a disappointing contrast to the Blue Posts. What effort would it have cost Frank to clean its interior? Or, at the very least, to have ejected the unsavoury sorts that had seemed quite at home in her snug.

She put the annoyance aside as Murphy returned with their drinks; a dainty glass of port for her and a tankard of ale for himself.

Easing himself into the cushioned seat beside her, he raised an amused eyebrow. 'So, Lizzie, this is a rare treat. We meet in favourable circumstances for once!' His handsome grin broadened. 'Your runner was most keen to get our date set.'

'Whippet's a decent lad,' she replied with a smile. 'I hope he minded his manners?'

'Oh, that he did,' Murphy assured her. 'My guess is the boy will be a fine addition to your ranks, given time.'

Lizzie gazed steadily into the Irishman's brown eyes. 'Time is what I don't have Murphy.'

'Ah, 'tis a common complaint affecting the population at large, I fear. The grey hairs and aching bones beset us mercilessly, though you Lizzie, have escaped such ravages and look even more beautiful than when we last met.'

Lizzie felt a stir of affection, for their previous meeting had been a happy one. Their rendezvous had been on the banks of the Thames on a fine summer's day almost six months before. They had strolled the embankment and eaten from a fish stall and talked of their lives since Chancel Lane. Of how Murphy now ran a legitimate business, or so he insisted, providing his fellow countrymen with employment in the security services.

As for herself, she had been about to take on the Mill Wall. Murphy had expressed his concerns but had not pressed the subject. They had enjoyed the day and indeed the evening together, parting closer friends than ever before.

'You're still as charming as ever yourself,' she teased, for neither of them had sought each other out since that day. 'But it's not your silver tongue or your wit that I'd value right now. It's more in the way of advice.'

He nodded slowly as if reading her thoughts.

'After last year, I'd hoped things might be easier,' she continued. 'For a while at least.'

'But you took down one of the biggest London faces,' he answered unsympathetically. 'Leonard Savage was no easy conquest. It was inevitable that others should fill his shoes.'

'If I took Savage down,' Lizzie retaliated, 'it was only with your help.'

A cold darkness filled the Irishman's gaze. 'When I first came to London that cold-blooded eejit robbed me of my hostelry. He stole my livelihood and murdered my friends. He would have despatched me if I hadn't escaped by the skin of my teeth.'

'He also made you into the successful businessman you are today,' Lizzie reminded him kindly.

He raised his tankard towards her. 'And you, Lizzie Flowers, into the woman you are now.'

Lizzie nodded with a brief smile. 'However, I owe you, Murphy. Don't think I've forgotten the debt.'

'Ah, 'tis endearing to hear it, Lizzie. But the transaction benefits me too. A deed, good or bad, is always returned by fate. We are now allies – and close friends.' Briefly his eyes twinkled. 'Now, in that state of rare grace, let us address your current problem. You have trouble with your recent acquisition, the Mill Wall?'

'How did you know?' she asked in surprise.

'I warned you the liquor trade would not be easy. The Mill Wall has a chequered history. A publican's role does not come easy.'

Lizzie knew full well that Murphy's story was a cautionary one. Like her, he had worked hard to make a success of his Chancel Lane tavern. And then the day had arrived when Leonard Savage had made his appearance. Murphy had refused to pay him his so-called protection money and Savage had taken his revenge. Not so far different from the night when Savage had lured her own kith and kin into a trap, intending to do away with the Flowers family forever.

'I may have taken your advice, Murphy,' she responded softly, 'but may I remind you that even a woman can think on her feet.'

'I have no doubt of that. But I've had the luck of the Irish with me,' he told her lightly, 'an advantage I can highly recommend – if you should be of a mind.'

She felt the colour rise in her cheeks. 'Is that so? Then I should be proud to share it.'

For a moment they held each other's eyes and Lizzie knew this rough, tough Irishman would never disappoint her.

'So, tell me,' he whispered at last, 'is it my soldiers you need?'

Lizzie posed her question carefully. 'I have made myself an enemy, Murphy. His name is Salvo Vella.'

Murphy stared at her incredulously. '*The Prince?*' he breathed, drawing away.

'Is he royalty then?' Lizzie asked in surprise.

'Only to his subjects,' Murphy replied disdainfully. 'The man is pure mischief; a leprechaun, a master at disguise. The women he runs would die for him, such is his charm. He is as lethal as the blade he is known for carrying in his belt and would have no hesitation to use on an adversary's throat.'

'Where does he come from? Who is he?'

Murphy's eyes narrowed. 'They say he is impossible to trace. A nomad. A shape-shifting gypsy who sets up camp in any unsuspecting hamlet on which he then leaves his mark. His whores frequent the taverns, his thieves and pickpockets work the streets and his cutthroats hide in the dregs of society where even the law refuses to venture.'

Lizzie took a long breath. 'But someone must know who he is.'

Murphy's smile was without humour. 'If there is such a person, they will not survive very long.'

Lizzie felt her heart race at the thought of how close she had come to disaster. 'So that's why he believes the Mill Wall belongs to him?'

'Is that what he told you?'

Lizzie nodded. 'As he held a knife to my throat.'

Murphy's face fell. 'Lizzie, 'tis not good news you bring

today.' He looked deeply into her eyes. 'This is not the place to discuss him, for he has spies in all directions.' He grasped his tankard and emptied it, his gaze quickly surveying the room. 'Come, Lizzie. Take my arm. Act as though we are lovers, enjoying our tryst. Which for me, is no great effort,' he teased, though his smile was fleeting.

Lizzie had barely touched her port; she had no desire for it now. Doing as he instructed, they left the Blue Posts and disappeared into the crowds of Soho.

CHAPTER 22

LIZZIE WATCHED Murphy and her brother carefully as they greeted one another in the shop. The smaller, leaner man held out his hand. 'Sure, it's good to see you again, Bert.'

'Likewise,' her brother acknowledged, returning the Irishman's warm greeting. 'What brings you to these parts, Murphy? Don't they keep you busy enough on the other side of the water?'

'Ah, too busy, in fact Bert.' Murphy grinned. 'Like yourself I suspect.'

'I thought you was meeting in Soho.'

'We've news to share, Bert,' Lizzie replied, eager to get down to business. 'Close the shop. Our customers will have to wait.'

Reluctantly her brother turned the sign on the door. Upstairs they seated themselves by the fire. 'Salvo Vella is known by his women as *The Prince*,' Murphy explained to Bert. 'He boasts blue blood. But he is no more royal than you or I. No one is sure who he is or where he comes from. It is thought his family - a band of circus performers - travelled from Europe, bringing their horses and whores with them.

But Vella's interests soon turned to more lucrative business. The mask has never left his face and it's rumoured he revels in his disguises. An arrogant actor of many parts, he will stop at nothing to get what he wants.'

Bert's heavy brow creased in a frown. 'I ain't heard of him down our way before.'

'But you have never run a tavern before,' said Murphy shortly.

'But surely the brewery would have turned him out,' Lizzie protested.

'Not at all. It would be like trying to rid the sewers of rats.'

'Which is why we got the lease cheap,' Bert muttered and Murphy nodded.

'Frank said he hasn't seen Vella before,' Lizzie said in confusion.

'Why should he?' Murphy expounded. 'If your manager had left the women to their business, Vella would not have made an appearance.'

'Hah!' snorted Bert. 'A coward, then!'

Murphy shook his head slowly. 'For all his vices, he is not.'

'So, what do we do?' Lizzie was anxious to find a solution.

'How many men have you?' asked Murphy after a moment's thought.

'Not even a handful,' Bert admitted. 'Elmo and Fowler and meself.'

Murphy glanced at Lizzie. 'And that man of yours, Danny Flowers. Can we count on him?'

Lizzie shook her head sadly. 'No, Murphy. Not this time.'

'It was Savage that done for Danny,' Bert interrupted. 'He got shot of his land at Chalk Wharf and pulled in a big earner. Soon after he moved up to Euston and out of trouble. 'The Euston Showrooms' he calls himself and doing trade with gents now.'

Murphy's face showed surprise. 'Euston indeed?' he

remarked, throwing up an eyebrow. 'Ah, so, I wish him luck. But trouble follows trouble as if waving hands were beckoning it! There's not a villain in the Smoke who doesn't know that Leonard Savage met his end by a Flowers. Danny is fair game now. He has a reputation, as you do, Lizzie.'

'There must be a way we can stop this chancer,' Bert said in confusion.

'Think back to the hostelry,' Murphy advised. 'Don't make the same mistake. You were outnumbered three to one there. You and Danny were disadvantaged from the off. So now, calculate! Have your soldiers ready, expecting attack. But I warn you, they will draw Vella's wrath.'

'When will he come?' asked Lizzie quietly.

Murphy sat back and lifted his palms. 'Maybe not this week. Or in six months. Or even a year. But come for sure he will.'

Lizzie felt a chill run through her. Could Salvo Vella really be as dangerous as Murphy insisted?

'I'll hire all the soldiers you have free,' she agreed. 'As many as you think fit.'

'They will be armed,' he warned her. 'A man cannot defend himself or his investment without a weapon.'

Lizzie fell silent at the thought. Weapons were not a prospect she cherished. Yet there was no choice if she wanted to fight *The Prince.* Without Danny by her side, it was only Murphy's men who could help her.

CHAPTER 23

IT WAS Christmas morning and Lizzie was stringing Polly's homemade paper chains across the front room. Despite the chilly day outside, the fire was roaring and filled the upper rooms above the shop with a hazy glow.

Lizzie awaited Polly who had gone to change into her new frock. Bert, was still down in the airey - his basement quarters below the shop. He was recovering from his late night at the tavern. Trade at the Mill Wall had passed peacefully enough and Lizzie had been tempted to return Murphy's men in the new year. Bert was more cautious. 'We'll do as Murphy suggests,' he had persuaded her. 'Let's see how it goes.'

'Perhaps Vella has given up,' Lizzie had suggested. 'And has other fish to fry.'

But Bert had shaken his head. 'No sense in taking chances. We'll keep two blokes on here at the shop. Put the other four with Frank.'

'It's six more wages to pay.'

'Every penny is worth it.' Her brother had not forgotten

the moment that Vella had held a knife to her throat. And if she was honest, neither had she.

Now, as she basted the chicken to a golden brown and slipped it back into the oven of the black-leaded range, she was relieved that Christmas Eve had passed without incident. She could enjoy the festivities wholeheartedly. All the vegetables were peeled and steaming. The fruit pudding awaited its dousing in brandy. There was nothing left to do except enjoy their meal in peace.

'Auntie Lizzie, I'm hungry.' Polly appeared, her copper ringlets bouncing on her shoulders. She was wearing her new pink party dress delivered by Father Christmas overnight.

'We'll eat when Uncle Bert arrives.'

'When are we going to Langley Street?'

'Later this afternoon.'

Polly was full of questions. 'Are we having a knees-up at Auntie Lil's?'

'It wouldn't be Christmas without a party.' Lizzie sat down on the settee and opened her arms. 'Come here and give us a cuddle. You look so pretty I could eat you. But I don't want to spoil me dinner.'

Polly fell into her lap, giggling and squirming. Then planting herself amidst the cushions she pointed to a bedraggled shrub that stood in an enamel pot. 'That tree Uncle Bert brought home ain't a real Christmas tree.'

'I know. But real Christmas trees are scarce.'

'Because of the Great Depression,' Polly volunteered with authority. 'Mrs Price said rich people can afford them, though. Ain't we rich, Auntie Lizzie?'

'We are rich in love, monkey, and that's what counts.'

Polly considered this carefully. 'Well, anyway, I got my dress. Father Christmas even knew my size. For a man, he's quite clever.'

Lizzie chuckled. 'Mrs Christmas might have helped him.'

'Or you did!' Polly laughed.

Lizzie laughed too, for she knew that Polly was a very grown-up eight.

'I'll bet Uncle Bert pinched our tree from the park,' Polly said after getting her breath back.

'I wouldn't be surprised.'

'It ain't got many branches.'

'You found your dress under it, so that's what counts.'

Polly jumped up, the tree quickly forgotten. 'Will we see Uncle Danny and Tom at Auntie Lil's?'

'I don't know, Pol.'

'I want Tom to see my new dress.'

'I'm sure Nelson and Callum will like it.'

'They're just babies!' Polly protested. 'Rosie and Timothy won't be coming neither. Auntie Lizzie, why don't my mum ever visit? I don't even remember what she looks like. I bet she'd walk past me in the street.'

'Oh, Pol, don't be upset.'

'She can't love me, I know she can't!'

'Of course she loves you,' Lizzie insisted, taken aback.

'Then why don't she send me a card?' Polly cried.

Lizzie drew Polly close. A torrent of tears and sobs followed. When at last they subsided, Lizzie said softly, 'I love you, monkey.'

'And I love you, Auntie Lizzie.'

'I know you do, Pol and we shall always love each other. But it's only natural you miss your mum. I miss her too.'

'Is she on her adventures?'

'Yes, that's it.'

'I 'spect she'll come home one day.'

'Yes, but for now we just have to trust it's all for the best.'

'That's what Mrs Price says about Jesus. That we have to trust in him.'

'And do you?'

Polly looked into Lizzie's gaze and shrugged. 'I like real people. Ones I can see.'

'That's a very grown-up answer.'

'Uncle Frank said it.' Polly blushed, then gave a giggle. 'But I do say my prayers.' She bounced to her feet, once again her old self. And when Bert appeared, suited and booted, she ran into his open arms.

But Lizzie knew that, although here, in the bosom of the family where there was more than enough love to go round for Polly, a mother's love was what she lacked – if only Babs had been able to provide it.

CHAPTER 24

THE AIR in Lil's front room was thick with cigarette smoke. Lazy clouds of nicotine hung in the air as Lizzie sat watching Polly. Her niece was playing with fourteen-month-old Nelson and Callum, a few months his junior. The children had made their camp under the extended dining table. Polly looked happy now, but Lizzie was concerned by her outburst this morning.

She was a dear little soul. Happy-go-lucky and eager to please. But now it seemed to Lizzie that as Polly grew older, there would be many such questions about her mother to which Polly deserved truthful answers.

'A penny for your thoughts,' a soft voice said in her ear.

'Oh, Ethel! Come and tell me your news.' Lizzie patted the settee. To her left sat Jenny and Madge, in conversation with Lil who, on Christmas Eve had visited the bakery. She had invited them to join the party since everyone now thought of Jenny and Madge as family. Lizzie could hear Madge and Lil discussing their ailments. Jenny was all ears, hoping to hear Bert's name dropped into the conversation.

Ethel nodded to the children. 'As you can see, Callum is spoiled rotten.'

'He's a bonny lad now.'

'Yes, I suppose so.'

Lizzie looked into her friend's eyes. 'You aren't still worried about his chest, are you?'

'No. It's not that.'

'What is it, then?'

'This morning I bumped into Edna Adams across the road. She looked into the pram and slammed her door shut. As if we was spreading the plague.'

'I hope you took no notice.'

'Mum was over there like a shot. Told her what she could do with her opinions. But it does upset me.'

Lizzie saw the hurt in her friend's eyes. 'There will always be tongues that wag.'

'I should have got used to the nudges and winks,' Ethel confessed. 'My baby is a different colour to all the rest, so what can I expect?'

'Have you heard from Rosie and Timothy?'

'A card arrived from Rosie. Didn't say much. Just sent her good wishes.'

'At least it's something.'

'Yes, a few crumbs to keep me happy.' Ethel's blue eyes looked wistful as though she was searching for something she'd lost. Lizzie noticed the dress she wore was rather staid, a dour grey and brown wool that didn't do her fair complexion justice. It was as if Ethel was still in mourning, afraid to let herself go.

'Ethel, have you thought of going to work?' Lizzie suggested. 'I'm sure Lil would look after Callum.'

'But who would have me? I've got no skills.'

'Jenny needs help at the bakery.'

But Ethel shook her head. 'I'd be useless talking to customers.'

'You liked working at Rickards.'

'That was different. I'd known Mr and Mrs Rickard for years.'

'Ethel, it would be good for you to get out and about.'

'Callum's too young to leave yet,' Ethel said at once. 'And Rosie and Timothy might turn up one day. I don't want to miss seeing them.' She quickly stood up. 'Let's help Flo with the food.'

Lizzie followed her friend to the kitchen. It was as if Ethel refused to start living again until Rosie and Timothy appeared. But Lizzie knew that all the wishing and hoping wouldn't bring her children back. Not if they didn't want to come.

'About time, an' all!' Flo scolded as they arrived in the kitchen. Her straight dark fringe was askew and her cheeks red. 'Have you two been at the port?'

Lizzie laughed. 'Chance would be a fine thing.'

Just then, they were joined by Jenny and Madge. 'Can we help?' Jenny asked shyly as she pressed down her pretty green dress. She glanced through the kitchen window, to the backyard where Bert stood smoking with the men.

'No ducks, it's your day off,' Flo insisted. 'Come and join the women of the family. You'll see your man soon enough.'

Jenny went bright red. Lizzie noticed that she had taken great care with her appearance. Her light brown hair was combed softly in waves around her face. She had tied a slim leather belt around her small waist and had replaced her lace-ups with fashionable court shoes.

'How did you manage to escape Mum?' Ethel teased. 'I'm sure she wanted to know all about you and Bert.'

'It's very kind of her to have invited us.' Jenny's gaze flew to the window again. 'Although there's nothing much exciting to tell. I wish there was.'

'Ain't he asked you out yet?' Flo demanded.

'Well, not in as many words. But he did come and pick me and Madge up today in the car. I felt like royalty sitting in the back.'

'Never had a ride in such a grand vehicle before,' said Madge, her gold tooth sparkling under the big smile on her plump face. She elbowed Jenny in the arm. 'I told you to sit in the front and show a bit of knee, but you wouldn't have it!'

Once again Jenny blushed to the roots of her hair. 'I don't even know if Bert likes me.'

There was a chorus of 'oh yes he does' and Jenny was showered in compliments.

'Well, he's only got to ask,' she said shyly.

'The world and his wife want to find Bert a nice little wife, just like you love,' said Lil, puffing away on her cigarette. 'But you might have to give him encouragement.'

'If it was me,' said Madge, with authority, 'I'd cook him a nice steak pie with plenty of veg. We all know he likes his spuds.'

'Luckily, I can make pies in me sleep.' Jenny blushed once more and Lizzie saw her steal another glance at Bert. Her brother did look very handsome as he chain-smoked with Doug and Syd in the cold winter's air.

'Well now, in anticipation of wedding bells, let's drink to the future.' Flo slipped a bottle of gin from a cupboard. 'Syd brought this home from the scrapyard. There's lemonade and sliced fruit on the table. Bung it all in together, Lizzie, and give it a good stir. We'll make ourselves a posh cocktail.'

'How much gin to lemonade?'

'On second thoughts, just make it gin and fruit,' Flo said thoughtfully. 'Save the lemonade for the kids.'

When the mixture was ready, Madge was given the big

kitchen ladle. She expertly spooned the cocktail into the tumblers.

'To us,' said Lil and they all drank in one gulp.

'Christ, this has a kick on it!' Flo exclaimed.

Ethel gasped. 'I don't want to get too merry.'

'Why not?' asked Jenny, licking her lips.

Ethel chuckled. 'I don't really know.'

Lizzie refilled the glasses.

'To a bloody good knees-up,' said Lil, coughing as she tried to smoke and drink at the same time.

'To Lil and your family, love,' wheezed Madge, thumping her chest with her fist to clear her indigestion. 'Thanks for making us welcome.'

'Yes,' whispered Jenny hoarsely, 'and thank you to everyone for being so ... so well, nice to me and Madge. We ain't never had ...' She paused her eyes filling with tears.

'Blimey, love, drink up,' blustered Lil, a little teary-eyed herself. 'Or you'll get us all going.'

The gin continued to flow and Lizzie was drifting into a pleasant haze when Flo asked the inevitable. 'Has that foreigner turned up at the pub again?'

Lizzie shrugged. 'No, and I hope he don't.'

'Who's this foreigner?' Jenny asked curiously.

'A right bugger,' Flo enlightened her.

'Really?' Jenny was wide-eyed.

'I hope you're not relying on Frank to protect the pub,' Flo giggled. 'He's about as much use as a sore bum without any lav paper.'

At this, everyone burst into laughter. 'I have Murphy to do that,' Lizzie replied with an easy shrug.

'Murphy?' Ethel asked blankly. 'Who's Murphy?'

'Get with it, Eth,' Flo chided. 'He's the Irishman who saved Lizzie last year from the jaws of death. Her knight in shining armour.'

'I thought Danny was.'

'So did we all,' Flo slurred. 'I mean, she is still Danny's girl by rights. He ain't done the deed with April Williams - yet.'

'Flo!' Lizzie went scarlet.

Lil smothered a giggle. 'We're only teasing you, love. But none of us wants to see you die an old maid.'

'Well, we're all gonna die sooner or later, ain't we?' Madge said, saving Lizzie's blushes. 'Now, while I'm a bit merry, I'll tell you all this. If ever I gulps me last breath, I don't want no bloody black 'orses. Or folk sobbing their hearts out around me grave. No, I don't want none of that. I'd prefer a good party like this one. As long as I've got a clean pair of drawers on in me box, I'll be happy.' She tossed back her drink, smacked her lips and fell back onto the kitchen chair. Her full breasts heaved and her double chins wobbled. 'Oh, bugger, I've got one of me dizzy spells coming on. But sod it, I'm going to enjoy meself while I'm still breathing.'

Everyone burst into laughter once again. The racket soon drew the attention of the men.

'What's going on in there?' Bert hollered from the yard.

Flo stuck out her tongue and shrieked, 'Never you mind!'

Lizzie raised her glass. 'To 1935,' she toasted. 'And the new year.'

'To the lovebirds Jenny and Bert,' called Flo.

'To those not here with us,' said Ethel wistfully.

'And to a bloody good knees-up tonight,' Flo jested. 'I want to wake up tomorrow with a well-deserved headache as well as my old man snoring beside me.'

At which point, Nelson appeared in the kitchen, dragging his nappy after him. Clutching his privates, he called out, 'See what a big willie I got!'

After which, there were hysterics second to none, echoing throughout the whole household.

CHAPTER 25

'AUNTIE LIZZIE!' Polly shouted above the noise of the party. 'Can I go and out to play?'

She was addressing Lizzie who was standing at the piano singing a duet with her Uncle Sydney. Polly was bored. All afternoon the adults had been trotting out the old numbers. The two boys had fallen asleep under the table, stuffed full of salt beef sandwiches and Christmas cake.

'What's that, monkey?' Lizzie bent down to slide an arm around her shoulders.

'I said, can I go out? My friends are playing in the street.'

'It will be dark soon.'

Polly missed Tom. He was the only one she really wanted to see on Christmas Day. Tom wasn't old enough to come on his own to Langley Street or visit the shop either. Mrs Williams, who had been Uncle Danny's landlady, disapproved of Uncle Danny and Tom coming here. She knew that because Tom had told her at school.

It seemed to Polly as though everyone she liked the most was absent. Uncle Frank wasn't welcome at Auntie Flo's either. Uncle Frank always made her laugh. But today he had gone to Granda's instead. So now she was on her own, while all her friends were outside.

Polly had got quite used to being around grown-ups all the time. She liked the customers at the shop and the two new men who helped Uncle Bert. One was called Maurice. He was short and had a long black beard. He did have nice white teeth, though, and he liked to talk a lot as he pushed the broom around the floor. The other was Ron, who was as tall and lean as a stick. Polly liked the way he smiled, for he had very few teeth and he pulled a funny face. But she had hoped today, Christmas Day, Tom would suddenly appear with his dad. And Uncle Danny would look at Auntie Lizzie like he used to. A special sort of feeling would fill the room that made everyone very nice to each other.

Instead, she had to play with the babies.

'Please, Auntie Lizzie,' Polly begged desperately. 'Me mates are out there having a good time.' The noise of the out-of-tune piano was so loud, Polly had to shout. She glared angrily at the rowdy company.

'Well, I suppose ten minutes won't do any harm,' Lizzie conceded. Put on your coat and leave the front door open. Stay where I can see you in the street, with your friends. I'll call you in when it's dark.'

'Oh, thank you, Auntie Lizzie!' Polly threw her arms around her aunt. Now she had got her way she felt happy.

'Don't forget what I've told you, monkey.'

'I won't. I promise.'

Polly disentangled herself from the many arms that tried to hug her and hands that attempted to pat her head as she struggled through the merrymakers.

At last she found herself in the passage and found her coat hidden under the many others hanging on the hall stand.

Doing as her aunt had told her, she stepped out into the

street, leaving the front door open. She ran excitedly towards the two girls she knew at school. They all began to talk about what had happened during the holidays so far.

It was a short while later when a boy she didn't know, tapped her on her shoulder. He had rough brown hair and two teeth missing in the front of his mouth. He wasn't from Langley street but Polly saw there were quite a few kids from different neighbourhoods.

'Come wiv' me,' he said, tugging her arm. 'I'll show you where you can get some free sweets.'

'Where?' Polly challenged.

'Not far.' The boy pointed to a crowd of kids at the end of the terrace.

Polly looked at the window. Auntie Lizzie wasn't there.

'I'm not allowed,' Polly declared firmly, but her two friends were talking with some others now. Free sweets were a temptation. Perhaps Auntie Lizzie wouldn't miss her.

'Quick,' said the boy. 'Or else they'll be gone.'

Deciding she would only be out of sight for a few minutes, Polly followed. They came to the crowd of children all standing round a man playing a mouth organ. The woman with him shook a tambourine. They were handing small brown bags to the children.

'Sally Army,' said the boy knowledgeably. 'They deafen yer first, then give you sweets so you'll go to church.'

'But they're wearing masks.'

'Yer, well it's Christmas, ain't it?'

That didn't make much sense to Polly. But she was attracted by the music and of course, the confectionary.

'Do we have to go to church if we take the sweets?' she asked doubtfully.

'Nah,' laughed the boy. 'Course not. You just grab what you can get.'

Polly found herself drawn towards the colourful group.

They looked more like the buskers she had seen outside the Queen's theatre in Poplar. The man had a soft scarf twisted around his neck. His short, dark hair stuck out in odd tufts and his smile, below the mask, was dazzling. The lady was gaily dressed, wearing a full skirt embroidered at the bottom. Her mask was frilly round the edges.

However, there seemed to be no prayers of any kind going on. The man was taking the bags of sweets from a pouch attached to his waist. Each bag was twisted at either side. Polly could just see a pink tip poking out enticingly.

She licked her lips. The boy snatched his and tore it open. 'Coconut,' he shouted and greedily pushed two in his mouth.

Polly edged her way past him and stood before the woman. She was very pretty with brown ringlets hanging to her shoulders.

'Here you are, child,' she said in a friendly fashion. 'Hold out your hand.'

Polly did so. A brown bag sank into her palm. It was full of coconut, Polly's favourite treat. 'Thank you,' she said politely.

'Merry Christmas.'

'My friend says you're from the Salvation Army,' Polly dared to say. 'But don't you usually wear a bonnet?'

'This is the day we put on something especially for the children,' replied the lady with a sweet smile.

Polly liked that. And she hadn't even been asked to go to church yet. She gripped her bag tightly.

The man looked at her. 'We are here to give gifts to God's children,' he said in a strange accent.

'What school do you go to?' the lady asked.

'Ebondale Street School.' Polly's eyes fixed on the plump bag that seemed to call her from the palm of her hand. Her mouth watered.

'Well, say hello if you see us pass by.'

Polly nodded. She could only think about the coconut. She wanted to untwist the corners of the bag and taste one. But she resisted the temptation. It might look too greedy in front of these holy people. And besides, Auntie Lizzie might be waiting.

'Now Jesus has given you your present,' said the man, 'you had better go back to your friends.'

Polly was quite amazed. He seemed to be reading her thoughts; she had been wondering if she dare reveal the bag to Nelson and Callum, who would grab sticky handfuls instead of just one. Now it appeared the sweets were meant just for her.

The woman rattled her tambourine. The man gave her a long, strange stare. As they moved slowly off down the street, they began to play and sing. Polly was relieved to find she wasn't expected to join in with the unfamiliar hymn.

Only this morning she had been talking to Auntie Lizzie about Jesus. Had Jesus himself sent the man and woman along to convince her he was real? It was Christmas, his birthday, after all.

Suddenly she heard her friends calling her. She hurried back, eager to see what had been going on in her absence. But the moment she arrived beside them, darkness began to fall.

Her heart missed a beat. She looked anxiously at the window. Auntie Lizzie was there, waving her in. Polly said goodbye to her friends and walked thoughtfully towards the open front door.

She was about to step inside when she came to a decision. She would tell no one about her little windfall from the Sally Army. After all, she hadn't done anything wrong. Accepting sweets from Jesus was like a bible story. Tom was missing, but she had been given her favourite treat instead. The more

Polly thought about what had happened, the more determined she was to keep the sweets to herself.

She quickly pushed the bag of pink coconut deep into her pocket.

As she hung up her coat, she felt a guilty excitement. She would wait until tonight when she was in bed to open the bag. After all, the sweets were meant for *her*. Jesus would have sent three bags if he meant any for Nelson and Callum.

Humming happily to herself, and in a much better mood, Polly rejoined the party.

CHAPTER 26

SYDNEY MILLER WAS SMILING; his broad, boyish face and regular features when he was happy, looked far younger than his twenty-six years. His muscular arms were folded across his chest as he reclined on his chair listening to Doug murdering a version of 'It's a Sin to Tell a Lie'.

Syd had not expected to enjoy Christmas quite as much as he was. Even Lizzie had joined him at the piano earlier, to sing a few requests. Ethel was playing the Joanna, forced into participation by Lil who had sternly reminded her daughter that her piano lessons had cost an arm and a leg.

Ethel had a good touch and with each tune came memories and wistful sighs of nostalgia from her attentive audience. But when someone had begun to belt out *A Long Way to Tipperary* and *Pack Up Your Troubles*, Lil had gone out to the backyard for a smoke. After all, both her boys had been lost in the war. The scars had never really healed, poor cow.

Still, *Fascinating Rhythm* and a few energetic Jack Hylton numbers from yours truly had got the party going again.

Syd was proud of his deep, tuneful voice; he knew he had an ear for music, although he couldn't read a note. He wasn't bad at the dancing lark either, though it was more like a free-for-all when Ethel started to knock out, *Knees Up Mother Brown*.

The high-jinks had gone on into the early hours. Everyone was pleasantly pickled. Oddly enough, he hadn't indulged much today; he wanted to make sure this Christmas would be one to remember, even though some of the old faces weren't present: Danny and Tom, Rosie and Timothy and even Richard to name but a few. But family was family. You made an effort at times like this. Therefore, he'd struck a bargain with Flo; Christmas Day spent with her crowd and Boxing Day with his. Tomorrow they were going to drive over to Hoxton and celebrate with the Missus.

Syd knew what a lucky man he was to have a woman like Flo as his wife. It had to be said, she possessed a mind of her own. This didn't always sit well with his family, since the Missus had a fine opinion on her, too. But Flo could give as good as she got.

Lucky that really. She had been the youngest of the Allens and he'd courted her after her dad had died. Without the discipline Tom Allen had imposed on his kids before the war, Vinnie and Babs had run wild. Lizzie and Flo were left to pick up the pieces of family, and that was where he had come in. Well, who else was there for the girl to lean on? Danny had sodded off to Australia. Frank had wheedled himself into Lizzie's affections. And to cap it all, poor little Pol had been conceived in a whorehouse!

He couldn't have just turned his back on Flo, could he? He loved her and considered it his duty to stick by her. Though he said it himself, Syd felt he'd done a pretty good job in his marriage.

Syd heaved a satisfied sigh. He smiled at Lizzie, who was well away with her port and lemon. For once, a flush coloured her pale cheeks and her green eyes were filled with laughter as she stood at the piano. She was a beautiful woman, a proper classic. Though he preferred his wife's homely good looks and easy countenance. You could always tell what was coming with Flo. Her face was an open book.

Not so Lizzie. She wasn't one to give much away. That was, until she got proper riled and then stand clear! As he'd learned first-hand when his brother had nicked Frank's watch and Lizzie had spotted it on his wrist. The fall-out on that little caper had only just begun to subside.

Syd eased his collar at the thought. Though he'd defended his brothers, privately, he wished Walter would keep his thieving hands to himself. He wished Clifford wasn't such an idiot as to boast to all and sundry that the Millers and the Flowers was joined at the hip. Hah, that was a good one!

Most of all, he wished his brothers and the Missus didn't keep on at him, claiming they could do a better job for Lizzie than the Irishman. But Syd drew the line at hanging, drawing and quartering, especially if perpetrated by his own family!

Christ Almighty, what if the law came knocking on his door in the middle of the night? No, Lizzie had warned him to keep out of her business and this time, he would as she asked.

Syd jumped when Lizzie tapped him on the shoulder.

'It's been a lovely evening Syd,' she said warmly. 'Thanks for making it one of the best.'

'I'm glad you enjoyed yerself,' he said guiltily and took a swig of his beer. 'Must be rotten without – well, you know ... Danny.'

Did he really just say that? Syd asked himself silently. What a twerp he was! Just when things were getting more cosy between him and Lizzie, he had to blurt out Danny's name. 'Sorry,' he mumbled. 'I've put me foot in it. Again. But you know what I think? I reckon that swanky car sales of his over Euston is keeping him busy.'

'It's Christmas, Syd,' Lizzie replied mildly. 'No one stays open on the 25th. Not even my shop.'

Syd felt he should say something, but what? She was right and they both knew it.

Lizzie sighed softly and spoke again, relieving him of the problem of what to say next. 'To tell the truth Syd, I've been hoping he'd show up. I thought he'd make an effort for the kids, if not for me. Tom and Polly have always been close, like brother and sister. He knows that and would normally put their interests first.'

Syd glanced at Polly who had fallen asleep on the settee, her head in Lil's lap.

'Just a bit of a hiccup,' Syd replied diplomatically. 'You wait and see. Christmas ain't over yet.'

'Did Flo tell you she met Danny up Island Gardens?'

'No,' Syd lied badly.

Lizzie looked at him and smiled. 'For what it's worth Syd, I know he's with April Williams.'

Once again, he kept silent.

Lizzie drained her glass of port of its last drop. 'Take no notice of me. It's probably the drink talking.'

'And why not? Come on, I'll have another one with you.' He began to stand up but she put her hand on his shoulder. 'No, thanks, love. Listen, I'm sorry we fell out about the watch. Sorrier still that it took Nelson's birth to bring me to my senses.'

'It's wasn't you. It was me.'

She chuckled. 'We're alright now though, ain't we?'

'More than alright,' agreed Syd fiercely. 'We're like this.' He held out two crossed fingers.

'That's good.'

Syd looked into her eyes and saw the sadness of all the past years, when she had fought for Polly and for Flo and tried to fight for Babs and Vinnie too. Only that had been a lost cause from the start. In the end the struggle had left her like this, without a bloke, or at least without Danny. Without any kids of her own and with a blooming great headache called the Mill Wall.

Nevertheless, his heart went out to her. Despite his earlier vow not get involved, he said earnestly, 'Lizzie, gel, you know you can call on me if the need arises. I mean just me, not my brothers, you understand?'

'That's decent of you, Syd,' she answered with a grateful nod. 'But you have a youngster now. You have to look out for him.'

'Which is why I don't plan to spend my life at the scrapyard,' Syd confessed. 'Just as soon as I've saved enough, I'm going to buy me own gaff. Not that I've said anything to Flo yet.'

'Well, I wish you good luck, Syd.'

'I want to show Flo I can do it.'

'We all have our reasons to succeed.' A loud clatter of dishes came from the kitchen. Looking over her shoulder she nodded. 'Better go and help. Time to start clearing away.'

Syd gulped the last of his beer down as he watched her go. What had he gone and said all that about owning his own place for? He'd not even thought it was possible before tonight, let alone probable.

But the moment the words had left his lips, he knew it was what he wanted. He just had to get away from the scrapyard and his brothers. It wasn't easy with the Missus always on at him to support them. But he was getting the feeling something underhand was going on. He knew that he was like an ostrich putting his head in the sand. One day there was going to be an almighty eruption. He felt it in his gut. It was the little things that bothered him. The nudges and the winks behind his back, the shifty characters who were attracted to to Clifford like moths to the flame. The old lags that sat in the office for hours on end, glorifying their prison days. The secret meetings behind closed doors that he was never privy to. He was left alone to flog the scrap, thank God. But one day he would be drawn in. And God help him then!

Syd sobered up a little as he always did when he thought of his brothers. And then it occurred to him – he should have asked Lizzie if she wanted in on his plans. After all, she was buying up the manor like there was no tomorrow!

Why not?

But what did he have to offer. No nest egg, no going halves. No working collateral. No investments to plough into a sound proposition.

A nice stable business with prospects – if only he had a plan up his sleeve.

But today was a beginning.

Perhaps tomorrow would bring something along. Syd always liked to look on the bright side. Even though he was a Miller.

CHAPTER 27

IN THE EARLY hours of 26ᵗʰ December, a light still burned above the greengrocery shop on the corner of Ebondale Street. Though Lizzie had tried to sleep after the party, she lay staring into the darkness.

What was Danny doing now? She wondered whether he was asleep beside April, his arm around her under the covers, his head close to hers on the pillow? Was Tom happy? Had all three enjoyed the company of friends on Christmas Day? Or had it been a quiet, intimate few hours, sharing a meal together?

'And why,' Lizzie asked herself out loud, 'haven't I accepted until now, that me and Danny are over?'

The thought was like a physical pain under her ribs. Every Christmas since Danny and Tom returned from Australia in 1931, they had shared time together. But yesterday, Danny hadn't walked into Lil's, his blue eyes searching for Lizzie across the room. There was no Tom to brighten up Polly's face.

Lizzie shivered, even though the bedcovers kept her warm. How could she have been so blind? Even Flo had tried to warn her. She swallowed down the tears. Danny had found someone else. It was a bitter shock. Her refusal to divorce Frank and her determination to remain in the East End had brought this about.

Lizzie dressed quickly and made a brew in the kitchen, listening without interest to the bubble of the kettle.

Eventually she threw away the cold tea. She stood watching from the window as dawn broke.

Softly she made her way past Polly's room and downstairs. All was silent in the storeroom where Murphy's men would return to from their families after Christmas. Examining the boxes of vegetables, sacks of potatoes, carrots and vegetables, all to be sold at half price on Thursday when the shop reopened, she scuffed away a tear.

Fleeting pictures came to mind of her past. Her brothers and sisters as children; resentful Vinnie, easy-going Bert, precocious Babs, loyal Flo. Sadness crept over her at the memory of her loving mother Kate, who, at only thirty-nine, had been taken too early. And Tom Allen, her disabled father, ending his own life in the Thames after.

She glanced out onto the slumbering street and gave a deep sigh. Her gaze fell on Bert who had just emerged from the airey. He stretched his muscular arms and puffed furiously on his roll-up. After throwing the dog-end into the gutter, she saw him look up to the sky and breathe in the crisp dockland air.

His routine never changed. And today would be no different. Though the shop was closed for Boxing Day and they would be driving to Bill and Gertie's for dinner, he would expect a hearty breakfast.

Lizzie smiled at the thought; a brother she could count on through thick and thin. The uncle to Polly who was always there when she needed him. He was their rock.

She hurried upstairs and lifted the big frying pan from its

hook above the stove. The eggs were sizzling in the fat as Bert plodded into the kitchen. A big smile appeared on his face when he saw his breakfast cooking.

CHAPTER 28

It was Boxing Day and a pale sun shone through the layers of thick cloud as the Wolseley drew up to the kerb in Gap End. Lizzie, wearing a new, deep blue suit, a dainty blue hat and matching gloves, climbed out and stood with Bert and Polly in front of a shabby, smoke-blackened building, one of many crowding the back streets of Poplar. Home to her father-in-law Bill Flowers and his partner, Gertie Spooner, the front door of the three-storey terraced home opened slowly. A very tiny figure, no more than five foot tall, peered out. As usual, Gertie wore her regulation darned woolly jumper and trousers with a thick brown hairnet draped over her straggly grey hair.

'Well then, who have we got here?' she croaked.

'Happy Christmas, Grandma!' Polly exclaimed, throwing herself into Gertie's arms.

'Well, I never did, how you've grown!'

'I'm almost bigger than you!'

'None of your cheek now, I can still throw a punch,' Gertie chuckled, hugging the little girl who looked on her as family, even though they were not blood-related.

'Do you like my new dress, Grandma? Father Christmas brought it.' Polly was already out of her coat before she sprang over the doorstep.

'He's got good taste, that bloke.' Gertie took Polly's coat and hung it on the hall stand behind the door.

'Where's Granda?'

'In the front room. He's been waiting to see you.'

Polly dashed off while Lizzie and Bert joined Gertie in the freezing cold passage.

'Dinner's nearly ready.' Gertie peered out into the street. 'Ain't Tom with you today?'

'Hasn't Danny called?' Lizzie asked in surprise.

'Not since October,' Gertie complained. 'He drove us up to see his new gaff at Euston. We was stuck twiddling our thumbs in that smart office of his all day. You youngsters are all so bloody busy, there ain't no time to talk.'

Lizzie looked at Bert who merely shrugged. Quickly he slapped his cap on the hall stand and hurried away.

'Right, what's up, then?' Gertie demanded, narrowing her small, beady eyes. 'You and Danny fell out?'

'Hasn't he told you?'

'We ain't seen him, ducks.'

Lizzie took off her hat and gloves. 'I'll explain after dinner.'

'Please yerself.' Gertie made off to the kitchen.

Lizzie gave a deep sigh. So Danny had left it to her to be the bearer of bad news! Gertie would not let her off the hook. She would want to know all the details. Trying to put her irritation aside, Lizzie followed Polly into the front room. 'Happy Christmas, Bill,' she said, smiling at the grey-haired man who reclined in an armchair by the fire. Polly was perched on his knee and Bert was sitting on the button-backed couch.

'Happy Christmas, ducks. Come here and plant a kiss on me cheek.'

Lizzie walked into his open arms, grateful to still have him in her life. He was a dear friend as well as her father-in-law. They had travelled a rough road together all through her nightmare of a marriage to Frank, his eldest son. Bill and Gertie had never married, but Gertie had helped Bill raise both his sons, as if they were her own.

'Granda, can we play dominoes?' Polly jumped to her feet.

'All in good time, youngster. I want to have a natter first.'

'Grown-ups always talk!' Polly pulled a face.

'That's what old blokes do,' Bill teased with a wry grin. 'Just like you will one day.'

'No, I won't!' Polly protested. 'Old people get grumpy and argue all the time. I'm never getting old – ever!'

'Polly, that's not very nice,' Lizzie reproved as Bill's jaw fell open in surprise.

'Don't care!' Polly sniffed and tossed her auburn curls. She ran from the room.

'What's got into her?' Bill asked in a puzzled voice.

Lizzie sat down beside Bert. 'Perhaps it's the excitement of Christmas, she don't seem her usual self. I thought she might cheer up after being at Lil's yesterday. But she was very quiet when we got home and went straight to bed.'

'Kids - who'd have 'em!' Bert tried to joke.

'Don't worry, I've got a thick skin,' Bill chuckled. 'I must look a hundred years old to a young kid. But there was a day not so long ago I could lift a sack of spuds to me shoulders. Don't suppose I'll ever see those days again.'

'Reckon you're still in with a chance, Bill,' Bert said easily. 'Why, on Saturdays you do as much work as me.'

'Wish that was true, son,' Bill said with a sigh. 'Just look at the size of you. Built like a bloody gorilla. Now, did you all have a good Christmas at Langley Street?'

The conversation took a happier turn as Lizzie told Bill about the party yesterday. Lil's Christmas knees-up was a regular event each year and Bill enjoyed hearing the gossip.

They were all still talking when Polly returned. 'Grandma says you're to come immediately. Dinner is on the table.'

'Then we won't waste another moment gassing,' said Bill ruefully, easing himself up from his chair. 'Lead the way, McDuff.'

With that, they all trouped along to the kitchen where Gertie had made an enormous meal. The table was set with the best china plates and Bill carved the sizzling roast chicken. Bert served the plump pork sausages and crinkly bacon, Polly and Lizzie, the veg. There were carrots cooked in butter, sweet green peas and crisp brown potatoes basted in fat.

It was not long before their plates were empty and the Christmas pudding appeared swamped in brandy.

'Who wants custard?' Gertie asked and everyone nodded.

The rich yellow dessert slipped down the sides of the pudding. Bert was the only one who had seconds.

'May I be excused?' asked Polly as the adults sat back to talk.

'Course gel,' Bill nodded. 'Go and amuse yourself while our dinner goes down.'

Polly scowled. 'There's nothing to do without Tom.'

'Polly!' Lizzie exclaimed. 'What's wrong with you?'

'I'm the only kid, that's what! I'm fed up with being on my own. It's been a rotten Christmas,' she declared and the tears burst forth.

'Now then, ducks,' Gertie said kindly getting up from the table to console her. 'Dry them tears. Christmas only comes once a year. You're supposed to be happy.'

Polly blinked her wet eyes. 'I know. But it's not like other Christmases.'

Gertie kissed the top of her head. 'No, it ain't, that's true. But we'll make the very best of it, won't we? Now why don't we play Happy Families? I'll throw in a half-crown as the prize. How does that sound?'

Polly smiled. 'A bit better.'

'You know where the cards are kept. Go and deal them out. I'll be along in a minute.'

With shoulders slumped, Polly walked slowly away.

Gertie turned her accusing eyes on Lizzie. 'So, what's it all about?' She asked again. 'Where's Tom and Danny?'

'Danny should have told you,' Lizzie tried to explain.

'Told us what?'

'We aren't together any more.'

'Another bloody row I suppose,' said Gertie impatiently. 'What's it over this time?'

Lizzie tried to steady her voice. 'The truth is, Gertie, Danny is with someone else.'

'Never!' exclaimed Bill, his eyes widening.

'Who is she?' Gertie demanded.

Lizzie took a deep breath. 'Her name is April Williams.'

'His landlady?' Gertie scoffed.

'She was - is, I suppose. But it's more than that now, Gertie.'

'Are you certain?' asked Bill with a bewildered frown.

But before Lizzie could answer, Gertie interrupted. 'I blame you, Lizzie,' she said accusingly. 'No wander Danny's gone off. He wouldn't have if you weren't so bloody wrapped up in that pub of yours.'

Lizzie felt the sting of tears. 'That's unfair of you, Gertie.'

'It's true, ain't it? Danny never wanted you to take the pub on.'

'He wasn't in favour, no. But I had my reasons.'

'I'd like to hear 'em!'

'Stop it, Gertie!' Bill yelled suddenly. 'This ain't an inquisition. We're supposed to be enjoying ourselves, not wailing at each other like a bunch of alley cats. What's happened to a bit of goodwill to all men? It's Boxing Day after all.'

Silence fell but Gertie's accusing gaze still lingered on Lizzie. Then, giving them all a scowl, she left the room.

'Don't take no notice,' Bill apologized. 'You know what she's like. Feels left out when she don't see her boys, like she ain't needed no more. Gertie will calm down in a minute.'

Lizzie tried to smile, but Gertie's words had stung. For there was a grain of truth in them. Danny, like Murphy, had been against taking on the pub. But she hadn't listened. Perhaps if she had made a different choice, Danny would still be with her.

CHAPTER 29

'That's it Pol, sit on the pouffe,' Gertie was saying as Lizzie walked in the front room. The coal fire was blazing and the drapes were drawn aside behind the old button-backed settee, shedding a dim light across the weathered leather. Gertie was sitting in one of the fireside chairs and Lizzie took the other.

'Are you playing with us too, Auntie Lizzie?' Polly asked.

'Yes, monkey. Deal me in.'

Polly expertly counted another hand and everyone studied their cards.

'Look who I've got!' Polly exclaimed. 'Mr Bones the Butcher, Mrs Pots the Painter's Wife and Mr Block the Barber!'

'You're supposed to keep them to yourself,' Gertie scolded gently. 'But we'll forget what we heard. Now Pol, you start first.'

Lizzie managed to avoid the frosty looks that Gertie threw and soon they were debating who was going to win Gertie's shiny half-crown. By the time the clock on the mantel struck three, Polly had claimed the prize.

They were debating what to play next, when a knock came at the front door. Polly jumped up excitedly. 'That might be Uncle Danny with Tom!' She ran to see who it was.

'Will his woman be with him?' Gertie asked Lizzie. 'What's she like?'

'April's been good to Tom.'

'Well, ducks, I may have been a bit hard on yer today,' Gertie acknowledged, 'but Danny won't get off lightly.'

Lizzie smiled. 'Bill's right, though. It's Christmas.'

'I don't appreciate being put on the spot. He could have come round to put us in the picture.'

Lizzie listened to the voices in the passage. Was it Danny with Tom and April? Her heart began to beat very fast. How should she react? Would there be more ructions to spoil the holiday?

'Happy Christmas one and all!' Frank came striding into the room, his arms full of packages.

Lizzie stared at him in surprise. 'Frank, it's you!'

'Who else?' His grin went from ear to ear as he bent to kiss Gertie and planted one on Lizzie's cheek. 'Have I missed the grub?'

'Yes, but there's plenty saved,' Gertie assured him. 'What have you got there?'

'Just a few surprises. Here, I'll put them on the table.'

'Is one for me, Uncle Frank?' Polly asked excitedly.

'You bet!' Frank swung her up into his arms. 'That's a nice dress. Do you reckon I should wear a pink tie?'

Polly burst into giggles. 'Course not. Pink is only for girls.'

Chuckling, Frank looked at Lizzie. 'Don't worry about the pub. I've left Murphy's men on watch and told Whippet to run over for me if there's a need. Shouldn't be though, as the pub ain't open. And I couldn't just sit there twiddling me thumbs. It's Christmas after all.'

Lizzie wouldn't normally be pleased to see Frank, but on this occasion she was relieved it was him.

'Where's Dad?' Frank asked as he put Polly back on her feet.

'In the yard with Bert,' Gertie told him.

'I'll go along and say hello.'

'You do that, son and get your father to pour you a drink.'

'I'm on the wagon, Mum, remember?'

'Good boy. You make me proud.'

Frank gave Lizzie a half-hearted smile. 'Don't your Auntie Lizzie look nice?' he said to Polly. 'Good job I washed and shaved me beard off this morning. It was so long I was tripping over it.'

'Uncle Frank, stop teasing!' Polly cried. 'Can I open me present now?'

'Yes, it's got your name on. But be careful it don't bite. I took all its teeth out before I came, but it's got a nasty suck.'

Laughing, Polly ran to the parcels. She undid the brown paper and pulled out a long, coiled skipping rope with bright red wooden handles. 'Oh, Uncle Frank, just what I wanted. Can I come out to the backyard to skip?'

Frank looked at Lizzie. 'Can she have a fag an' all?'

Polly fell about laughing. Grabbing Frank's hand, pulled him into the passage.

Gertie looked at Lizzie. 'Pol thinks a lot of Frank. It's a bleeding shame she don't know he's her father.'

'I'm waiting for the right time to tell her.'

'Well, don't wait too long. It could all go tits up if you dither. And you've got to give Frank some credit. He's turned over a new leaf. And that was what you asked of him. A man can be forgiven his sins if he tries as hard as Frank has.' Before Lizzie could respond, she added, 'Now, let's go and put some food on the table.'

Lizzie followed Gertie to the kitchen She was thinking

about what Gertie had said. It was true Frank was trying to reform, but it was Polly's happiness that counted. She needed to know that Frank could be trusted, and had a father to rely on through the years ahead.

So far, Frank had shown his better side. Was this genuine Lizzie wondered? His voices could be blamed for the bad he had once done, but what if they returned? Time alone would tell.

'You could do a lot worse than Frank,' Gertie said mildly, as they brought plates of cold cuts and pickles out from the larder. 'He thinks a lot of you, you know.'

'Frank is family, Gertie,' Lizzie replied as she looked through the window to the backyard. Polly was skipping with her new rope and Frank, Bert and Bill were watching. Lizzie's heart warmed at the sight, for Polly was happier than she had been all through Christmas.

'He's your old man, love.'

'I know that. But we can't live together.'

'Why, if Danny ain't in the picture?'

'Gertie, you know the answer to that, we just ain't right for each other,' Lizzie replied firmly. 'But if it makes you feel better, the reason I took on the pub, was to give Frank a chance at making something of himself. Polly is his daughter and he needs to her earn her respect as well as her love.'

Gertie put down the plate of egg and cress sandwiches. 'You took the Mill Wall on for Frank?'

'Why wouldn't I? Polly means the world to me.'

'So must Frank if you done that for him.'

Lizzie gave Gertie a rueful smile. 'We get along alright now. I'm hoping it stays that way.'

'Well, good luck to you both. Sorry I had a go at you about the pub.'

'You were right in a way,' Lizzie admitted. 'The Mill Wall isn't easy to run and we do have some problems.'

'I know,' Gertie admitted shortly. 'That bloody foreigner!'

'Did Frank tell you?'

'He said he's a smart dresser.'

Lizzie couldn't help herself and laughed. 'What Salvo Vella wears is the least of our problems.'

Gertie frowned as she sliced the fruit cake. 'The bugger sounds a handful. I hope Frank can handle it. He's not got a lot of bottle.'

'That's why I hired protection.'

'A bloke named Murphy?' Gertie asked, narrowing her beady brown eyes. 'The Irishman who got you and Danny out of hot water at Chancel Lane?'

'Yes, the very same.'

Gertie put down the knife and looked out of the window. Very slowly, she turned back to Lizzie. 'Straight up, gel, does this Murphy mean something to you? Is he the reason why our Danny strayed?'

Lizzie took a sharp breath. 'Whatever gave you that idea?'

'I put two and two together.'

'It's true I've done business with Murphy since Chancel Lane,' Lizzie admitted. 'Without his men, we wouldn't stand a chance of keeping the Mill Wall clean. Frank is vulnerable as both you and me know. But Murphy is a friend who I trust. And without Danny's help, I need one. So does Frank. Believe me, Gertie, whatever the grapevine says, you have heard the truth from me.'

Gertie nodded. 'That's all I wanted to hear, love.'

Just then Frank came in with Polly. Their faces were rosy and flushed. Lizzie found herself thinking for the first time, *two peas in a pod*. Polly, as a younger child, was like Babs, all big brown eyes and curly auburn hair. But now, as she was growing older, she was changing. Her expression was Frank's, his wide smile and charm. The resemblance was unmistakable.

'Who's for a game of hide and seek?' Frank said enthusias-tically.

'Me!' cried Polly. 'Oh, Uncle Frank, I love it when we hide upstairs.'

Gertie chuckled as she looked across the table. 'First, sit down and eat your tea.'

Everyone gathered in the kitchen; the stout and sherry appeared from the cupboard. Glasses were filled to the brim, except for Frank's who drank lemonade with Polly.

Lizzie saw that Gertie was in a better mood now. Her eyes never left Frank, who was happy to be the centre of everyone's attention.

'Can we play hide-and-seek now, Uncle Frank?' Polly asked, as she finished eating. 'There's a lot of creepy, dark rooms upstairs.'

'Blimey, gel,' gasped Frank, downing the last of his lemon-ade, 'you'll have to hold me hand or I'll get the collywobbles.'

'Don't be daft, Uncle Frank!' Polly giggled until tears rolled down her cheeks.

Lizzie was looking at Gertie who couldn't take her proud gaze from Frank. Now she knew that her beloved boy had been accepted back in the family, she was content. In Gertie's eyes at least, he was a reformed character, and no one could tell her any different.

CHAPTER 30

LIZZIE WAS SITTING QUIETLY in the kitchen at Ebondale Street. She was pleased to be home at last, after the long day at Bill and Gertie's. Bert had retired early and Frank had surprised her, calling by to say goodnight to Polly.

His deep voice echoed from the bedroom as he read to Polly and Lizzie's mind wandered. The peaceful atmosphere was very different to the past. There were very few happy memories of the time when she and Frank had lived here as man and wife. What little joy there was in the marriage, had soon vanished. For Frank's involvement with crooks and bookies had left them almost destitute. Had it not been for Bill standing by her, then she may not only have lost her livelihood but Polly, too.

Now, all these years later, it was difficult to believe that Frank was so changed. Not that she dared to trust him again. But seeing him through Polly's eyes, had allowed the bad memories to fade.

'Pol's nodded off,' a voice said, jarring her suddenly back to the present. She glanced up to see Frank watching her, hovering at the kitchen door. 'I better be on my way, I suppose?'

It was more a question than a statement. Lizzie nodded to the teapot. 'There's a fresh brew on the table before you leave, if you want one.'

'Never say no to a cuppa,' he replied and pulled out a chair.

Lizzie poured two cups and they sat without speaking. She wondered if her smiling husband could remember the unhappiness he'd brought to her here. Or if he'd turned a page on the past, rewriting history with his own version.

When at last she met his eyes, she saw a reflection of Polly again, and her heart softened. Yet a chill swept over her.

'Like old times,' he said, turning his cup on the saucer. 'Sitting here, in the kitchen with you.'

'When did you ever do that?' she asked. 'You preferred the whorehouse, the pub or the bookies.'

This stung and she saw him pale. 'Christ Lizzie, I'm sorry. You know I had a screw loose. It took all them months in the loony bin to get rid of the - '

'Voices,' Lizzie provided. 'Yes, I know, Frank. You've told me many times they were responsible for the bad things you did. But what if these voices of yours come back again? It's Polly I worry about.'

'I've got them conquered now. I take proper pills from the 'ospital. I've chucked the booze and the last time I went with a woman - '

'Frank, I want you to be happy. I don't ask you to live like a hermit.'

'That little girl in there is my daughter,' he said and cleared his throat. 'She's changed my life. And you have.'

Lizzie felt the tears sting. This man was her husband. She'd made her vows to him and had thought she could learn to care. But perhaps he had always known that she could never love him like she loved Danny.

'You're still the only gel for me,' he murmured. 'I know I've put you through hell and I don't expect you to understand why I lost me marbles. I don't even know myself. I'm a bloody freak of nature. Yet you've given me a chance at the pub and I'll not let you down. I'm no hero, but I want to do it right this time. I'm giving it all I got.'

For all his failings, Lizzie thought sadly, Frank knew himself and freely admitted his faults. Could she say the same of herself? She loved Danny but had never thought he would leave her. She'd imagined they would always be together. How wrong she was.

She smiled to herself at the ironies of life. Danny had gone and instead it was Frank who remained. Perhaps that was why she was sitting here now and why she had never divorced him.

'Frank, we were over after Polly was born.'

'I don't even remember when me and Babs - ' He stopped, shamefaced. 'I didn't know what I was doing.'

'But I did. I can forgive you for Polly's sake. Because you and Babs made a beautiful, innocent child who has given me so much happiness. But as for the past, I still can't forget.'

'I know. That's why I'm trying so hard ... to prove to you - ' He reached for her hand and drew it towards him. 'To prove I love you.' Before she could catch her breath, he kissed her, a kiss that brought back so much and made her feel achingly vulnerable. A kiss that was not like the kisses he had once demanded at the start of their marriage, but now, a gentler, tender offering that made her shiver with regret.

She pulled away. 'Frank, I think you should go.'

'Let me stay a bit longer. I was someone else all those years ago. I've changed.'

'And I have too, Frank.'

'Is it still Danny?' he asked.

She did not answer and he nodded, heaving a sigh as he rose slowly to his feet. His blue eyes were full of remorse and his shoulders slumped. Then turning slowly at the door, he held out his palms. 'I've got nothing to offer you, Lizzie, not like Danny has. But I won't run out on you or the pub and that's a promise.'

'I'll expect you to keep it, Frank.'

His lips parted on a hesitant grin. 'You deserve your pound of flesh, and I'm willing to give it.'

She listened to his footsteps on the stairs and heard the click of the storeroom door below.

Her thoughts and body felt numb. Frank was a reminder of the past, for good and for bad. He was a man she kept at arm's length and yet in some way they were still attached.

Lizzie went downstairs and drew the bolt on the storeroom door. Then she returned to sit by the fire. The Christmas decorations spread gaily around her, yet it was the end of another year. 1934 had brought many surprises, some welcome and some not. Was she so starved of affection that she had allowed Frank to kiss her?

Her thoughts turned to Salvo Vella. Was the danger over? A new year would soon be dawning. The year had ended without seeing Danny. Was the old saying true? *Absence makes the heart grow fonder.*

Her eyes closed in the warmth and she fell asleep.

CHAPTER 31

CHRISTMAS WAS OVER – almost – and Danny sighed with relief. Just one last excursion and it would all be over.

'We'll meet some very important people tonight, Daniel,' April enthused. 'I'm so proud of you. I want to show you off.' She was about to kiss him when Tom walked in.

'Can I stay home?'

'No, Tom,' April replied. 'Get dressed now.'

'Tom, go along, there's a good lad,' Danny urged gently for he knew how Tom must be feeling. Christmas had been a whirl of engagements with people they hardly knew.

'Tom's been left to run wild,' April complained when they were alone. 'Although you are a very capable father, he needs a firm hand.'

Though Danny didn't regret for one minute his decision to adopt and raise Tom, at times he had felt inadequate as a father. Though there had been Lizzie and Pol. Had things been different, they would be a family by now.

Danny pushed the thought from his mind. Putting on his coat he waited alone in the car, soothed by the familiar leathery smell of the interior. Yet much to his annoyance he couldn't escape the memories of Christmases past.

Half an hour later they arrived at the Murdoch' house in Granter Square. He shook hands with any amount of Gerald Murdoch's colleagues all of who worked in the City. Stock-brokers, bankers and investors, financiers who gave a wink and nod over their whisky. Most of the exchanges had gone over his head. Even the expensive wine at dinner had not eased the boredom.

We could be a million miles away from home, he thought as he watched Tom perched on a seat in the corner. The Murdoch's boy, Ralph, was standing a few feet away with his friends. Every now and then Tom met Danny's gaze with an imploring look. It took all his willpower to resist making an excuse to leave the Murdoch's. But how could he let April down?

At last the guests began to leave. But not before Gerald Murdoch insisted on giving them a tour of the house. Up and down all five floors they marched, with an anecdote on each!

Finally, it was time to go. Danny saw that April was flushed with excitement as she sat beside him in the car. She looked a picture of elegance in her long dress, with her crepe-de-chine stole folded over her shoulders. She gazed up at him with such gratitude that this seemed to make all the effort worthwhile.

'What a wonderful evening we spent at the Murdoch's,' she cried. 'Edith has promised to give me the name of her decorator when we move to our new house. We're sure of a discount if Edith puts in a good word.'

'A little way off yet,' Danny replied amiably. 'But yes, it was kind of her.'

'Dad,' said Tom from the rear seat, 'I don't want to move.'

'We shan't yet, son. Not for a while.'

'Tom,' said April firmly, 'don't pester your father.'

Danny looked in his driving mirror at the pale face solemnly regarding him. 'Really, Tom, nothing is settled yet.'

'I don't want to go to boarding school either,' pleaded Tom. 'Especially the one that Ralph and them kids go to.'

At this, April interrupted. 'Ralph Murdoch was very kind to you, Tom. He included you with his friends – his manners are impeccable. Edith thinks he is very bright and might even go to Oxford.'

Tom mumbled under his breath. 'They said they're gonna keep me under a cold shower till I freeze.'

'Tom,' laughed April dismissively, 'it was only a joke. It's upper-crust humour, that's all. You'll soon get to understand, my dear.'

Tom wriggled to the edge of the seat. 'Don't send me away, Dad,' he begged. 'I promise to mind me manners.'

'We'll discuss this later,' said April curtly. 'Now sit back on the seat or we'll have an accident.'

Danny heard the choked sob of his son. He knew that he would have to harden his heart and hope that as time went on and Tom would adapt to their new way of life. He'd brought Tom up on the land, living rough and ready and without the respectability that gave a man his standing in society. April was right. He could no longer let Tom run wild. His life would take a different turn when he left Ebondale Street and Danny knew it would not be easy at first. But with April's guidance his son would have the education and standing that would make him a good fit in society.

He glanced at April now and saw the clean cut of her face. Neither handsome, nor plain, but proud and resilient. It could not be easy for her to take on another woman's child. She was trying her best, he knew.

After supper, when Tom had gone to bed, April kissed Danny lightly. 'I think I shall retire too,' she told him.

'Tomorrow there's early communion. I think I shall go. Will you and Tom come with me?'

Danny held her in his arms and smiled. 'Yes, why not?'

'Don't stay up too long, Daniel.' She kissed him again, fully on the mouth and pressed herself against him. 'I've turned down your bedcovers.' She looked into his eyes and stroked the hair from his forehead, her fingers glancing his scar. 'Sleep well, dearest.'

'April - '

She placed her fingers over his mouth. 'Hush. Not tonight Daniel.'

He sighed, for he had been about to dip in his pocket for that velvet box.

Danny watched her leave the room. The light from the lamp flickered over her straight-backed figure, her elegant poise and composure. Listening to her footsteps, he heard her go up the stairs. Did she think of her late husband, George, when she lay alone in bed?

Danny admired and respected her. He was grateful for the guidance she gave to Tom. For Danny felt himself ignorant in the world of educated men and women. Wealth had brought him many opportunities, but if he were not to take them, then what would his struggles have been for. April fitted well into this new way of life. For Tom's future, Danny wanted more than he had ever wanted for himself.

He eased himself into the comfortable fireside chair and stared into the dying embers of the fire. The soft orange glow gave the room a solid feel; carefully arranged drapes and embroidered soft furnishings were all of April's choosing. He thought again of his predecessor George Williams. An older man, he had been an executive with the railways. Danny knew that April had suffered when he'd lost money in the Depression. Forced to sell their Hampstead home, they had moved to the better part of Poplar and this villa. But the couple remained childless. April had never spoken of wanting a family. Yet Danny hoped for children to complete his family. He yearned for the close ties that he'd had with Lizzie and Pol.

'Dad?' The soft whisper came as the door opened. 'I can't sleep.'

Danny's heart clenched as he saw his son's pale face and hollowed eyes. 'Tom, my boy, what's up?'

'Has Aunt April gone to bed?'

'Yes, she has.'

Tom stumbled over and Danny reached out, hauling him into his arms.

'Can I stay with you for a while?' Tom curled himself into Danny's lap.

'Is something worrying you?'

'Are you going to work tomorrow?'

'Perhaps, in the afternoon.'

'Can I go with you? I could wash the cars like I did at the garage. Bring 'em up all nice and shiny. That's what I want to do when I leave school Dad, sell cars like you.'

Danny pushed back his unruly blond hair that April insisted on combing neatly with a centre parting. 'Selling cars is not a sound job, Tom.'

'But you like it.'

'I can do nothing else.'

'You can mend engines,' Tom said proudly. 'You taught me to mend 'em too, remember? I don't have to go to boarding school for that.'

Danny pressed the damp hair away from Tom's blue eyes and grinned. 'We're both a bit out of our depth in these new circles.'

'I didn't like it at the Murdoch's, Dad.'

Danny heaved a soft sigh. 'Aunt April is trying her best for us.'

'I wish we was at Auntie Lizzie's,' said Tom holding his arms tight around Danny's neck. 'It don't seem like Christmas without Pol.'

Danny threw caution to the wind and said, 'Chin up now. I'll take you to Island Gardens tomorrow, after communion.'

'Do we have to go to church?'

'Best we do, Tom.'

Danny held his son closely, feeling the bump on his hip of the small velvet box in his pocket, that he had yet to give to April.

PART II

April 1935

CHAPTER 32

LIZZIE WAS STANDING in the snug of the Mill Wall as Bert restored order to the public bar. The broken chairs and tables had been thrown out, and most of the shattered glass and sawdust was swept into soggy piles. After the long quiet of three months, Salvo Vella had left his calling card.

'We was caught unawares,' said Frank beside her, with one eye completely closed under a purple swelling above his bloodied nose. He looked downwards to pull together the torn sides of his jacket.

'Are you hurt?' she asked in concern as a thread of blood oozed from his ruffled hair.

'The buggers did us over,' he growled as he inspected his buttonless waistcoat. 'This suit cost me a fortune.'

Lizzie felt a moment's sympathy as he dabbed at his head with a bloodied handkerchief. Even though Whippet had pedalled as fast as he could to alert her, Vella's thugs had long since departed.

'We wasn't expecting it,' he continued wearily. 'There's been no trouble since last year; not what you'd call trouble. Just incidents, like. A few tarts try their luck and before you know it, they're on the pull. Then there's he usual effing and blinding when they're shown the door. But not real aggro.'

'Are you certain they were Vella's women?' Lizzie enquired.

'Not stab-meself-in-the-heart certain,' replied Frank, running his tongue of his swollen lip. 'But they are crafty as a cartload of monkeys. They snuck in today when the geezer on the door was having a pee. Now, if I was a betting man, which as you know, I ain't, I'd put a pound on them watching this place.'

'Do you keep a man on watch outside?'

'Yes, but how are they to know when Vella's about? It could be anyone coming in the pub to drink. If they're dressed ordinary, like a docker, my man would let 'em in. What's he to do? As for credentials? No, we don't stand a chance if a geezer has a pint, sizes up the pub, then goes out and gives the nod to someone.'

'How many came today?' Lizzie enquired.

'A couple of women with blokes at first. They drank quiet like, at the tables. Didn't even try for the snug.' Frank raised his hand to his injured eye. 'Before we knew what was happening the cows went out, then brought in more blokes. Could've been a dozen or more. All our usual punters vanished. Anyway, me, Fowler and Elmo was soon in the thick of it. They was all over us and I found meself on the floor looking up into the ugliest mug I'd ever seen. He was as big as Bert, with arms the size of houses.'

'All right, Frank, I get the idea. Where were Murphy's men?'

'Down in the cellar helping the brewery's navvies to unload. I managed to get away and went down the back to tell them. I'll give them their due. They were up in the bar in a blink and sorted out Vella's lot. But the draymen did a bunk, leaving us short on ale. A right mess it was by the time we got rid of the troublemakers. The cellar drop-doors were broke open and someone emptied our barrels. We was swimming in muck. We'll have to send Whippet over the brewery for replacements. What a bloody waste of good booze!'

'It must be Vella,' Lizzie said thoughtfully.

'If it was, we didn't see him.'

'Who else would do this?'

'Only him,' agreed Frank. 'But he's too much of a bloody coward to face me.'

'I doubt that,' reasoned Lizzie. 'Murphy said he would come. And I believe he has. He's sending his men first to put the wind up us.'

'He did that an' all.' Frank swiped a trickle of blood from his cheek.

'Let's have new locks and chains fitted,' Lizzie decided. 'If he tries the cellar again, he'll be disappointed. We can't leave the front door unoccupied again, not even for a minute. It's the only way the women can get in.'

'Do we turn them out? I mean what if a regular arrives with his wife, say?'

'Then you'd recognize them, wouldn't you?'

Frank nodded doubtfully. 'Could do.'

'Let them in if you're sure they're legit.'

Frank nodded. 'We'll have to take shifts.'

'If that's what's needed, then yes.'

Lizzie paused in the bar, where Lenny was cleaning the spilled ale from the floors. A gleaming mirror hung behind him and fortunately had not been damaged.

'The usual punters have cleared off,' Frank said following her gaze. 'But don't worry, their thirst will drive them in soon.'

Despite his assurance, Lizzie felt uneasy. Once more, Salvo Vella had left his calling card for all to witness.

CHAPTER 33

IT WAS the Monday before Easter when Lizzie saw a navy blue uniformed man outside the shop window.

'Rozzers!' Bert exclaimed and bolted to the storeroom where Maurice and Ron were working. 'Scram,' he yelled. 'The law's on the prowl.'

'Mrs Elizabeth Flowers?' The policeman was addressing her as he made his entrance.

'That's me.'

'You are the owner of the Ripon Street bakery?'

'Yes. Why?'

'There's been a fire.'

'What do you mean a fire?' Lizzie repeated. 'Where?'

'At your premises at Ripon Road.' The bobby adjusted the strap under his helmet. 'My gaffer told me to inform you. Started early this morning by all accounts.'

'But how did it start? Has it been put out? Are my staff safe?' Lizzie wanted to know.

'You'd better get over there if you want to find out. Sorry missus, but I'm on my bike, so I'd better be off.'

The policeman left as Bert walked from the storeroom. 'What was that all about?'

'He said there's been a fire at the bakery. But he didn't know more. Just said I'd better get over there.'

'It's probably nothing. Them bluebottles are always up for a bit of drama. Someone's just burned a few pies.'

But Lizzie knew that couldn't be so. The law wouldn't have bothered to alert her if it was not serious.

A few minutes later they were seated in the Wolseley and Bert had his hand on the horn. The traffic seemed thicker than ever, with hold-ups and detours along the dock road. Lizzie knew she must stay calm and prayed that Jenny, Madge and Elsie were safe. She didn't care how many pies were burned, or cakes ruined. Or even if they'd had to extinguish a fire in the kitchen and left a mess. She just wanted her staff to be there safe and sound when they arrived.

When the Wolseley was parked at the end of Ripon Street, Lizzie's heart sank. Grey funnels of smoke twisted into the air and spread over the houses. There were snaps and crackles from burning timber. The fire engine and its crew were working frantically with their hoses. A crowd had gathered but there was no sign of Jenny, Madge or Elsie.

'What happened?' Lizzie called out as she hurried towards one of the firemen. 'Where are my staff?' She wanted to go closer, but it was too hot.

'Stay back! The fire is still burning,' he warned. 'If you want any information, see the constable over there.'

Bert led her towards the policeman. 'What's going on?' He demanded.

'Are you the owners?' Coughing, the constable took out his notebook.

'I'm Mrs Flowers. What happened to my bakery? How did the fire start?'

'Dunno. I only just got here myself.'

'I'm worried about my staff.' She looked around. 'Have you seen them?'

'How many worked here?'

'Three,' Lizzie said hoping he would say they had all been rescued and taken somewhere close by.

Instead he shook his head. 'The house to the right was empty, and the shop on the other side closed up. Only one was brought out from the bakery.'

'One?' Lizzie cried in distress. 'Who?'

'Don't know,' the policeman shrugged again. 'The ambulance took her off.'

'You don't know much then, do you?' Bert said, beginning to lose his temper as the smoke grew thicker around them.

'Listen, son,' the copper snarled, 'don't take that tone with me. I'm doing me best.' He coughed again.

'I'm sorry but this is a shock,' Lizzie intervened. 'Which hospital was the person taken to?'

'Poplar,' he croaked.

'We'll go to the hospital if there's nothing we can do here,' Lizzie decided.

'I need to take a statement,' objected the law. 'If this is your gaff, I've a long list of questions to ask.'

'They'll have to wait.' Bert pointed a finger in the copper's face. 'We ain't hanging around here if you can't tell us nothing.' Bert propelled Lizzie through the smoke and back to the car.

'Oh, Bert, who is in hospital and what's happened to the others?' Lizzie gasped as they climbed inside. 'And how did the fire start?'

'Gawd knows,' Bert muttered as he drove them out of Ripon Street. 'Fat lot of good the copper was. Couldn't even say who went in the ambulance!'

Lizzie wiped her eyes. The smoke had made them smart. She knew Bert was thinking of Jenny. But there was Madge - dear Madge to consider - and little Elsie who was no more than a child. Where were they if they hadn't been rescued?

Surely they couldn't be caught in that inferno?

CHAPTER 34

LIZZIE WALKED with Bert along the hospital corridor, thinking of the plans that she and Jenny had been making only last week. They had set aside a day to visit the women's hostel and offer a job to any soul in need. She and Jenny wanted to help those who, like Jenny and Madge, had had a hard deal in life. Jenny knew only too well what it was like to be battered and abused. She had escaped death by a whisker and found her calling at the bakery. She wanted to help others, as Lizzie did. But their dreams now lay in ruins. The shop was a burning wreck, but it was Jenny, Madge and Elsie who mattered.

Lizzie told the casualty nurse who they were and asked which one of her staff had been rescued.

'Her name is Jenny Maguire.'

'Thank God,' Bert breathed, unable to contain himself. 'Is she alright?'

'No, I'm afraid not.'

'What's wrong?' Bert boomed.

'A number of things. She is in no state to be visited.'

'Can we see her for just a few minutes,' Lizzie begged. 'We are the only family Jenny has.'

The nurse finally gave in. 'Just a short while, then.'

They were shown to a side room and Lizzie tried to hide her shock. Jenny's head and hands were swathed in bandages. A cage was propped over her legs.

'Jen?' Bert whispered as they stood beside the bed. 'It's us. Bert and Lizzie.'

'Please don't touch her,' the nurse warned as he went to take her hand. 'Her skin is very sensitive. Remember, just a few minutes.'

Lizzie forced back her tears. 'Oh, Jenny, my dear. I am so sorry.'

'What happened to me?' Jenny whispered so softly they could hardly hear her.

'Can't you remember?'

'No. Only the smoke and I started choking.'

Lizzie wanted to ask about Madge and Elsie but she knew this was not the time. Jenny's face was red and blotched. Her eyes were red, peering out of their sockets as if through a haze. She began to cough.

'I'm sorry, but you'll have to leave,' the nurse said, gently propping the pillows behind Jenny. 'Wait in the corridor and I'll speak to you.'

Lizzie and Bert left the ward. They waited silently together until the nurse joined them.

'Smoke inhalation has affected her lungs,' she explained. 'And for a while her burns will be very uncomfortable.'

'Will they heal up?' Lizzie asked anxiously.

'It's early days yet. We'll do all we can for her.'

'We'll come tomorrow,' Lizzie said quietly.

'Just one of you, please.' The nurse walked quickly away.

Lizzie looked up at her big, brawny brother with whom

she had shared so many misfortunes. She had seen him weep only once before, at their mother's grave.

Now he stood and hung his head as his tears fell.

THEY LEFT the hospital with heavy hearts as Bert drove them back to Ripon Street. They found the fire was now under control but once again there was no sign of Madge and Elsie.

'Has anyone turned up?' Lizzie asked the same policeman who was mopping the soot from his forehead. He had moved down the street to avoid the firemen and their long hoses.

'No, I'm sorry to say no one has been found. Did you find the person who was taken to hospital?'

'It's Jenny Maguire,' Lizzie explained. 'My manageress.'

'Is she expected to live?'

'I bloody hope so!' Bert interrupted.

'She is very weak,' Lizzie said, trying to keep the peace. 'She only remembers the smoke.'

'So, she don't know where the other two are?' the constable asked, keeping his distance from Bert.

Lizzie shook her head.

The policeman licked the tip of his pencil. 'Names and addresses of the missing and their relatives please.'

'Madge Hobson, my cook, lives here - did live here - at the bakery,' Lizzie said sadly. 'She has a son called Ted but I don't know where he lives. Elsie Booth, our kitchen help, might know. She looks after her sick husband over at Lavender Court in Bow.'

The copper took a long time writing his notes. Bert paraded around the blackened building, pestering the firemen and looking very annoyed.

'You'll be notified of any developments,' the policeman said when Lizzie hd answered all his questions. Then he quickly stuck his notebook in his pocket and cycled away. She knew Bert must sound very intimidating as he tried to get information from the firemen.

'What are the uniforms gonna do about Madge and Elsie, then?' Bert grumbled when he returned. 'Other than wasting time writing a lot of nonsense.'

'He was only doing his duty, Bert. What did the firemen say?'

'He asked what sort of insurance there was on the property. I said we're with the Prudential.'

Lizzie stared at what was left of the bakery. 'Insurance? All I can think of is poor Jenny, Madge and Elsie.' Lizzie wiped a tear from her eye.

Bert put his arm around her. 'Madge and Elsie might have got taken in somewhere round here.'

'Perhaps,' Lizzie said doubtfully.

'Come on, chin up.' Bert waved his hand to clear the smoke still in the air.

'What if it was Vella that started the fire?' Lizzie said suddenly.

'Don't think he would know you owned it,' Bert said but his face went white all the same. 'Tell you what, let's knock on some doors. Ask a few questions.'

Lizzie nodded. At least it was an action to take. But after an exhausting hour going round the houses, they drew a blank. 'No one's talking,' said Bert wearily. 'They're only worried about the dirty marks on their curtains.'

Lizzie stared at the unrecognisable building that only yesterday had been her prosperous bakery.

'Come on, we're going home,' Bert said dismally. 'Nothing more we can do.'

They made their way back to the car as the black smoke continued to curl over the street. When they arrived home, Maurice and Ron were busy serving. But Polly was upstairs, sitting in the front room.

'I missed you, Auntie Lizzie.' Polly threw herself into Lizzie's arms.

'Why are you sitting alone up here?'

'I didn't want to talk to Maurice and Ron.'

'Why not?'

'I wanted to be by meself.' Polly was rarely unhappy when she came home from school, but Lizzie could see the tears were close. 'I had a horrible day.'

'Did you get in a fight?' Lizzie asked as she sat beside Polly.

'It was worse than that.' Polly sniffed.

'You'd better tell me, monkey.'

'Bad things sometimes happen to kids, they get taken away,' Polly whispered as though she didn't want to be overheard.

'Oh, Pol, who told you that? One of the children?'

Polly looked away. 'A man and a lady came to the school. He grabbed my arm through the railings. It hurt. Mrs Price had to shoo them away.'

'Who were these people?' Lizzie asked in alarm.

Polly's cheeks went red. 'I saw them before, at Christmas. They was in our street when I went out to play with my friends. This boy said they was from the Sally Army cos of the funny clothes they wore. They had masks on their faces like the buskers outside the Queen's.' Polly wiped a tear from her cheek. 'They were giving the kids sweets and told us they were from Jesus. I never told you because I thought you'd be cross.'

'But Polly, how did they come to find you at school?'

'I told them I went to Ebondale Street. They said I should say hello if they passed by.' Polly suddenly burst into tears.

Lizzie drew her close. 'Now, now, Pol, you've had a nasty shock.'

'He hurt my arm.'

A cold shiver went through Lizzie. 'These people weren't from the Salvation Army.'

'I know. I'll never talk to them again.'

'Don't trust strangers, monkey. Even if they offer you sweets. You must tell Mrs Price straight away if you see them again. And you must tell me too. I'll never be cross.'

Polly nodded. 'Will the cops catch them?'

Lizzie kissed the top of Polly's head. 'I'm sure they will.'

Lizzie was relieved that Polly was unharmed. But she was very afraid. Her thoughts were in a whirl. Could this man Polly had described be Salvo Vella?

Tomorrow she would have a heart-to-heart with Mrs Price.

CHAPTER 36

'Sit down, breakfast's ready,' Lizzie told Bert the next morning when he appeared, all bleary-eyed.

'After yesterday's goings-on,' he grumbled as he slumped at the table, 'I've got no appetite.'

However, Lizzie cooked him two eggs, sunny-side up with rashers of well-done bacon. All of which he devoured in minutes.

'Now your stomach's full,' she said joining him, 'Polly told me last night that some strangers turned up at school. They spoke to the children through the railings. I believe it was Salvo Vella and one of his women.'

Her brother's head came up with a start. 'You what?'

'He grabbed her arm through the railings and told her bad things could happen to children.'

'Turn it up, Lizzie, are you kidding?' Bert roared, dropping his knife and fork with a clatter.

Lizzie told him all that she had learned from Polly.

Bert looked furious. 'I'm putting a stop to his nonsense once and for all.' He crunched his big knuckles together. 'I'll go down the school and wait for him. He'll wish he never set foot near the place!'

But Lizzie shook her head calmly. 'He won't go there again. Why would he? Mrs Price saw him and sent him off. He just wanted to frighten Polly enough so she would tell me.'

'You mean …? ' Bert hesitated as the truth dawned on him. 'He planned this deliberate like?'

'He wants the Mill Wall.'

'I'd like to know where he is!' Bert fumed. 'The East End is full of crooks now! How are we expected to fight them? We're costermongers, not thugs or criminals. We don't tote shooters around like the Murphy crew does. Why can't we be left in peace?'

'I walked into a trap when I bought the lease from the brewery.'

'They sold us a pup!' Bert agreed 'So, what do we do now? This bloke is no nutter. He's one step ahead of us every time.'

'He's not the first ruffian we've fought,' Lizzie said resolutely. 'We've been though bad times and survived.' She looked at her downcast brother; he had a dark growth of beard and was wearing an old shirt with a threadbare collar. She knew he was heartbroken over Jenny and wanted to vent his anger.

'Go and shave, Bert. Better smarten yourself up before you visit Jenny.'

'Someone has to pay for what's been done to her.'

'I know how you feel. But Jenny needs you to comfort her now.'

Her brother stood up and lumbered to the door. His huge form dwarfed the kitchen.

'Tell her that when she's well enough, we'll bring her home.'

'She ain't got one, has she?' Bert said bitterly. 'The bakery went up in smoke.'

'She's got us, Bert. You love her don't you?'

'Yeah, but will she still want me after what the fire done? I was no bloody use to her then.'

Her brother slouched off and Lizzie sat listening to his heavy steps on the stairs. Her thoughts were of Jenny in the hospital, but what of Madge and Elsie? Where were they?

And then she thought of Elsie's husband. He was sick and must be alone and distraught. But had Elsie managed to escape the fire and go home? Had the police investigated yet?

After speaking to Mrs Price tomorrow, Lizzie decided to drive to Bow and find Lavender Court herself.

CHAPTER 37

Lizzie searched the street as she drew the car up at the school. There were mostly mothers and small children leaving the school gates. There were no men and unless Vella was in disguise – and a very good one at that – it was clear he hadn't put in an appearance this morning.

'Auntie Lizzie, I hope that man don't come back again,' Polly wailed from the seat beside her.

'Don't worry Pol,' Lizzie told her niece. 'I'm going to speak to Mrs Price to make sure the playground is watched.'

'Can I come with you?'

'No, you'd better be at your desk for the register.'

Polly looked upset, but walked with Lizzie into school, then after a little more reassurance, left for her classroom.

Lizzie found Mrs Price in her office. 'Good morning, Mrs Price. May I speak to you about Polly and the disturbance yesterday?' she asked.

'Good morning.' Mrs Price gestured to a chair. 'It was an upsetting incident.'

'Polly was in tears when she came home from school.'

'Sometimes we attract beggars who play on the children's generosity, hoping for a windfall.'

'This man is no beggar,' Lizzie replied as she took a seat.

'You know him?' Mrs Price asked in surprise.

Lizzie nodded. 'From Polly's description, I believe the man was Salvo Vella, a man who trades in prostitution and who has attacked my tavern in order to do business there, At Christmas he befriended Polly in the street in order to threaten me. And the visit he made to the school was a deliberate attempt to put pressure on me to get his way with the Mill Wall.'

Mrs Price lifted a critical but unsurprised eyebrow. 'Mrs Flowers, I must be direct with you. I think that becoming involved in the nefarious world of alcohol is the cause of your problems. Prostitution has always flourished in taverns. Wouldn't it have better to keep Polly away from such an influence in the first place? Now the damage is done. And it's Polly and the school who are paying the price.' Mrs Price folded her hands together on top of the desk.

'There are reasons why I'm in business at the Mill Wall, Mrs Price,' Lizzie replied coolly. 'As I've told you, Polly's father, Frank, is manager there.'

Mrs Price looked disapprovingly down her long nose. 'It's common knowledge that Mr Flowers has always had criminal leanings. And though he's Polly's father - and Polly calls him her uncle - we have taken care at school never to complicate matters any more than they already are.'

'I'm grateful for that,' Lizzie replied. 'Though Frank may not have been the best father in the past, he's reformed now and works hard at the pub.'

'I hope that will remain the case, but I feel it's unlikely,' said the teacher doubtfully, standing up. 'However, you can be assured that Polly is in safe hands at school from any outside influences including the man and woman who appeared yesterday. I've given the caretaker orders to call a policemen should they return.'

Lizzie rose to her feet. 'Thank you.'

'Good day, Mrs Flowers.'

After the abrupt dismissal, Lizzie went into the playground. It was deserted, as was the street outside. She sat in the car thinking about what Mrs Price had said. The lecture she had just received had at first annoyed her. But on reflection there was more than a grain of truth in what she had said. Mrs Price had known Polly ever since she'd begun school at Ebondale Street and had always been a stern, but caring teacher. She had taken on the role of headmistress but still taught the children. She knew the name of every child and the background to their families. It could not be an easy job to undertake. She also knew that Babs was Polly's mother and understood that Polly had been too young to understand that her Uncle Frank was really her father. Mrs Price had been very discreet. She always had her pupils welfare at heart.

Slowly Lizzie regained her composure as she drove to Bow. Lavender Court was in a very run-down area. The tenement slum was four storeys high. The dirty brickwork and stone steps were neglected. When she climbed them, an army of cockroaches spilled out from every nook and cranny. Grimy, battered doors along the passages were worn down to wood. She held her breath at the smell rising up from the latrines below.

The door of number sixty-six on the second floor had a small, broken window with a hole in it the size of a fist. The knocker had fallen off and left a splintered hole in the wood. Lizzie bent close to the window. 'Mr Booth, it's Lizzie Flowers,' she shouted. 'Is Elsie there?'

She waited, listening for movement. When no one came, she shouted again. 'Mr Booth, please I must speak to you!'

After a few minutes there was a shuffling noise. Lizzie's heart raced. What was she to say to the bereft husband? Obviously Elsie wasn't there or she would have answered straight away. Did he know of the circumstances of the fire and what might have happened to his wife?

The door opened an inch. Lizzie peered into the foul-smelling blackness.

'Come in,' a voice whispered.

Lizzie stepped inside. She jumped as the door quickly closed behind her. Blinking her eyes, she tried to adjust them to the dark shadows. Eventually a face formed in front of her. To her great surprise there stood Elsie! Thin, pale and grubby-looking, she was very much alive.

'Oh, Elsie! Thank heavens!' Lizzie hugged her tightly. 'I'm so pleased to see you.'

Elsie nervously stepped back. 'What do you want?'

'I thought you might have perished in the fire at the bakery.'

'As you can see I didn't.'

'Have the police called?'

'Yes,' Elsie retorted. 'The buggers was banging on the door so loud it nearly gave me hubby a relapse.'

'What's wrong with him?' Lizzie asked.

'It's his lungs. Has to stay in bed.'

'Do you know the bakery has been burned to the ground?'

Elsie gave a non-committal shrug.

'What did you tell the police?'

'Nothin',' Elsie declared. 'Give the coppers a chance and they'd pin the fire on me.'

'Why would they do that?'

'I've got previous, ain't I?'

A man's voice shouted from behind one of the closed doors. 'Elsie, get your arse in here. I need me pills!'

'That's my old man,' Elsie croaked, glancing over her shoulder anxiously. 'You gotta go.'

'Elsie, I must speak to you. Please! Just a minute or two.'

Elsie gave a soft groan. 'Keep yer voice down then. Come into the scullery while I see to him.'

Once taken to the scullery, Lizzie stood listening to the raised but muffled voices coming from another room. The man seemed very agitated, swearing and cursing. The kitchen was cramped and cluttered and smelled of stale food. The grime-ridden stove stood next to a brown-stained sink overflowing with dirty pans. There were no chairs, or table on the unswept floor; just a broken three-legged stool propped in the corner. The single curtain at the window was torn and ragged.

'So, what do you want to know?' Elsie said in a shaky whisper when she reappeared.

'How did the fire start?'

'Dunno, I wasn't there.'

'Didn't you go to work that day?'

'I did, but I left. There was this almighty row in the shop. Jen sold a pie to a bloke who took a bite, spat it out and said it was pig-swill. Madge was ear-wigging through the hatch and before I knew it, she rushed out to confront him. I tried to stop her but when she threatened to call the law I done a bunk.'

'Did you see this man?'

Elsie looked away. 'I told you, I was in the kitchen.'

'Did he sound foreign?'

'Gawd knows, there was too much shouting going on.'

'Elsie, is there anything else you can tell me?' Lizzie pleaded. 'Jenny's in hospital and don't remember what happened and poor Madge has gone missing.'

'I'm sorry to hear that,' Elsie replied truculently. 'But there ain't nothing more to say. Now, I'll see you out.' She scuttled from the scullery. 'Don't send the coppers again,' she warned in a hushed voice as they stood at the door. 'If you do, I'll deny everything.'

'But Elsie - '

The loud shouting came again and Elsie pushed Lizzie out. The door slammed in her face and Lizzie stood at the broken window through which she could hear Elsie's husband's angry roars. For someone with bad lungs, he seemed to have no trouble in yelling at his wife.

Lizzie went slowly down the many steps of the tenement. What was she to do now? There was no one she could ask for advice. Except perhaps one.

Starting the engine, she drove towards the bridge that would take her across the river to Deptford.

And Murphy.

CHAPTER 38

LIZZIE BANGED on the big wooden gates, under the weathered sign that announced, "Murphy's Haulage and Transport". She had never been here before, but she could hear activity beyond the gates. The yard was situated a little way off the busy High Street where the engineering factory sat close to the rows of terraced houses. Many barrows – laden with just about anything you could wish to trade – lined the road and led down to a branch of FW Woolworth.

Slowly the gates creaked open. A very tall, muscular man with a bull-neck peered out. Beyond Lizzie glimpsed a group of men of similar build talking together, but when they saw her they quickly dispersed.

'I've come to see Murphy,' Lizzie said a trifle nervously. 'My name is Lizzie Flowers.'

'Wait here.' The big gate closed and she heard shouting. A minute later it opened again and Murphy stood there.

'Lizzie!' he cried. 'Come in.'

She stepped towards him and jumped when two more burly men appeared. At Murphy's command they hoisted a long wooden plank and slotted it securely onto the back of the gate.

'Just a precaution,' Murphy said with a gracious smile.

Lizzie hoped she could get out again. The yard and its outbuildings were built like a fortress. There were lookouts stationed above on a platform that wound around the yard and men positioned in every section.

'Follow me, Lizzie.'

Murphy led the way into a long, narrow building. Lizzie was surprised to find this part quite light and airy.

'My office,' he told her, urging her into a large, well-furnished room that reflected very good taste. She supposed the beautiful paintings of rural landscapes on every wall must be from Murphy's beloved Ireland. Although there were bars at the window, these were disguised by heavy, crimson curtains tied with thick, woven rope. There were books of all shapes and sizes arranged in a tall bookcase, and a long desk equipped with a comfortable looking half-chair.

'Sit here,' said Murphy, guiding her to a long, low-backed leather settee. Its small, stout legs stood on a thick rug and as she sat down, she gazed admiringly at the highly polished boards of the floor. Then her eyes fell on a glass cabinet in the corner of the room. Her heart gave a little jerk.

'The firearms are securely locked away,' Murphy dismissed as he took the half-chair. 'As you know, we must protect ourselves.' He opened a drawer in the desk. 'Will you take a drink?'

Lizzie shook her head as Murphy stood a small tumbler and a bottle of whisky in front of him. 'You don't mind if I do?' He poured a hefty measure. 'Now, Lizzie, you have travelled across the river today. How can I help you?' He eased his shoulders, staring at her from under his tangle of brown hair. To Lizzie he looked much the same as he always did. He wore his trademark leather waistcoat still and his bright brown eyes were alert, taking in every detail. But now she saw tiredness in them. His jaw showed more than a few nights' stubble and he made quick work of his drink.

'My bakery burned down,' she began. 'I believe it was Vella.'

'Are you certain?'

'Who else could it be?' Lizzie explained all that had happened since their last meeting. His eyes never left her face as she spoke of her constant fears for Polly's safety and her mistake of not protecting the bakery. She confided her guilt at Jenny's injuries and Madge's disappearance and the concern she had for the Mill Wall.

A kind of an uneasy silence descended. 'You have paid a heavy price for your tavern,' he agreed.

'What am I to do Murphy?'

'Our turf is threatened, too,' he said with a regretful sigh. 'Salvo Vella is a cuckoo in London's vast nest. He's moving across the city with his thieves and his pickpockets, his painted women and a gang of pantomime artists. They favour belts and buckles, razors and knives and they'd clout a man round his head with a fire iron or take out his eyes with stones. Just a month ago, in the dead of night they came to my gates with their tricks and taunts. They are a new breed, Lizzie, without faces, vultures thirsting for blood.' He turned the glass thoughtfully. 'It took the resourcefulness of all my soldiers to hold them off. I cannot advise you to fight them. 'Tis no disgrace to know when you're beaten.'

'Murphy, I can't give up now.'

'But you know the score?'

'I do, but what choice is there? They will come, just as they've come in the past, wherever we do business.'

'Then you have work in front of you. I have lost good men in recent months. My numbers are depleted.'

Her spirits sank as she thought about the Mill Wall. She

had come to Murphy to ask for his help. But he had told her what she didn't want to hear. Was she capable of resisting Salvo Vella alone?

'If you want to stay in this game, unite your soldiers, Lizzie. Danny Flowers is the man you should have at your side.'

Lizzie listened with a sinking heart. 'I don't think that's possible, Murphy.'

'Listen to me now!' Murphy exclaimed as he poured himself another measure. He threw it to the back of his throat. 'I would fight shoulder to shoulder with you, Lizzie Flowers and not turn a hair that you wear a skirt. But my captains and lieutenants ain't likely to go into battle with Vella or his likes, for a woman. No disrespect, for I admire your mettle. But my men are fighters. They listen for the sound of a battle cry that don't come in soft whispers.' He pushed his broad hands over the table, flexing their joints. 'But if they were to see the man ... the man who foiled Leonard Savage, then that would be another thing altogether ...'

Lizzie looked into the deep brown eyes that seemed to be challenging her. They were asking her to sink her pride and beg Danny for help. Then perhaps Murphy would join her? But even as she took her leave, Lizzie knew that this would be one favour she couldn't call in.

CHAPTER 39

'WE CLEARED ALL the rubbish outside the shop,' Maurice said, swiping the sweat from his black beard with a muscular forearm. 'It's Easter termorra. Do we get a day off?'

Lizzie hung her apron on the peg. Her hands were filthy with dust from the spud sacks and her hair had fallen untidily to her shoulders. 'You both have families,' she told them. 'Me and Bert can manage till Tuesday.'

Ron looked at Lizzie. 'You sure?'

Lizzie reached into the till. She had wrapped their wages and a bonus in brown paper.

'What's this?' Ron held out his package.

'It's a bit extra for the wife.'

'You've always been fair, Mrs.'

'You will come back?' she said anxiously, thinking of what Murphy had told her.

'Yeah, we'll be back. Ain't got nothing better to do.'

Lizzie smiled. 'Thank you.'

The shop seemed very quiet after they left. Bolting the shop door and turning the sign to "Closed" she thought about Danny. What was he doing this minute? Was he with April?

Murphy had great respect for him and she could understand the Irishman's thinking. But Danny had another life now. He had warned her about staying in the East End. She could have gone with him ...

It was a beautiful spring evening. Polly's voice drifted down from upstairs where she was playing with her friend. The two little girls had asked to skip in the street. But Lizzie was still nervous of Vella's whereabouts.

With a deep sigh, she sat on the stool. Ebondale Street lay bathed in the sunshine. Children of all ages were playing in the fresh air. The boys kicked stones and fought with each other. The girls played hop-scotch or tag and looked after their baby sisters or brothers.

Poor Polly, she thought once more. How long would she have to stay indoors while her friends had so much freedom? Lizzie's thoughts grew very dark as she wondered if, and when, Madge would be found. Elsie had been of no assistance at all and could not be persuaded to help. And Jenny, how long must she languish in hospital? Though Bert said Jenny was still only allowed one visitor, would the nurse allow two?

Her thoughts went round and around, making her dizzy.

Just then a small figure on a bicycle rode up to the shop. Dressed in his jaunty cap, jacket and shabby trousers, Whippet jumped off the bike and banged on the shop window.

'Trouble at the pub?' she asked as she opened the door.

Pushing back his cap, the young messenger grinned. 'Frank sent me to tell you the punters are in short supply. He ain't taking any money.'

'Then tell Frank to mark down the beer.'

'They don't like it when Frank chucks the dollies out.'

'The Mill Wall isn't a brothel, Whippet. The sooner they learn that the better.'

The boy just shrugged as Lizzie filled a brown paper bag with apples. She took a silver coin from the till and dropped it in his dirty palm.

'Ta very much,' he said with a wink. 'Do you like me new pedals? I'll run yer messages quicker now. If I hear anything about old Madge you'll be the first to know.'

'There's half a crown in it if you do,' she promised.

When Whippet had cycled off, Lizzie sat on the stool again, her thoughts returning to the Mill Wall. She was trying to make the pub a clean business. But was all this worry worth her efforts? The trade was slow because there were no distractions; the women had attracted the men. Shaking her head, she tried to clear her troubled thoughts. It was Easter Sunday tomorrow. Time to take Polly for an outing to Lil's and forget her worries.

But after her friend had left, Polly was in no mood for the visit. 'I'll have to play with the babies again.'

'They are nice little boys, Pol.'

'But I'm a girl and much older.' Polly was not happy at all and went off in a huff.

But the next morning, Lizzie was pleased to see her mood had improved. The sun was shining brightly through every window, church bells were pealing and the shop was closed for the day. When breakfast was over, Polly changed into her party dress and Lizzie tied a pink ribbon in her hair.

'You look very nice, monkey.'

'Is Uncle Bert coming with us?' Polly asked.

'No, he's sleeping in.'

'He stinks of hospital these days,' said Polly tossing her curls. 'And he's always grumpy.'

'Don't be rude, darling. He's doing his best to cheer Jenny up.'

'He's lucky. He can go out on his own,' Polly retorted and bolted down the stairs. Lizzie sighed. These days Polly was very unpredictable. Where was the sweet little girl she used to be?

'Pol, you look very pretty,' Lil welcomed as they arrived.

'Where's are the boys?' Polly asked airily.

'Next door. You'd better go in and see them.'

'I suppose I don't have no choice,' Polly sniffed and ran off.

'Little Miss, ain't she?' Lil grinned as they sat down at the kitchen table. 'Don't worry, she'll grow out of it.'

Lizzie smiled as they sat down at the small table. 'Lil, did you hear about the fire at the bakery?'

Lil nodded as she poured the tea. 'Did your girls manage to put it out?'

'As a matter of fact, no.'

'What?' Lil looked alarmed. 'Me and Doug thought it might be one or two of Madge's pies that caught light.'

Lizzie shook her head. 'Jenny is in hospital. Madge has disappeared.'

'Christ almighty!' exclaimed Lil. 'The poor cows.'

'I'm worried about Madge. No one has seen her.'

'You mean she might have died in the fire?'

'Oh, Lil, I hope not. If it wasn't for me taking on the pub, Jenny would never be in hospital and Madge wouldn't be missing. I think it was Salvo Vella who did it.'

'Come on, now, love,' Lil consoled. 'You're imagining things.'

'I don't think I am.' Lizzie's voice broke.

'Blimey, you are in a bad way, gel. Tell me what happened.'

Lizzie poured out her story. Eventually Lil folded her arms and muttered, 'I have to agree with you. It's too much of a coincidence - the fire and him seeing Polly at school. Almost as if he's pushing you to yer limit.'

'Yes, and he's doing it.'

'I reckon young Elsie knows more than she's saying.'

187

'She might,' agreed Lizzie who had thought the same herself. 'But she won't tell, Lil. I begged her. But it was no use.'

Lil lit up and took a long drag. 'How's yer brother? He must be worried over Jenny.'

Lizzie nodded. 'He says she's lost a lot of her hair.'

'I'd do meself in if all my hair went,' Lil commented unhelpfully. 'It's a woman's crowning glory.'

A remark that Lizzie could have done without!

CHAPTER 40

DANNY HELPED April into the smart Sunbeam saloon he'd parked outside of April's mid-Victorian semi-detached house. The car was rather ostentatious but April liked it. They were travelling up to Regent's Park to meet up with the Murdochs for a stroll, then on to other friends for tea. And finally, a soiree back at the Murdochs'. Though it would be a long day, Danny reminded himself that April had gone to great trouble to arrange it.

As April seated herself beside him and Tom climbed into the back, Danny's thoughts were preoccupied. Perhaps he was a little on edge. He and Hugo had endured a rather worrying episode a few days ago. He had been out demonstrating a car one morning when a band of hooligans had stopped outside the showrooms.

Hugo had ventured out and explained that the forecourt was private property. But the cavorting had continued and when a stone had been lobbed at the glass, Hugo had protested fiercely – for which he'd received a rather nasty knock on the nose.

Danny had returned with his customer, to find a bobby

taking notes and Hugo holding a handkerchief up to his bloodied nose. Danny's customer, and several others who had been admiring the stock, had made off in haste.

'Those damned idiots,' Hugo had snarled, 'God knows where they appeared from. Even threatened to return after they attacked me.'

'Go home and rest up,' Danny had offered as a consolation and Hugo had quickly accepted.

But Danny was keenly aware that his business had a reputation to keep. His well-heeled customers expected an hour or two of luxury and light-hearted conversation when purchasing a vehicle. Certainly not a constable prowling the premises and a wounded salesman. He was worried, too, that Hugo might not stay the distance if there was a repeat performance.

With all this in mind, Danny drove towards the city, half listening to April as she described the Murdochs' recent holiday. 'Edith and her husband stayed near Balmoral,' she was explaining, 'cost an absolute fortune of course. But they have friends there. By the sound of them they could be royalty! You know, Daniel we should try the Highlands, or Edinburgh. Or perhaps somewhere a little warmer. Edith speaks very highly of the Cunard Line cruise ships.'

'Dad and me have been on a big ship, haven't we Dad?' said Tom from the back seat.

Danny smiled, recalling their long and memorable voyage from Australia back to Britain. 'We have indeed son.'

'We was in a storm. The ship lifted us right up and threw us off our seats,' Tom expounded. 'The captain had to put chains on all the chairs.'

'Now Tom, don't let your imagination run away with you,' April reproved.

'I'm not, am I Dad?' demanded Tom indignantly. 'That really happened, didn't it?'

Before Danny could answer, April pointed to the stream of motorised vehicles, trams, horse drawn carriages and carts rumbling and chugging in front of them along the Commercial Road. 'Daniel, isn't there another route to take? It's very hot inside the car.'

'Can't we go to Island Gardens instead?' asked Tom.

'Another day, Tom, when you and your father go out together.'

'But we're always with you,' Tom retorted and Danny glanced warningly in the mirror.

'I only meant we ain't ever on our own,' replied Tom truculently.

'Tom,' said April half-turning, 'please try to speak the King's English.'

Danny felt his heart twist as Tom curled his legs up on the seat and sank his chin to his knees. He had never corrected Tom about the way he spoke. It was the manner they always conversed in. But lately April had been on at the boy. She intended it only as a help, but Danny felt for his son.

'When you go to your new school,' April continued, 'you will have to mind your p's and q's.'

'I'm not going to a new school, am I Dad?' Once again Tom sat forward. 'You promised!'

'Your father made no such promise, I am certain,' April disagreed, glancing sharply at Danny.

There was a moment's silence before Danny gathered his thoughts. As he moved the car only inches forward, he said, 'April, I told the lad there were no plans yet. We haven't even found a house.'

'Then you misinformed him,' April said curtly. 'I have a very nice house in mind, quite near to Edith. I saw it only last week.'

Danny took his eyes from the road in surprise. 'You never said!'

'I wanted to make certain it was what we wanted.'

'How could you, without me?' Danny demanded, beginning to lose his composure.

'You're always at work,' April accused. 'We would never move if it was up to you.'

Danny misjudged the gears and the engine stalled. The car shook and shuddered. He cursed under his breath. He wanted to answer that not moving would be perfectly acceptable to him. In fact, it would be the very best outcome he could hope for. But, as he looked into her face and saw the hurt there, he swallowed on his irritation.

This Easter was when he had planned to ask April to marry him. To give her the ring in the velvet box that he kept in his pocket.

Perhaps April was right. Work consumed most of his time. And it seemed to him, the Murdochs occupied the remainder!

He set the car going again and the traffic picked up speed. An orange sun splashed its way through lumpy grey clouds. Steeling himself, Danny took a deep breath.

He studiously avoided the tear-filled blue eyes that he knew were staring at him from the rear seat. He turned the car off the Commercial Road and motored towards the city, hoping that a breath of fresh air and a change of scenery would lighten all their moods.

CHAPTER 41

AFTER POLLY HAD TAKEN Callum into Flo's, Lizzie and Lil sat together on the yard wall, discussing the bakery fire. Lil smoked another cigarette, drawing the nicotine deep into her lungs as she offered an opinion on the unfortunate events that had befallen Lizzie.

Lil's voice drifted in and out of her head as Lizzie breathed in the strong smell of the the docks; the dirty, flotsam-filled water and the polluted wharfs banked by mossy green walls. The aroma reminded her of the days when she would mudlark with Vinnie and Bert and take Flo and Babs to the park to play under the dark, damp railways arches. If she was blindfolded now, she would know where she was; the horse dung left on the cobbles to dry, the brewery men's carts that clattered up and down, the pie shops' kitchens and the coffee canteens and the throb of East End activity that brought with it a smell that was like no other. Everyone she knew and loved lived within a stone's throw of Langley Street. Except one. Her mind wandered to Danny and Murphy's advice. She understood his reasoning, and trembled a little at the thought of facing Vella alone.

Lil tapped her on the shoulder. 'A penny for your thoughts, ducks.'

'My thoughts don't amount to much lately,' Lizzie confessed. 'Is Mrs Price right? The fire might never have happened if I hadn't took on the pub. Jenny wouldn't have got burned and Madge wouldn't be missing.'

'Listen, what's done is done,' Lil replied firmly. 'Count your blessings. Jenny ain't dead and will get better. And Madge will probably turn up.'

'Somehow I doubt it.'

'Didn't no one see her?'

'Apparently not.'

Lil put an arm around Lizzie's shoulders. 'Don't like to see you so down. You know, your mum used to say, it will all come out in the wash.'

Lizzie nodded. 'I hope she was right, Lil.'

'Kate was a good neighbour, the best. I wouldn't be here if it wasn't for her. And I hope you know I'd do anything to help you.'

Lizzie smiled. 'That's why I'm here now, telling you all my worries. Speaking of which, how is Ethel?'

Lil rolled her eyes. 'Upstairs, no doubt. Gazing out of the window looking for Rosie and Timothy.'

'Has she heard anything from them?'

'Not a word.' Lil narrowed her eyes. 'There's been times I've wanted to drag her into the car and get Doug to drive us over to Lewisham. That's what I would do, if left up to me. I'd bang on Cora Ryde's door until she opened it, then demand to see my kids.' She heaved a sigh. 'But Ethel ain't me. And Doug says I'm to behave meself.'

'He's probably right.'

Lil laughed. 'Now let's go in and I'll call Ethel down.'

Lizzie followed Lil back through the kitchen. When Ethel

appeared, Lizzie hugged her friend close. 'Ethel, how are you, love?'

'Oh, you know.'

Lizzie saw her friend was still well and truly in the doldrums. Her blonde hair was scraped severely back from her face. She wore no make-up and hadn't bothered to put on a clean dress. Even when Lizzie explained about the fire and Madge and Jenny, she showed little interest.

It was not until Syd arrived at the back door with the two little boys, that Ethel managed a smile.

'Come in, son,' invited Lil with a smirk. 'You must have smelled the tea. We was just having a chat.'

'Ta,' Syd said eagerly. 'The two lads have turned me place upside down. They wanted to come in and see their Auntie Lizzie. Young Pol is out in the yard with her skipping rope.'

'Where's Flo?' Lizzie asked as Nelson and Callum made off to the front room.

'She's gone to the doctor's.'

'What for?' Lil demanded as Syd sat down. 'She ain't ill is she?'

Syd shook his head. 'No, the opposite.'

Lil almost choked. 'Flo's not up the spout again?'

'Think so.'

Lil cackled. 'Blimey, you two didn't waste no time!'

'Mum!' cried Ethel indignantly.

'Congratulations, Syd,' Lizzie told her brother-in-law. 'That's wonderful news.'

'Do you want a boy or girl?' Ethel asked quietly.

'Wouldn't mind either.' Syd's smile faded. 'I am a bit worried, as the doctor told Flo she might not be able to have another kid. Even if she does, she'll have to stay in bed. And you know Flo. She won't be happy about that.'

'She'll have to do as she's told,' Lil said archly. 'Does the Missus know?'

Syd looked even more downcast. 'I'm biding me time. Think we'll leave it a while.'

'Why's that?' asked Lil as she poured him a cup of tea. 'The old girl will be over the moon.'

'Yes, but I want to have plan A - and B - ready.'

'Syd, you ain't making much sense, ducks.' Lil screwed up her eyes.

'It's me job,' he muttered. 'I've decided to jack in the scrapyard.'

'What? With another kid on the way? You must be nuts,' spluttered Lil.

'I ain't told Flo, not in her condition.'

'So, you're telling us instead,' Lil said acidly.

'Mum, just let him speak,' Ethel pleaded.

Lizzie felt her heart jerk. Something was wrong. 'Go on, Syd,' she urged.

'The Missus wants me to take over the business. And that's bad news.'

'Why?' said Lizzie, Ethel and Lil together.

He pushed his hands over his face and sighed. 'Last night the Missus's house was raided. The coppers found swag under her floorboards. Walter and Clifford was nicked.'

All went silent until Lizzie found her voice. 'What kind of swag?' she enquired, a sinking sensation in the pit of her stomach.

'Gold, silver, diamonds,' replied Syd with a gulp. 'My brothers done over a jewellers' up West. Cleaned out all the sparklers and blew open the safe. Took the whole ruddy lot.'

'Oh, Gawd,' Lil breathed. 'They'll get a long stretch for that.'

Syd nodded dismally. 'That's not the worst. They done over a guard. Put the poor bugger in hospital.'

To which there was a united gasp.

CHAPTER 42

THE HOSPITAL WAS VERY quiet on Easter Monday as Lizzie made her way along the narrow corridors. The unpleasant smell of disinfectant grew stronger as Lizzie neared the ward. When she entered through the doors, all the beds were full and the nurses scurrying round to make sure the few visitors did not tire their patients.

Lizzie made her way down to the last bed on the left. She was shocked to see it was empty and the frail figure slumped beside it in a chair, was Jenny. The bandages had been removed from her head and she wore a sort of white cap instead. Her long hospital gown covered her burned legs, and her bandaged hands were placed, very still, on her lap. When she saw Lizzie, she tried to smile, but her lips were still swollen and cracked.

'Jenny, how good it is to see you! I didn't expect to find you sitting up.'

'They put me in the chair because it's bad for my chest to lay down.' Jenny saw the oranges that Lizzie had brought. 'They look nice.'

Lizzie put them at the end of the bed, then drew up a small wooden chair. 'Jenny, are you in pain?'

'Only a little,' Jenny said through her sore lips. 'I try to keep still while the burns heal.' She gave a raspy cough.

'Can you sleep?'

'Yes, they give me a pill.'

'What about your hair?'

Jenny raised her bandaged hand. 'They cut it all off, even the good bits. It's to stop the infection.'

'It will grow again.'

'I don't know about that. But the nurses are very kind.'

'What does the doctor say?'

Jenny coughed and tried to catch her breath. 'What he always says. Only time will tell.'

'Bert is very upset,' Lizzie assured her. 'And so am I.'

'It wasn't you that caused the fire. Have you seen Elsie?'

'I was worried about her so I went to Lavender Court where she lives. When I got there, it was Elsie who answered the door. I was relieved to see her, but she wasn't as pleased to see me.'

'It's that husband of hers. He treats her badly.'

'I thought he was sick.'

Jenny moved slightly in her chair. 'That's what Elsie says, so people don't ask any questions.'

Lizzie heaved a deep sigh. 'Well the long and short is, Elsie shut up as tight as a clam.'

'I'm sorry, but Elsie is a strange one.'

The sat talking for a while until it was time for Lizzie to leave. 'Jenny, you must come home to us when you leave this place. The airey is very large. You'll have your own quarters and be quite private.'

Jenny lifted her sore eyes. 'What does Bert think about that?'

'Hasn't he told you?'

Jenny shook her head.

Lizzie smiled. 'He's very fond of you.'

'But I won't have any hair,' Jenny sobbed.

Lizzie looked at this brave little woman and her heart went out to her. 'Jenny, it will grow back wait and see. Now try to rest.'

The visitors in the ward began to leave and after kissing Jenny goodbye, Lizzie joined them. When she got to the door, she turned back. The nurse was helping Jenny into bed. She looked an old woman. A lump came to Lizzie's throat. Jenny hadn't deserved this. She was so very brave.

Lizzie couldn't hold back her tears.

CHAPTER 43

THE NEWS that Lizzie was dreading came a week later. The same policeman who called before, arrived at the shop. He dismounted from his bicycle, strode in and took an official looking document from his breast pocket.

'This is from the coroner's office,' he boomed.

Bert peered over Lizzie's shoulder. 'What does it say?'

'We have to attend an inquest,' Lizzie explained and sank down on a stool. Her knees felt very weak.

'Why?' demanded Bert.

The policeman shifted from foot to foot. 'The fire investigators have found some remains.'

'Is it Madge?' cried Lizzie.

'You'll have to wait till the inquest to find out.' The policeman snatched back the paper. 'Anyone who can shed light on the matter has got to give evidence.'

'Did you ask Elsie Booth to attend?' Lizzie enquired.

'She's been shown the letter, same as you. Maintains she wasn't at the bakery that day. We went after the missing son too. There's no trace of him either. As for the survivor in hospital, we took her statement, but that was no help as she don't remember nothing.'

'It's a ruddy miracle she's even alive!' Bert cast the broom angrily aside. 'Don't go pestering my Jenny again!'

'We are only doing our duty,' the constable answered fearfully, backing away from the threatening figure.

'What if someone started the fire on purpose?' yelled Bert, his anger overwhelming him. 'You should be trying to find them.'

'Are you making an accusation?' the policeman ventured.

'What if I was?' Bert challenged. 'I might be!'

'Then I suggest you come down the station and bring your evidence with you.'

Bert looked so red in the face that the copper hurried out of the door and jumped on his bike.

Lizzie sank down on the stool. 'Bert, you shouldn't have said that. Without Elsie voluntarily giving evidence, there's nothing we can do.'

'I know. But I lost me rag.'

Lizzie thought of the terrible death that Madge might have suffered. How would the coroner identify Madge? Would anyone ever know for sure?'

'Listen, Lizzie,' Bert said desperately as he pulled up another stool and sat beside her. 'I've been thinking. Maybe Danny's got a point about leaving. No reason why we couldn't start afresh somewhere else.'

'What, you'd leave the island?' Lizzie said in great surprise.

'It's not too late to get shot of the Mill Wall.' Bert lifted his great shoulders. 'Or the shop. I mean, it's not out of the question ...'

'Do you really mean that Bert?'

Suddenly he growled like a big bear and closed his eyes

tight. When he opened them, Lizzie could see the hurt, anger and confusion in them.

'Oh, Bert, don't be upset. If you want to leave the East End, then so be it.'

'You'd do that for me?'

Lizzie nodded slowly. 'You are the only one in the world I would do it for, if it means that much to you. We are brother and sister, but sometimes I think we're joined at the hip. We think and work the same way. You are my best friend and closest ally. There's never been an occasion that you've let me down.'

Bert gave her a long stare, then slowly shook his head. 'I dunno what I'm saying, gel. Vella is messing with me mind. It's just that I can't get hold of him and knock seven bells out of the bugger. But I know I couldn't live with meself if I quit now.'

'Are you sure?'

Bert grinned and wiped the moisture from his eyes with his big fingers. 'Dunno what got into me. It's Jenny, I think. Seeing her in that 'ospital bed day after day, with all her lovely hair gone.'

'She *will* get well, Bert.'

'I know, gel. I want to make good for her. Settle down, have a family. And I want to do it here, on the island.' Bert tilted back his cap and looking directly at Lizzie, he said in a heartier voice, 'How much have we left in the kitty?'

Lizzie shrugged. 'Enough for a rainy day.'

'Let's get our thinking caps on. The bakery's a write-off. But that don't mean to say we can't try our luck with something else. And to hell with Vella!'

Lizzie heard Maurice and Ron coming in from the back-yard and whispered, 'we'll talk later tonight.'

Bert nodded, a wide grin parting his lips.

CHAPTER 44

IT WAS LATE at night and the interior of the shop was lit by Tilley lamps, shedding a glow over the crates of fruit and vegetables piled high against the walls. The blinds were lowered against the warm May evening and Bert had opened the storeroom door to allow in the breeze.

Maurice and Ron had left and Lizzie paced slowly up and down, across the gnarled, uneven floorboards. The shop on the corner of Ebondale Street had been part and parcel of the island for over a century. She thought about her father-in-law and the many occasions they had sat talking after a long and tiring day's business. If Bill was here now, he would refuse to be beaten by the likes of Vella and she took comfort from this.

Bert, with his big hands twisting the brown tobacco into thin papers, crooked an eyebrow as he followed her movements.

'We can sit tight and wait for Vella's next move,' Lizzie suggested as she paused her movements. 'Or we can take action. You and me cut our teeth in the East End. We know that when one door closes another opens.'

'I'm glad to hear you say that, gel.'

'1935 is a good time to be in business,' Lizzie continued. 'This month the King and Queen are celebrating their Silver Jubilee. It's a very special year.'

Bert's smile widened. 'I'm with you all the way, gel.'

'Time to talk to family.'

Lizzie had an idea forming. But it would take a great deal of planning with the help of those she knew she could trust.

CHAPTER 45

IT WAS Monday 6th May and the King and Queen's Silver Jubilee. Bert was driving Lizzie and Polly to Langley Street to celebrate. On every street in the East End there was a party planned. The kids had been given a day off school while the men climbed ladders to string bunting from roof to roof. The women were setting out the buffets on the long tables beneath, shoved end to end and laden with food.

Bert nudged the Wolseley into the gutter and Polly bounced excitedly on the back seat. 'Oh, Auntie Lizzie, I won't have to stay inside today, will I?'

'No,' Lizzie assured her as they clambered out of the car. Every front door was open, spilling out children of all ages. Lizzie knew she couldn't keep Polly inside any longer.

'Auntie Flo, when are we going to the party?' Polly asked when Flo appeared on the doorstep.

'Very soon, ducks. Now run along to the front room with your Uncle Bert and see Nelson.'

When they were alone Flo lowered her voice. 'Lizzie, I wanted to break the news to you the other day, but Syd said he told you already.'

'Yes,' Lizzie replied in a hushed whisper. 'What was the doctor's verdict?'

'I'm three months gone,' explained Flo. 'The baby's due in October.'

'I'm very happy for you, Flo.'

'But Syd is out of a job. He packed in the scrapyard, though the cops think he was doing a bunk after Walter and Clifford were collared.'

'Have they questioned Syd?'

'Yes. It was awful, but he'll probably tell you all about that. My big problem is we don't have no money coming in and we'll soon have another mouth to feed. Oh, Lizzie, it's all getting on top of me.'

'It's not the end of the world, Flo.' Lizzie squeezed her sister's arm. 'I'll see you never go short. Now, come on, cheer up, you are a mother-to-be. What better news is there, than that?'

Flo sniffed. 'Here's me, going on about my own troubles when what happened at the bakery was terrible. Is Jenny still in hospital?'

'Yes, Bert visits every day.'

'What about Madge?'

'Still no news. They're holding an inquest soon as they've found some remains.'

Flo gasped. 'How can they tell if it's Madge?'

'I don't know. But who else can it be?'

'She was such a nice little woman.'

Once again Lizzie felt guilty over Madge's death.

'Let's forget about our troubles and put out the food,' Flo suggested eagerly. 'The King and Queen will be celebrating today and so should we.'

It didn't take long before the Sharpes arrived with Ethel and Callum. They brought trays piled high with salt-beef sandwiches, pickles and crusty pies. Union Jack flags were stretched over the tables directly outside the front doors. One by one, the plates were added to the newspaper party hats and homemade crackers.

Lizzie could barely hear herself think. The children's screams of delight were deafening. The racket echoed up to the rooftops, together with a pounding on an old piano that had been carted out into the street. The flags and bunting waved in the breeze as the nation celebrated twenty-five years of the King's rein.

The beer flowed freely. More sandwiches were cut to replace the ones gobbled up by the kids. Then came the jellies, jam sponges, ice creams and lollies. Tummies were filled to bursting point.

After bawling out, 'God Save the King' many times over, the men cleared the tables, leaving room for the dancing. More patriotic songs were belted out on the piano. The children hurled themselves into the fray and the adults began to drink in earnest.

Lizzie watched Polly as she played with the other children. She looked so pretty in her pink party dress with her long copper ringlets bouncing over her shoulders. Nelson, up to mischief as usual, seemed to be twice as wide as he had been only a week ago. He was pushing and shoving with the best of them, using his strong arms and sturdy legs to fight off the competition. Callum at fifteen months was as tall as Nelson but very slight. He sat on his grandmother's doorstep, his big, dark eyes fixed on the children at play. Every now and then Polly would run up and cuddle him as Nelson received more than one clout round the ear from his mother.

It was late afternoon by the time the women left the kids to enjoy themselves. The men soon followed and tea was served indoors.

Lizzie was joined by Ethel on the settee, who gave a

noticeable sigh. 'It worries me that Callum doesn't join in with the other kids.'

'He's just a toddler yet.'

'I forget his age because he's so tall,' Ethel agreed wistfully.

'Just like his father,' remarked Lizzie. 'Have you thought about writing to Cal?'

Ethel shrugged. 'What good would it do? If he was interested, he would have written to me. I wonder if Rosie and Timothy are celebrating like we are?'

Lizzie couldn't help but grin. 'I can't imagine Cora enjoying a knees-up.'

This brought a reluctant smile from Ethel.

Just then, Lil called from the kitchen. 'The booze is served! We'll toast the King and Queen again before we go out.'

The off-the-back-of-a-lorry bottles of stout, sherry and gin flowed into glasses, mugs and any free receptacle.

'To King George and Queen Mary!' everyone shouted, after which they all sat down again, exhausted.

'Well, Syd,' said Doug after a brief respite, 'did you have any luck at Billingsgate?'

'I asked for my old job back, but they knew about my brothers. It was like I had the plague. Everyone steered clear of me.'

'That don't seem fair,' said Bert staunchly. 'It wasn't you who clocked the guard.'

'Course it's not bloody fair,' agreed Flo plonking herself down beside Ethel. 'But Syd is tarred with the same brush as the rest of the Millers. If he had stayed away from his perishing family, none of this would have happened.'

Syd looked critically at his wife. 'You didn't complain while I was bringing in the money.'

'No, because it made up for my rotten in-laws.'

'Have they charged Walter and Clifford?' Lizzie asked.

'Yes, with burglary and GBH,' growled Syd. 'They've been refused bail as the guard is fighting for his life.'

'That's the kind of people Syd's relatives are,' said Flo accusingly. 'We were foolish enough to believe they were going straight. When all the time they were using Syd as a front.'

'I'm sorry, Syd,' Lizzie said genuinely.

'And that's not the end of it,' Flo continued relentlessly. 'Tell 'em, Syd.'

Syd gazed down at his empty glass. 'They found more loot hidden at the scrapyard.'

'Did you know it was there?' Lil shouted from the settee as she puffed on her roll-up.

'No, 'course not,' Syd replied indignantly. 'But that didn't stop the law from carting me down to the station.'

'It's true,' Flo nodded with tears in her eyes. 'They turned up in a van and shoved Syd inside. I was left to face all the nosey parkers. He should have got out of the Missus's grasp before it was too late.'

'I tried,' Syd insisted. 'There was always some reason she needed me. But when she told me to lie to the cops and say Clifford and Walter were with me and Flo on the night of the robbery, it was the end of the road.'

'Christ lad, you wouldn't do that, would you?' said Doug in alarm.

'No, Doug, 'course I wouldn't. I'm not that much of a sucker.'

'She wanted to have a hold on us,' Flo said angrily. 'Draw us in so we could never get away.'

The room fell silent as everyone thought of the outcome of such a possibility.

'If you don't go back to portering,' Lizzie said, 'what will you do?'

'I tried the docks,' Syd replied half-heartedly. 'But I'd have to sign on as a casual. The work is very limited.'

'There's always the factories,' suggested Lil.

Syd shrugged. 'I went to the rope works and the boiler makers, but they only need skilled workers.'

Once again, the room was hushed.

'In that case, I do have an idea,' said Lizzie, breaking the silence.

'He ain't doing pub work,' Flo cried before Lizzie could explain. 'So, if you're thinking of offering him a job at the Mill Wall - '

'No,' Lizzie interrupted. 'I wouldn't do that.'

'It would be like jumping from the frying pan into the fire.'

Lizzie looked hard at her sister. 'Flo, it don't help you keep criticising. I'm trying to clean up the Mill Wall.'

'No chance with Frank at the helm,' Flo muttered under her breath.

'Now the bakery has gone,' Lizzie continued, ignoring the insult, 'me and Bert have decided to start again. Why don't you come in with us, Syd?'

'We ain't got a penny to spare,' complained her brother-in-law. 'I'm flogging the motor next week just to get us by.'

'You can chip in later,' Lizzie offered. 'It's manpower we need. Look, we are family. We trust each other. But it's your choice. I'm not twisting your arm.'

At this, Flo began to look interested. 'What have you in mind?'

'A decent gaff,' Bert began. 'That we can do up.'

'A shop, I suppose, to flog more bloody spuds and bananas,' moped Flo.

'No.' Bert raised his eyebrows. 'A factory.'

'What!' everyone cried.

Lizzie turned to Syd. 'You once said if you had the chance you'd leave the scrapyard.'

'Yes, but I didn't think you took me serious,' Syd protested.

Lizzie leaned forward. 'It would be a business we could all invest in. If we found an old place near the docks big enough to accommodate equipment.'

'What sort of equipment?' queried Flo.

'I'm not sure,' Lizzie said thoughtfully. 'But whatever it is, we need the accounts kept. When you met Syd, you were a clerk at the pickle factory.'

Flo nodded hesitantly. 'Yes, but I'm a bit rusty on figures.'

'First I've heard of it,' grumbled Syd. 'There ain't a day goes by without you totting up our expenses.'

'What about Nelson?' Flo asked ignoring her husband. 'I couldn't let him run loose in a factory. He'd have the whole lot arse upwards.'

'I'll help,' said Lil suddenly. And everyone turned to stare. 'I mean, Callum and Nelson get on like a house on fire. They'd be no trouble at all.'

'And if there was any way I could help …?' Ethel murmured.

'Gawd blimey,' gasped Syd, 'I never thought I'd get a chance like this. Are you sure, Lizzie?'

'I wouldn't make the offer, otherwise.'

'You and me, Syd,' said Bert eagerly, 'we'll do the labouring. If things go well, we'll take on more hands. Doug, would you be up for a few hours supervising?'

'Me?' said Doug, looking surprised. 'What good would I be?'

'You're still as sharp as you were when you worked for the PLA. You knew all the rules of the docks. You could liaise with their offices for us. In a sort of advisory capacity. Make sure we keep to the straight and narrow.'

'Well, I never did,' laughed Doug. He turned to his wife. 'What do you think, Lil?'

'It would get you out from under my feet for a few hours,' Lil chuckled. 'But where is all this big business going to take place?'

'The East India Docks,' suggested Lizzie. 'Somewhere like Chandler's Wharf where's there's a lot of factories and warehouses standing empty. It will take time to find the right one. But if everyone is on board, then Bert and me will start looking.'

'Well now,' said Doug, grinning. 'This is a cause for celebration.'

'Too true,' cried Lil exuberantly. 'We'll drink to the family firm. Who knows where this could lead?'

'As long it ain't up the garden path, who cares?' Cried Flo, refreshing the empty glasses.

'To a new start,' said Syd, lifting his beer.

'To prosperity and good health,' said Doug.

'To the family firm,' said Bert and polished off his beer in one.

After which, everyone else followed suit.

Lizzie smiled for this was a new start; Salvo Vella had not weakened their spirits, he had strengthened them. Prosperity and good health would not come easily, she knew, but today everyone was happy.

CHAPTER 46

IT WAS EARLY on a fine May day when Danny strolled along the pavement outside his showrooms, nodding to the passers-by as he went. Some of the faces he knew well and after a few cordial nods and greetings, he returned inside, studying the line-up of cars that were now on display. The festivities of the Silver Jubilee were over but there was still a feeling of excitement in the air and the public's mood was buoyant.

His gaze lingered on a two-tone Cabriolet with a full-length roll-back fabric sunroof that would knock the socks off any competitor's stock in this vicinity. Beside it was parked a sleek tourer, fitted with a twin overhead camshaft and a four-cylinder engine that was top of the range.

He was considering a smaller model for himself, so that he could teach April to drive. Though the reason she'd mentioned it was not much to his liking. They had disagreed once again on Tom's future schooling. Danny was reluctant to consider boarding him. But April had insisted that Tom would do very well in his education if given the opportunity.

Danny heaved a thoughtful sigh and returned his attention to the well-shod punters beginning to arrive on the forecourt. Several men browsed round the cars, but then a couple stopped to gaze in. The young woman wore a fur stole draped around her shoulders. One grey-gloved hand was firmly attached to an elderly man's arm. The gent sported a tailored Edwardian-style jacket and leaned heavily on his cane, though every now and then he remembered to straighten his shoulders.

Danny nodded slightly in their direction and received a brief acknowledgement back. It was often the case in such affluent circles that the luxury car would be purchased as a gift. The woman was at least thirty years younger than her companion. But just as they were about to enter the showrooms, a child of about three or four years of age, dressed in clothes that were almost too shabby to call clothes, with curly ginger hair matted to its scalp and a face so filthy he could only guess it was a boy, ran up to the couple. He held out his cupped hands, begging for coppers.

Oh, dear, thought Danny, could this be the return of the troublesome travellers? He held his breath, waiting to see if more arrived.

Danny watched intently as the young woman recoiled. But the gent dipped into his pocket and threw a coin. Then without warning, the beggar child's mother appeared. In contrast to her boy, she was half-decently, but oddly, dressed in a white blouse and colourful skirt, much like a street performer might wear. Gold hoops swung from her ears under her dark, curling hair. Bracelets shimmered on her wrists. Smiling at the couple, she attempted to engage them in conversation. However, whatever it was must have distressed them for they made off in great haste.

Annoyed that the incident had driven off a potential

customer, Danny made his way out. His eyes surveyed the scene to left and right, although he could see no travellers, and since the pavements were crowded, the woman and child were lost to sight. He was about to retrace his steps when suddenly he spotted them.

Just a few paces away, the boy was howling, refusing to give up his coin. His mother, appallingly, did everything in her power to relieve him of it; with a push, a shove, and a clout round the head – Danny was incensed.

Forgetting himself almost, he strode towards them just as the woman delivered another blow with such force that the boy was knocked off his feet. Should he help the child first, Danny wondered, or severely reprimand the mother? But before he could move another step, a hand landed on his shoulder.

He turned to find himself staring into the face of a stranger, a man he had never seen before accompanied by a smaller man who stared up at him with challenge in his small, sly eyes.

'Don't resist,' said the taller of the two and before Danny could object, he was pushed headlong into a vehicle that had drawn up to the kerb. Struggling to free himself, he saw the beggar woman staring through the window. She was smiling now, the child's hand in hers, before a hood was pulled roughly over his head.

Danny tried to listen for sounds he knew or some indication of where he was being taken. The voices he heard led him to believe he was accompanied by three men at least; one to drive the vehicle, the other two to restrain him. His hands were bound behind him and his protests all ended with a sound punch to the belly.

He felt the sweat stick to his collar. Who were these people and why had they taken him?

He didn't have to wait long for an answer. The car's engine finally rattled to a stop where a sharp jolt ended the journey. With pushes and thumps he was dragged along. More blows followed as he fell to his knees.

A command was shouted and he was grasped under his arms. His captors thrust him onto a hard seat. Here he sagged forward, once again attempting to catch his breath. Silence fell. This seemed even more menacing than the voices.

He sat very still, straining his eyes to see through the filthy hessian covering that reeked of engine oil. But it was pitch black. He knew this odour well and wondered if he had been brought to a garage. For all his senses told him that he was now shut in, hidden away from the world.

A sound of footsteps came close, light on the ground and slow, as if the person was assessing him. Or was there another beating to come? The steps were mingled with the brush of sawdust; that fine, gravelly mixture of wood shavings he'd used in his workshop.

'Where am I?' he demanded. 'Who are you?'

Again, followed the uncanny silence. Sweat oozed down Danny's back. His wrists were tied so tightly, he was forced to sit at un unnatural angle. His shins pounded and his ribs ached. Whoever this was, they knew about hurting. Just as Leonard Savage had. But Savage was dead. None of this made sense.

Suddenly the hood was removed. He blinked several times to adjust his eyes to the dim light. He was seated on a chair, a rope tied around his chest and fastened to his hands behind his back, so that every movement increased his discomfort. In front of him was some kind of painted wooden article, covered by tarpaulin. Beside this, what looked like a generator. Perhaps he was right about the garage. Could this be a competitor? Someone who resented his starting up in Euston? Yet he had made no enemies as far as he knew. The expensive stock he sold set him apart from back-street dealers.

Blinking hard, he strained to see to his right and left; but those corners were in total darkness. One smell was pervasive throughout - *horses*! Animal sweat, oils and liniment. Straw bales baked under a hot sun.

'And so we meet,' a male voice said and Danny's attention was drawn to a figure standing in the gloom by the only door he could see. It was however, bolted, barred and offering no chance of escape.

'Where am I?' Danny addressed the shape. 'Do I know you?'

'I know you.'

'Then tell me your name.' All Danny could see was the silhouette of a tall figure, with an odd looking feathered hat on his head. A cape of some sort was slung around his shoulders, giving him a theatrical air.

'I could be a friend,' came the strange accent. 'I could be your enemy.'

Danny saw the glint of metal at the man's waist. A weapon! Cold air seemed to blow into Danny's lungs and freeze his insides.

'Chancel Lane earned you a reputation,' the voice continued.

'How do you know about that?' Danny demanded.

'You have come up in the world,' continued the man, 'and, after Leonard Savage, have discovered great wealth in the city.'

So this person knew about Savage! Danny pulled back his head in an effort to ease the pain of his shoulders. 'What do you want of me?' he asked again.

This was ignored. 'I have heard that you have abandoned the East End and your friend and ally, Lizzie Flowers.'

Icy fingers clawed at Danny's ribs. Just as they had in the barn at Chancel Lane when death had awaited him only inches away, at the bottom of that stagnant well.

'What's Lizzie got to do with this?' he gasped, trying to stay calm.

'She is why you are here,' said the man in his soft, musical voice. 'You must persuade the lady to see reason.'

'I haven't seen Lizzie in a long while,' Danny protested. 'I couldn't persuade her, anyway, of something she didn't want to do.'

As unmoved as marble, the man's face showed no reaction. And then, to Danny's alarm, he saw it was a mask. Half a face, so cleverly sculptured that it could be mistaken for skin and bone. Eyes hidden behind slits, below finely curved eyebrows. An aquiline nose above a mouth that must be real for it smiled so cruelly.

'Running away like a frightened cur, will bring you no gain, Danny Flowers,' said the twisted lips. 'Do you know that a man carries his past like a cross? Even great wealth will not ease your burden.'

In anger, Danny yanked his arms, only to feel an agony shoot through his limbs. The chair beneath him moved and for a moment he thought he would topple. He gasped for breath and found himself choking.

'Remind Lizzie Flowers that the Mill Wall is mine,' said the whisper. 'Ask her about me. She will tell you.'

Danny struggled against his bonds but they tightened on his chest, breaking the flow of air to his lungs.

'And one day in the not too distant future, we shall speak again of your fine investment,' continued the speaker. 'We shall admire your fortune together, and how it has raised you above the common man. Above jackals like me!' Laughter trickled into Danny's ear; a breath fanned his cheek. And all at once, Danny remembered a tall, black-haired man wearing a dark beard and the sound of his lilting voice. But more distinctly he recalled the tell-tale trace of mud on the heel of a polished brogue. And the fact that this swaggering stranger visiting his showrooms for the first time, had known he was Danny Flowers.

'Bring in the law and you are doomed,' came the husky threat. 'We shall meet again, Mr Flowers!'

Before Danny could take a breath, the hood came down over his head again. He was dragged from the chair, pushed and punched, and finally thrown into a vehicle. He gasped for breath, straining to hear any voices or sounds that he might recognise. The vibration of the engine shuddered through him and he painfully wriggled himself upright. This time, he gathered, he must be alone with the driver.

He wondered if he could pull off his hood somehow, but his hands were still tied behind his back. He knew now they weren't about to kill him, so they must be returning him, but to where?

It was a good half hour later when the car came to a halt. He tensed and waited, while his heart beat a tattoo inside his chest. The click of the car door made him start and someone pulled him into the open. He was sent sprawling, his head hitting the ground. There was a woman's scream and the roar of an engine. Tyres screeched and a horn blasted.

Danny rolled on his back, the bonds around his hands digging mercilessly into his skin and tried to sit up, but he was dazed.

'Danny! What in God's name has happened?' The voice was Hugo's and Danny blinked as the hood was removed. He stared around him and saw first a blur, then a vague impression of the street, people stopping to stare at him and Hugo's concerned face.

'Untie me,' Danny muttered. 'Quick as you can, Hugo.'

As his salesman clumsily tore at the ropes binding him, Danny felt his head swim. A trickle of warm blood ran down by his ear.

It seemed an eternity by the time Hugo managed to free him and awkwardly hoisted his arm around his shoulder. 'Not far now, old man,' Hugo said as he dragged Danny towards the open doors.

'Shouldn't someone send for the police?' called a man from the crowd of onlookers.

Danny stopped briefly and forced himself to smile. 'We'll take care of that, thank you.'

But as they stumbled into the showroom, he knew that the very last action he would take, would be to involve the law. He had taken the masked man's threat seriously. He was not about to fill the street with blue uniforms.

'What happened?' Hugo asked as they reached the safety of the office and Danny sank onto a chair.

'I barely know,' Danny said, nodding to the decanter. 'Pour me a whisky will you Hugo?'

'Is that wise? You should have that head wound seen to.'

'A drink will do the trick. And make it a stiff one.'

Danny drank thirstily and felt the alcohol kick through his system.

'Was it those meddlers?' Hugo asked astutely. 'The ones I had trouble with?'

Danny nodded. 'I fear it was, Hugo.'

'What were they after?'

Danny slung back his whisky. 'What every scoundrel is after. Money.'

Hugo stood in his fine tailored suit, his immaculate

appearance only marred by the fear in his eyes. 'Protection-ists?' he said in his cut glass English and Danny nodded.

Much more than that, Danny thought to himself but didn't say. For Salvo Vella was a league apart from the refined social circles in which Hugo mixed. *The Prince* was an opportunist who would stop at nothing to get what he wanted.

CHAPTER 47

IT WAS a rainy morning at the end of the month when Lizzie and Bert drove to a large municipal building in Walthamstow. They were told when they arrived that the inquest was to be held in an office normally used for council meetings. As they filed in, along with others, Lizzie looked around for Elsie. She was disappointed to see that she hadn't attended.

Bert fidgeted on his chair as the room filled, prising his finger under his collar and stretching his neck. Lizzie knew he was uncomfortable in his rarely worn suit, but they had both dressed up in Madge's honour. Lizzie wore her navy-blue suit and white blouse and had coiled her dark hair up on top of her head. As she gazed around, she saw the policeman who had taken her statement. He sat in his uniform, looking very stern.

'This is a very unfortunate case,' began the coroner, a Dr Nolan, who had his name written on a white card placed on the desk in front of him. He studied the people who sat before him, then turned to the official on his right – a severe-looking man in a dark suit. 'The clerk will now read out the details that we have been given by the police regarding the fire in April this year at the bakery in Ripon Street.'

The clerk shuffled his papers then, in a very low voice, told everyone of the events of that day that were known to the police. It was hard for Lizzie to listen to as she thought of poor Jenny in hospital and Madge who had lain under all that debris from the blazing fire. Eventually the clerk announced that Madge's only relative, her son Ted, could not be found by either the police force or the insurance company. He quickly finished his summary and sat down.

'From the investigation results,' said Dr Nolan, 'it is clear that the blaze started in the kitchen of the bakery on Ripon Street, owned by one named Mrs Elizabeth Flowers. Is this lady present?'

Nervously standing, Lizzie nodded. 'That's me.'

'First my condolences, Mrs Flowers. I understand that you were on close terms with the deceased?'

'Madge was a good friend and employee,' agreed Lizzie in a soft voice.

'You had two other employees, Miss Jennifer Maguire and Mrs Elsie Booth?'

Lizzie nodded again. 'All my staff led very hard lives before they came to work for me. I offered Madge and Jenny accommodation above the bakery. Elsie lives at home and looks after her sick husband.'

'I see,' said the coroner, bending his white head to study his notes. 'I understand Miss Maguire is in hospital as a result of her injuries. But what of Mrs Booth?'

Lizzie paused before she spoke. 'Elsie's husband depends on her.'

'But if she managed to get to her job at the bakery each day, why couldn't she travel here?' he asked abruptly. 'I am told she refused to be interviewed by the police. Instead, she shouted at them through a broken window.'

Lizzie felt her cheeks burn as all heads turned to stare at her.

'Mrs Flowers, may I ask,' continued the coroner, 'in your opinion, is Mrs Booth a person to be relied on?'

'Yes, of course,' replied Lizzie quickly.

'And, she was on good terms with the other two women?'

'Yes, she was.'

'Is Mrs Booth in good health?'

Again, Lizzie hesitated. 'I believe so.'

'Then I can see no reason why she couldn't make some arrangement for her sick relative and attend today.'

Lizzie swallowed as she thought of poor Elsie's fear of the law and the sick husband who seemed to dominate her life. But how could she explain these circumstances without throwing Elsie into a bad light?

'Mrs Booth has a police record,' the corner said sharply. 'Are you aware of that?'

Lizzie took a breath. 'Yes, but Elsie is a good worker and I trust her.'

'You trust her?' repeated Dr Nolan with narrowed eyes. 'Trust her enough never to smoke a cigarette in your bakery and drop a match near a source of gas? Or leave a pan on the hob to burn? Or the ovens to overheat?'

'No, she wouldn't do that!' Lizzie protested, aware of the insinuation. 'Elsie didn't cause the fire. It was someone else.'

At this, a hush fell on the room.

Lizzie stared into the curious eyes surveying her.

'And who may that be?' came the silky, soft question.

Lizzie's palms were damp. 'I believe it was a crook named Salvo Vella, known as *The Prince*. He has a grudge against me and could easily have started the fire.'

Dr Nolan sat back in his chair and studied Lizzie with a mocking smile. '*The Prince*?' he repeated with contempt.

'Yes,' Lizzie murmured, aware of the muffled giggles around her. 'He and his women have used my tavern for prostitution.'

At this there was a sudden rush of whispers. 'Quiet!' cried the coroner and frowning at Lizzie he mocked, 'both a prince and a pauper? Surely it must be one or the other?'

Bert jumped to his feet. 'It's true,' he hollered, 'you should be after him, not poor bloody Elsie!'

There was sudden chaos in the room. It seemed to Lizzie that papers flew in the air, the clerk dropped his files to the floor and Dr Nolan jumped to his feet. 'Be quiet!' he roared at Bert. 'Or I'll have you thrown out!'

Lizzie was terrified that Bert would be dragged off. She grabbed his arm. 'Please Bert, don't lose your temper. It's no use. They won't believe us.'

'If there is any more disruption, I shall close the proceedings,' threatened the coroner. 'Now, let us have quiet and we shall resume.' He sat down with a thump and glared at Lizzie. 'Mrs Flowers, you have made a serious accusation. Have you any evidence to support your claim?'

Lizzie could only shake her head.

Dr Nolan folded his thin hands together on his desk. 'It is a very serious thing to accuse someone of a crime. And as this is an inquest into the death of the late Mrs Hobson, and not a criminal investigation, I shall overlook your outburst. But if there is any further disorder I shall stop the proceedings immediately. Which means there will be no resolution to a very tragic event.' He took in a long breath. 'I would like to remind everyone present that an inquest is held only to ascertain how, when and where a death occurred.'

Lizzie glanced at Bert.

'The old codger don't know what he's talking about,' Bert muttered under his breath.

'Now let us move on,' said the coroner. 'We have statements from the police and the fire department and a report from the insurers of the property. Apparently the late Mrs Margaret Hobson had no living relatives other than a son. It appears we can't find any trace of him. Is that right, Mr Spencer?'

Mr Spencer, the clerk, was a tall, thin man who nodded his head many times with an inscrutable expression. 'Yes, Dr Nolan. The police made enquiries as did our office, but no relative was found.'

'Very sad,' said the coroner formally. 'In which case, we shall hear what the police have to say and let us all remember we are listening to evidence and other information gathered about the how and when of this incident at Ripon Street, Isle of Dogs.'

Lizzie listened, her breath held as the same constable who met them at the fire, read out his notes. He spoke in a very laboured fashion, referring to "the deceased" many times over and describing the conflagration that had consumed the Ripon Street bakery.

'And Miss Jenny Maguire's statement, I understand you have it?' said Dr Nolan.

Jenny's short statement, that she remembered nothing after blacking out in the fire, was read aloud.

The coroner examined another file of papers then looked at a small dumpy man sitting to the rear. 'The pathologist, I believe, has the results of the post mortem. I do have your notes, Doctor, but would be grateful if you'd read them out for the benefit of the assembled.'

The pathologist made his way to the front. Lizzie listened intently, learning that Madge's remains had been identified by her one gold tooth, which Lizzie had described to the policeman. The test results showed the remains to be female and of middle age.

'And the cause of death?' the coroner asked.

'Failure of the heart,' said the pathologist and Lizzie gasped.

'Therefore, this lady did not die as a result of burns or suffocation?'

'Her lungs were not impaired, but the heart had suffered a sudden arrest.'

'Can you enlarge on that?' enquired the coroner. 'Would the shock of the fire have caused her heart to fail?'

'Possibly,' returned the pathologist. 'But in my opinion, the victim was suffering from the last stages of coronary artery disease. The heart showed an underlying and irreparable damage.'

'Not caused by the fire?' the coroner repeated.

'This person would already have been displaying symptoms of ill health in my opinion. Such as dizziness, fatigue, indigestion or pain in the chest, arms or shoulders.'

Lizzie sat up with a start. Although Madge had never said she felt ill, she had often complained of her 'turns'. Could these be what the pathologist was referring to?

'Mrs Flowers,' called the coroner. 'I have more questions for you. Please come to the front.'

Lizzie made her way forward, passing the pathologist to stand by the desk where the coroner sat.

'Mrs Flowers, did you know your employee suffered from a bad heart?'

Lizzie shook her head.

'She never complained of feeling ill?'

Lizzie hesitated before answering, causing the man to frown at her.

'Well?'

'Madge sometimes had a dizzy spell. She would call it one of her 'turns'. But she never mentioned a bad heart.'

'Did she visit a doctor?'

'I don't think so.'

'How often did she have these 'turns'?

'I … I don't really know.'

'Every week, every month, what would you say?'

Lizzie felt confused. 'I only heard her complain three or four times.'

'Then it was not a single occasion?'

Lizzie shook her head.

'Thank you. You may sit down now.'

The coroner bent towards his clerk and soft muttering could be heard as Lizzie took her seat again.

'What was all that about?' growled Bert.

'I don't know, but I wish,' whispered Lizzie, 'that I hadn't taken Madge's turns so lightly.'

The coroner addressed the pathologist once again. 'So you can confirm this lady did not die as a direct result of the fire?'

'As I have said, sir, the shock may have contributed, but the victim would not have survived another year, in my opinion.'

Lizzie felt numb. She couldn't take it all in. Madge had died from a bad heart, which no one had suspected.

The next person called by Dr Nolan was a representative from the insurance company. He explained that they were no nearer drawing a conclusion as to how the fire had started. An engineer from the gas company spoke next who was just as vague.

'Could the ovens be at fault?' the coroner asked. 'I understand they were there when Mrs Flowers took over the property from a Mr James?'

'They was old,' said the gas engineer, 'been there donkey's

years when there was rooms rented out. But there was nothing to say they was faulty.'

'Could there have been a leak from the mains?'

'We cannot be certain, sir,' said the man; a short, thin man with a permanent frown. 'The fire damage was extensive.'

Dr Nolan sighed a deep sigh. 'In that case, I cannot come to a satisfactory conclusion about the circumstances that caused such a sudden and unexplained death. I have interviewed everyone concerned bar one.' He looked accusingly at Lizzie. 'Unless the police wish to take matters further, I believe I can do no more. Do I have an opinion on this?' he demanded of the constable who jumped to his feet and shook his head firmly.

'No sir. We have concluded the investigation.'

'Very well, I am recording an open verdict,' decided the coroner. 'The body may now be released for burial. Good day to you all.' He stood up and waved his clerk before him, striding out of the room, followed by his grey-suited and grey-faced officials.

Lizzie sat in silence, watching the people file out. She gazed at Bert who sat open-mouthed. 'Well we ain't none the wiser, are we?'

'Strikes me, he'd like to put the blame on Elsie.'

'But it wasn't her.'

'You and me know that, but I reckon he would have got her in a right tangle just to get a result.'

'It's hard to believe that Madge was dying of a bad heart.'

Bert pulled on his cap. 'She couldn't have known herself or else she'd have told someone.'

'At least we can bury her now. We'll stop at the undertakers on the way home.'

'Will it be the full works, horses and all?'

'Madge didn't want to be buried with fuss,' Lizzie answered. 'Though she did say she'd like a party and no tears.'

'I like the idea of that.'

As they left the building Lizzie thought about all that happened since Madge's death. The investigations by police and insurers had turned up nothing new. Nobody was any the wiser after the inquest. If Salvo Vella, or one of his gang was the cause of the fire, they had certainly fooled the authorities.

CHAPTER 48

THE STRAINS of *The Day Thou Gavest Lord Has Ended* soared up to the vaulted ceilings of the Church of Our Lady of Grace. The robust voices of the small gathering echoed throughout the Roman Catholic Church and onto the street outside where passers-by were mopping their foreheads in the sultry June weather. However, it was cooler inside the church. The congregation sat quietly listening to the parish priest and tried to decipher the Latin that they were unfamiliar with.

Lizzie was wearing a black, two-piece costume and black lace mantilla over her drawn back hair. Bert sat to her left dressed in his best, and only, dark suit. Polly on her right, wore a deep green summer dress, black patent shoes and white ankle socks.

Those who had come to pay their last respects at the Requiem Mass were mostly Lizzie's family as Madge, it appeared, had very few friends. But a handful of customers and residents from Ripon Street had arrived at the last minute to swell the numbers.

Lizzie had seen to it that the coffin had been carried into

the church the evening before when she had attended the Benediction. Her one regret was that Ted, Madge's son had not been found. Despite the funeral arrangement notice she had posted in the local newspapers, Ted remained absent.

Mindful of Madge's wishes, there was to be no gathering at the graveside. There were, however, a handful of floral tributes on the wooden casket; marigolds, white chrysanthemums, cream-coloured lilies, purple, sweet-smelling violets and a spray of summer flowers.

There were very few dry eyes in church that day. As the organ began to play *Abide With Me*. Lizzie listened to Polly's sweet voice as she sang from the hymn book. Bert boomed out the loudest, his towering form dwarfing the rest of the mourners.

The priest, Father Bergen, had not known Madge as she had been a lapsed Catholic. But after the hymns and much ringing of altar bells, he stood in the pulpit and spoke of Madge's hard life and industrious spirit. He also gave an account, provided by Lizzie, of the welcome and safety that she found at the bakery on Ripon Street.

'I didn't know Mrs Hobson personally, but I understand she was a kind and caring soul,' said the young priest in his soft voice. 'She suffered, I have been told, from a weak heart. Despite her ill health, she made a very fine cook. She was beloved by all and enjoyed a rare sense of humour. Let us pray that she finds peace in the Life beyond, where we shall all travel one day and where our creator holds each one of us in the palm of His hand.'

Madge was indeed a brave soul, Lizzie reflected. She would always be considered of as one of the family.

Father Bergen began to distribute the Holy Communion. Lizzie thought again of Ted Hobson, the missing son. Madge had once said that the drink had been responsible for his violence. But if only he could be here now to bid goodbye to his mother.

Slowly, heads bowed, the communicants returned to their pews with a quiet shuffling on the polished boards of the floor. The aroma of incense filled the church.

When the organ struck up, it was to play the first bars of Rachmaninov's *Ave Maria*. A young female voice from the choir loft began to sing. The notes were so pure and true that many handkerchiefs were dabbed under eyes and noses blown.

The pall bearers stepped forward and took hold of the oak casket's gleaming handles. Syd and Frank, at Lizzie's request, had agreed a truce for the day and supported the rear. Bert and one of the funeral parlour's own staff lifted the front. Lizzie held Polly's hand and followed the small procession. Outside, in the sunshine, the casket was slipped into the rear of the hearse.

Slowly, people took their leave.

'I know we ain't invited to the grave,' Gertie said, adjusting her black beret. 'But there's beer and sandwiches at our place. Frank's driving us back, so come when you've done your bit.'

Lizzie watched Frank's car leave the church grounds, closely followed by Doug's little Morris in which was squeezed Lil, Flo, Syd and Ethel.

At last Lizzie stood alone with Polly in the church grounds.

'Is Madge happy now?' Polly asked in a dignified manner.

Lizzie smiled. 'Yes, I'm sure she is.'

'Then why do people cry?'

'Because they miss seeing that person.'

Polly frowned. 'Uncle Frank said he almost died once. But he don't think people cried about him.'

Lizzie looked into Polly's big brown eyes. 'You care a lot for your Uncle Frank, don't you, Pol?'

'He makes me laugh and he don't tick me off. I wish I had a dad like Uncle Frank.'

Lizzie knew this was the moment. 'Pol, what would you say if he could be your dad?'

'You mean, he's not my uncle?' replied Polly, looking alarmed.

'Would it matter if he wasn't?'

A pair of small shoulders lifted. 'Dunno, really. But if my mum is me mum and Uncle Frank is me dad, why didn't they get married?'

'Not everyone gets married,' Lizzie explained. 'Your mum and Uncle Frank were close friends.'

'But she went away.'

Lizzie bent down. 'When people are friends, that's what matters.'

'Like you and Uncle Danny?'

Lizzie nodded.

'Do I have to leave you and live at the pub if Uncle Frank is me dad?'

Lizzie gave a firm shake of her head. 'Not if you don't want to. Nothing will change, except what you call him.'

Polly traced the toe of her shoe in the grass they were standing on, then looked at Lizzie with a mischievous smile. 'You know what Uncle Frank told me?'

'What?'

'He showed me these little white pills and said they stop people from jawing in his head. He said, they rabbit on so much, he can't get a word in edgewise. He ain't barmy is he?'

Lizzie chuckled. 'No Pol, he's not.'

'He said he's on the wagon.'

'Do you know what that means?'

'He said if he falls off it, you might never speak to him

again. And he don't want that. Neither do I. Cos I love you both.'

Lizzie held back her tears. This little girl was such a joy. She had her own way of reasoning out her life and so it seemed, had her father.

'Polly, you are a very grown-up young lady. I didn't think we would be talking about your father today.'

'You ain't gonna get all upset are you?'

'No. I'm very happy.'

It now seemed to Lizzie that Frank had already found a place in his daughter's heart and Polly had accepted the facts that Lizzie had been afraid to disclose.

'Look, Auntie Lizzie, look who's over there!' cried Polly suddenly.

Two figures approached. Lizzie wondered … could it possibly be? Was she dreaming? The cheeky-faced boy was a little older than Polly. The tall, broad-shouldered man wore a dark suit. His thick, fair hair deepened to gold in the rays of the sunshine. Strangely, it seemed a lifetime since she had last seen Danny. Yet somehow, it felt like yesterday.

'LIZZIE,' Danny murmured softly and took her hand in his. 'It's good to see you.' He grinned at Polly. 'My word, Pol, you've grown!'

'Uncle Danny! Tom!' Polly cried. 'Why haven't you come to see us?'

'Ah,' he said glancing at Lizzie. 'That's a long story, Pol.'

'Grown-ups always tell long stories,' Polly answered matter-of-factly. 'I'm quite used to having to listen to them.'

'Well I ain't,' Tom disagreed matter-of-factly. 'They bore me stiff. Aunt April is always saying that children should be seen and not heard.'

Lizzie looked at Danny who remained silent.

'You should have come to Mass, Tom,' Polly continued in her authoritative manner. 'There's lots of candles you can light and make a wish. And one of me wishes came true, almost the minute I'd wished it.'

'What was that?' asked Tom.

Polly looked at Lizzie, her brown eyes sparkling. 'Me and Auntie Lizzie know. But I can't tell you yet.'

'Can I light a candle and make me wish, Dad?' Tom said eagerly.

'Well, I'm not sure … ' Danny hesitated.

'The church is still open.' Lizzie smiled at the two youngsters. 'Don't drip wax on your nice clean clothes.'

Tom and Polly ran off and Lizzie returned her gaze to Danny. She wanted to ask why he was here. The day had been full of emotion; first bidding goodbye to Madge and then came the moment when, as if it was by Madge's own hand, Lizzie had found the moment to tell Polly about her father.

And now there was Danny. Standing before her, unchanged and just as she remembered. When he eventually spoke, he chose his words carefully. 'I was very sorry to hear about the bakery,' he murmured quietly. 'And the sad loss of Madge's life.'

Lizzie nodded, digging deep to make her reply. 'Thank you. Madge was very special. We miss her.'

'How are you, Lizzie? It's been a long time.'

'I thought we would see you and Tom at Christmas.' She tried to keep her voice steady, for seeing him again so suddenly was bringing back old memories.

He hung his head, pushing his hands into his trouser pockets. Lizzie thought how immaculate he looked, a man of distinction in his dark suit, white shirt and plain dark tie. How different he was to the person she once knew, at his happiest when covered in oil and grease. 'I'm sorry, Lizzie, truly sorry. It was … ' he stopped, frowning as he lifted his sad blue eyes to hers, 'another long story.'

Lizzie had thought their friendship meant more to him than belated apologies. 'Christmas wasn't the same for Polly without Tom.'

'No, nor for him – or me,' he answered. 'I should have made more of an effort.'

Lizzie wondered what was going through his mind as he tugged the cuffs of his jacket. Gold cufflinks sparkled in the sunshine and the breeze lifted his hair gently. Raising his fingers to the scar just below his hairline, he asked, 'How are Dad and Gertie?'

'Ask them yourself,' she invited quietly. 'I'm going there after I've been to the graveyard.'

'Would I be welcome?'

'You know better than to ask that.'

He paused. 'Can I drive you?'

Lizzie shook her head. 'But you can take Polly.'

'Lizzie, we need to talk about Murphy. I've been to see him and I think you should know what we discussed.'

Lizzie didn't ask more as the children came running towards them. But whatever it was had brought Danny here and must be of great importance.

CHAPTER 49

It was now late afternoon and a cooler breeze blew across East London Cemetery. Lizzie's thoughts were still with Danny as she stood at the graveside. Father Bergen, dressed in his cassock and surplice, sprinkled the lowered casket with holy water from the aspergillum.

Lizzie's hoped Madge would be happy with her resting place under the shady branches of a small hazel tree. The patch was not far from Lizzie's mother's grave, where almost fifteen years before, Kate Allen had been laid to rest. It consoled Lizzie to think that Madge and Kate might be together on another plane, smiling as they watched today's proceedings. The priest, though, was solemn-faced and accompanied only by the gravedigger. The blessing and prayers were short, the final offering made by Father Bergen in a quiet, respectful tone.

'For dust thou art and unto dust thou return ... ' Father Bergen's words joined the song of the sparrows, nestled in the tree's branches above. Lizzie bowed her head as she looked into the void below where Madge's mortal remains now rested.

'May this soul and the souls of all the faithful departed through the mercy of God rest in peace.'

I hope you are happy wherever you are, my dear Madge, Lizzie thought silently. *You are always in my thoughts.*

Father Bergen continued as Lizzie threw in a handful of soil. Madge had been given the send-off that she had asked for, but would it be more proper for that missing son to be here? She looked around, at the many headstones and long grass and the winding path that led out of the cemetery. A single female figure lingered some way off. She wondered if someone had turned up who had not been to the church. But as the figure moved off, she returned her attention to Father Bergen.

He closed his prayer book and smiled at Lizzie. 'I hope you approved of the service?' he asked.

'Thank you. It was what Madge wanted.'

'We shall say prayers this week for the repose of her soul.'

'Can I drive you back to church?' Lizzie asked.

'No, I have my bicycle. God bless, my dear.'

Lizzie watched him walk away very serenely through the untidy graveyard. Once again, the wind caught the leaves of the tree over Madge's resting place as the gravedigger began his work.

Slowly Lizzie turned, only to come to a sudden halt. The figure she had seen down the path appeared in front of her. A scarf was tied over the woman's head, coming down almost to her nose. The coat she wore was a shabby tweed and her flat shoes were dull with age. There was something familiar about her and Lizzie took in a sharp breath. Stepping slowly forward, she said cautiously, 'Elsie? Elsie? Is that you?'

The figure nervously retreated a few steps. Lizzie called out again.

'Elsie, please don't go!'

The hunched shoulders began to jerk with sobs. As Elsie looked up, Lizzie saw her eyes were swollen with tears.

'Lizzie, oh Lizzie, is Madge really dead and gorn?'

Lizzie hurried forward to take the sobbing girl in her arms. As light as a feather, Elsie fell into them, shivering and shaking.

'Elsie, what's happened to you?'

But Elsie couldn't reply. Her loud sobs echoed throughout the churchyard. Lizzie took her gently by the shoulders and guided her towards a nearby bench.

CHAPTER 50

GERTIE OPENED the door and gasped. 'Blimey, look who it ain't!' She stared at Danny, blinking. 'Is it you or an apparition?' Her startled eyes descended to Tom and Polly. 'Just look at you two! The terrible twins! There won't be no gloomy faces this time, eh Pol?'

Polly flung her arms around her grandmother's neck. 'Grandma, I had a ride in Uncle Danny's posh car. Auntie Lizzie's gone to the cemetery.'

'Then you'd better all come in.' Gertie smothered the two little faces in kisses. 'Go along with you both. The grub's in the kitchen.'

Danny stepped into the dark passage. 'Hello, Gertie.'

Gertie's eyes filled with tears. 'Hello, stranger.'

'Long time no see.'

'Last bleeding October it was,' retorted Gertie. 'Why didn't you visit at Christmas?'

Danny held her close. 'Sorry,' he whispered.

'I was beginning to think the next time you showed up it would be to bury me or your dad.'

'Don't say that, Gertie.'

She smiled in a forgiving manner, her wrinkled face under her thin, grey hair reminding Danny of the hard life she had led bringing up two young boys that were not her own. It felt good to be close to her once more.

'Your brother is here,' she warned. 'Don't start any fights.'

'I didn't come for a fight,' Danny assured her. 'At least, not with my brother.'

'That's good, then.'

She led him into the front room where his father and Doug Sharpe were sitting in the comfortable armchairs beside the hearth.

'Hello, Dad. Doug.'

'Well, bless my soul, if ain't Danny,' Doug cried. 'Good to see you, my lad.'

Bill stared in a bewildered fashion at his son. 'Danny! What are you doing here?'

'I asked him the same meself,' chuckled Gertie. 'So, don't tear him off a strip.'

Danny embraced his father. 'How are you, Dad?'

'Better for seeing you, boy. Were you in church?'

'No. But I saw Lizzie.'

Bill's lips parted in a smile. 'Is everything all right with you two?'

Danny didn't answer but drew up a chair. 'Sorry it's been so long.'

Doug touched Danny's shoulder. 'Like a beer?'

'You bet, Doug.'

'Well now,' said Bill when they were alone. 'You'd better spill the beans.'

'There's something on my mind, Dad. I need to speak to Lizzie.'

'Is it this other woman?' Bill stared at him with watery eyes. 'I never thought I'd see the day when you two split up. Thought you would work it out somehow.'

'Dad, I've been a fool.'

'I've dropped a few clangers in me time as well,' grinned Bill. 'But it's never too late to put them right.'

Danny nodded. 'It's about the pub that I've come.'

'The Mill Wall? Your brother ain't doing a bad job. He's doing the best he can for Lizzie.'

'I know.'

'I hope it ain't sour grapes,' said Bill looking anxious. 'You was never up for the likes of running the Mill Wall in the first place. You figured you'd do better with that posh place in Euston.'

'No Dad, it's not sour grapes.'

'Must say, your showrooms was an eye-opener. We spent half a day gassing with that that fella of yours, what was his name – Hugo? Didn't understand a word he spoke, mind, but he cut quite a dash. Me and Gertie reckoned you were on to a winner even though you'd turned your back on the East End.'

Danny heaved a sigh. 'After Leonard Savage, I'd had enough.'

'He was a bastard, no doubt about that.'

'I figured I'd get a square deal up West with the gentry. Better class of vehicle and customer, clean money.' Danny laughed emptily. 'But I've found it's a better class of crook, too.'

Bill's jaw dropped as he listened to his son's tale of woe.

'We've been having agitators outside the showroom. Hugo got threatened and then I did, too. And it's not just a threat against me. It's the pub as well.'

'Is Lizzie in danger?'

Danny knew Lizzie was like a daughter to his father. Bill had protected her the best he could from the early days when Mik Ferreter, the bookie, had tried to steal the shop. Leonard Savage, both thug and murderer, had followed and had so very nearly succeeded, where Ferreter had failed.

'A few weeks back,' Danny explained, 'I was pushed inside a car and driven somewhere. They put a hood over me head so I couldn't see. When we arrived, the welcome party put the boot in. They want the Mill Wall and my showrooms.'

'Does Lizzie know?'

'That's what I need to tell her.'

'Did they rough you up bad?'

'Nothing I couldn't handle. But I'm worried about Lizzie.'

'She's got Frank and a few of Murphy's boys.'

'But is that enough?'

Bill looked up as Doug returned with the beers. 'Do you know who took you?' Bill asked gruffly.

'His name is Salvo Vella.'

At this, Doug sat down with a thump. His face turned white. Beside him stood Frank.

'You're joking,' Frank gasped, having overheard what had been said.

Danny shrugged. 'I wish I was.'

'I was going to say it's good to see you again, brother,' Frank muttered. 'But after hearing that I've changed me mind.'

Danny forced a smile. 'At least this time we're on the same side.' A remark that everyone present agreed with.

CHAPTER 51

LIZZIE LISTENED as Elsie poured out her sad story. 'I met Madge years ago when we both lived in Stepney. She was a cook in a cafe and I was her skivvy. She was like the muvver I never had. I'm an orphanage kid, see.'

Lizzie gave Elsie a hanky and she wiped her tears. 'I thought you first met Madge at the bakery.'

'When Madge got the job with you, she told me you was a nice lady. But by then I was shacked up with Ted, Madge's son. He was a real charmer at first. Madge said I'd regret the day I ever set eyes on him. And she was right. He pinched all me money and bashed me about. So me and Madge ran away from Stepney. While Madge fell on her feet and started at the bakery, I kipped at the Sally Army. We thought he couldn't find us. But he did. He said if I didn't go and live with him at that pigsty in Lavender Court, he'd do us in.'

'Oh Elsie, you should have told me.'

'Daren't.'

'Is that why you said he was sick?'

Elsie nodded. 'It was the only thing I could think of.'

'Did Jenny know about this?'

'No, 'cos she would have told you. Ted threatened to rough her up, too, if we didn't take money from your till. But Gawd's honour we didn't.'

'Elsie, you and Madge must have been very scared.'

Elsie nodded and slowly pulled off her scarf. A red line showed round around her neck and there were bruises on her throat. 'This is what he done to me last night. I thought it was me end.'

Lizzie stared at the dreadful marks of strangulation. 'Oh, Elsie, he almost killed you.'

Elsie nodded. 'I can't go back there. Ted will come after me.' Her tears plopped onto her shabby coat. 'It was Ted who started the fire because we wouldn't pinch any money.'

'What?' Lizzie gasped.

'Ted came in the bakery and hit Jenny. He must have knocked her out. Madge went to help but he done her over, too. I was too scared to stay and scarpered. But, oh, Lizzie, if I had tried to stop him, Madge might still be alive.'

Lizzie drew a sobbing Elsie into her arms. She understood the guilt that Elsie was feeling, for she had felt it, too.

But the fire was down to one man only. Not Salvo Vella as she had thought. But a perfect stranger called Ted Booth whom no one had suspected.

'You'd better come with me, Elsie.'

'Where to?' Elsie croaked.

Lizzie took Elsie's arm as she climbed unsteadily into the car. 'My in-laws live in Poplar. You'll be quite safe there.'

The front door to Gertie and Bill's house stood open. Elsie peered out from under her scarf. She looked up and down the street, refusing to move. 'I don't want to cause no trouble, especially as it's the day of Madge's funeral.'

'Elsie, you've nowhere else to go,' Lizzie protested. 'We can't stand out here in the road all day.'

Just then a small figure wearing a black beret tottered out

from the house. 'Lizzie, gel, we've been waiting for you.' Gertie stared at Elsie. 'Who's this?'

'Elsie worked at the bakery with Madge.'

'Oh Gawd,' cried Gertie, taken aback. 'You was the one who don't like the cops!'

At this, Elsie burst into tears.

'Now, now,' said Gertie sternly, 'don't upset yerself. We ain't fond of the rozzers round here, so you're in good company.'

The two children came running after their grandmother. 'Auntie Lizzie,' cried Polly excitedly, 'Tom and me have been playing hide and seek and ' She stopped in alarm when she saw Elsie's tear-stained cheeks and frightened face.

'Come along all of you,' said Gertie, taking Elsie's wrist and pulling her along. 'We'll sit in the kitchen and finish up them currant buns, kids.' As she herded them together, Gertie looked over her shoulder at Lizzie. 'The others are waiting for you in the front room. We'll join you later.'

Relieved that Gertie had taken charge of Elsie and the children, Lizzie walked into the front room. Danny was standing at the big, unlit fireplace. One arm rested on the shelf above and his blue eyes met hers with an unspoken welcome. Doug and Bill reclined in the big easy chairs whilst Frank and Syd sat opposite one another on the dining chairs. Flo, Lil and Ethel all looked up from the settee.

'You'll be surprised to see we ain't killed each other yet,' cackled Lil, the first to break the tense silence.

Flo chuckled. 'Those two over there came close.' She nodded to Syd and Frank who deliberately avoided each other's gaze.

'We waited till you arrived, love,' greeted Bill in his wheezy voice. 'Danny here has something to tell you.'

Lizzie smiled. 'And I've something to tell you, too.'

'Then we'd best get on with it,' said Doug officially. 'The

last time we had a pow-wow like this was almost three years ago.' He looked at Frank. 'When you walked back into our lives on Lizzie and Danny's wedding day and buggered everything up.'

Frank shifted uncomfortably on his chair. 'You don't have to rub it in, Doug.'

'I'm just giving a sense of proportion.'

'As Danny said, we're all on the same side this time,' Frank agreed, glancing at his brother.

'We all have an interest in the future,' Syd chipped in.

'Yes,' agreed Lil, 'are you still up for the factory, Lizzie?'

Lizzie walked to the dining table and sat beside Syd. 'More than ever, Lil. But first, I'd like to thank everyone for turning up today. Madge would have appreciated the effort.'

'Poor mare,' said Flo and Lil nodded.

'That bloody foreigner needs stringing up for what he done to her,' Lil muttered as she sipped her sherry.

'The fire wasn't started by Salvo Vella,' Lizzie announced. All heads swivelled towards her. 'Elsie was at the churchyard today. She's in the kitchen with Gertie.'

Bert sat forward. 'Did she come clean?'

Lizzie nodded. 'It was Madge's son, Ted, who started the blaze. Ted is the man she's been living with. She lied about him being sick so people wouldn't find out he beat her and Madge on a regular basis.'

Bert jumped to his feet. 'She could have told us!'

'He swore to kill her if she did.'

'I'll soon sort him out!' Bert strode to the door.

'Bert, come back and sit down.' Lizzie shook her head firmly. 'Time for that later. We have a bigger problem to deal with.'

'Salvo Vella,' Danny interrupted as Bert returned to his seat. 'A thug who may not be responsible for the bakery fire but he does have other plans to take over the Mill Wall – and my showrooms.'

'How do you know all this?' Frank asked suspiciously.

'I know because I was at the wrong end of his boot when he gave me the warning.'

'But how did he know where to find you?' Lizzie asked in alarm.

'You and me have a reputation, Lizzie. Leonard Savage ain't forgotten by a long shot. You were right,' he admitted, facing her. 'You can't leave your past behind, not with what we've done.'

Lizzie gazed around her at the expectant, if solemn, faces of the only people she trusted. Murphy's words went through her mind. Family and friends, gathered together as they always had through the trials and tribulations of the passing years. But she had never expected Danny to be present. Nor Syd and Frank to sit at the same table together.

'United we stand, united we fall,' muttered Syd, glancing across at Frank. 'But you better be on your bloody toes this time, cocker.'

Frank ignored this and looked at Lizzie. 'Vella will only take the Mill Wall over my dead body.'

At which Lil roared with laughter and spluttered, 'And do us all a favour!'

But Lizzie spoke in Frank's defence. 'Lil, if we are all in this together, then Frank don't need knocking. He deserves credit for sticking it out at the pub.'

Just then the door flew open and Polly and Tom burst in. 'I lit a candle at church,' Polly said to Frank, 'and made a wish that you was me dad.'

Frank looked surprised. 'Well now, Pol, if that's your wish, I reckon it's granted.'

'But I still want to live with Auntie Lizzie.'

'Sound thinking, gel' Frank replied looking at Lizzie. 'There ain't no place like home.'

'Dad, if Uncle Frank is Polly's dad when he was her uncle,' interrupted Tom, 'what do I call you, if I'm adopted?'

Danny slipped his arm around his shoulders. 'You call me what you've always called me, Tom. You're my son, and I'm your dad.' Danny looked at Frank and gave a brisk nod. 'And this is your Uncle Frank. We ain't seen much of him lately, but all that's about to change.'

Flo took out her hanky and blew her nose. Ethel smoothed a tear from her eye.

'Now we've got all that sorted, then,' said Bill unsentimentally, 'can we all get on with business?'

'I second that,' said Gertie as she walked into the room. 'Get your thinking caps on the lot of you. Like Bill says, you have to decide what's to be done about this foreign bugger.'

At which everyone hurriedly nodded.

CHAPTER 52

DANNY CLEARED HIS THROAT; he hadn't expected to be standing here, pouring out his heart. But he found himself explaining what had happened at the showrooms and, looking at Lizzie, told of his meeting with Murphy. 'We've made a plan. It's not foolproof. But it's worth considering.'

'Are you sure Murphy is on the level?' said Lil and lit yet another cigarette. 'I mean, he's no saint himself.'

'That's true Lil,' Danny agreed. 'But neither is he a devil.'

'What made you go to Murphy?' asked Lizzie.

'It was when I was face down in the dirt at Vella's feet,' he growled. 'I saw myself back at Chancel Lane and my best mate Cal was drowning in a stinking well not fifty feet away. Frank and Bert were expecting a bullet to their brains and you were hooded, Lizzie, just like Vella did to me. So, I asked myself one question. How many more times are you going to end up a mug making the same mistake again, Danny Flowers? I decided then, if I got out of Vella's alive, I would do whatever it takes to make him pay.'

Once more there was a stunned silence until Doug spoke.

'There's an alternative to violence, son. You could turn him into the law. There's a chance he's on their books.'

'But how could he be, Doug?' Danny asked. 'No one knows what he looks like, or where he operates from.'

'What's your plan then, Danny?' Syd asked eagerly.

'It's the Mill Wall he wants, Syd. And we are going to give it to him.'

Once more there was not a whisper.

'We give him exactly what he wants,' Danny repeated. 'And this is where Frank comes in.' He turned to his brother. 'From now on you let Vella's women trade on the condition you get a backhander.'

'But I've been kicking them out,' Frank protested.

'Not any more you won't. Instead, let them know you're dissatisfied, that life under Lizzie Flowers ain't worth living. You've taken to drink again and woe betide anyone who tries to stop you.'

'But I'm off the booze.'

'Use a tankard. They won't know what you're drinking.'

Frank opened his mouth and shut it again.

'Tell them you're all bitter and twisted and thinking of jacking the pub in. Vella will soon come sniffing around.'

'But they'll see the blokes on the door and Elmo and Fowler out the back,' Frank argued. 'They're loyal to Lizzie and them women know it.'

'You won't have them,' Danny answered steadily. 'You'll be on your tod.'

'I'll be left alone you mean?'

'This has got to look authentic, Frank.'

'So, it's me who's the patsy?'

'There's no other way.'

'I ain't even got Lenny. He did a bunk last week.'

'Just keep tipping the ginger beer down your throat and falling over. The women will believe you're kosher and Vella will show up. You doing the dirty on Lizzie is too good a chance to miss.'

'It's a risk, Danny,' warned Bill with a frown. 'Frank might put dynamite up Vella's arse instead of fooling the bleeder.'

'It's a risk I'm willing to take, Dad. The question is, are you Frank?'

'I dunno!' Frank protested in panic. 'What if he smells a rat?'

'He won't if you convince him you're eager to take revenge for the lousy way Lizzie has treated you. Your voices have come back. They're in your head, driving you mad.'

Frank gasped. 'Don't tempt bloody providence, Danny!'

'Syd will call by each evening. Vella knows me and Bert but he don't know Syd. He will buy a pint and suss out whether or not Vella has moved in. When we've got a result, we'll use Murphy and his crew.'

'I ain't having my Syd in no dust-ups,' cried Flo in alarm. 'I'm in the family way, don't forget.'

'I understand,' answered Danny quietly. 'Syd doesn't have to be part of this if you don't want.'

'We're family, Flo,' Syd said loyally. 'Remember what it was like when I first met you? We had our backs to the wall then and put up a bloody good fight against Ferreter.'

'Yes, but we wasn't married,' argued Flo tearfully. 'We didn't have a kid and one on the way to consider.'

Syd lifted the palms of his hands. 'It's for our kids and you I'm doing this, love.'

All was silent once more as Danny studied the faces of the assembled. 'Best everyone go home and think about what I've said.'

'No need, mate,' Bert cried. 'I'm in all the way.'

'Me too,' said Doug. 'Syd won't be on his own. I'll go with him.'

Lil sat up in her seat. 'You're too bloody old for this lark!'

Doug smiled at his wife. 'I ain't past having a pint with my mate, love.' He nodded at Syd and winked.

Bill croaked a laugh. 'Well, I *know* I'm past it, but if I was ten years younger I'd be alongside you and that's a fact.'

'Thanks, Dad.' Danny looked at Frank. 'A lot will depend on you, brother.'

Frank loosened his tie and pushed a hand over his sweating forehead. 'Count me in,' he muttered.

Danny smiled and thought of all he hadn't spoken about and of the luck they would need to put paid to Salvo Vella once and for all.

CHAPTER 53

After the Sharpes and Ethel had departed, Lizzie stood with Gertie as Polly and Tom played in the road close by.

'I gave Elsie a good dinner,' Gertie said as they watched Frank help the pathetic little figure into the back seat of his car for it had been decided in the absence of Lenny, that Elsie was available to be his replacement.

Lizzie was doubtful about the idea, but as Gertie observed, where else was Elsie to go that could offer her both job and accommodation?

'She'll have to spruce up,' Gertie remarked as Frank drove away. 'She can't pull pints with a scarf on her Uncle Ned.'

'She's a bag of nerves,' said Lizzie worriedly. 'But who wouldn't be, living with that monster?'

''We'll get Elsie to tell the cops,' Gertie assured Lizzie. 'Just as soon as she's on her feet.'

'I hope so.'

'Leave it to me, love. I've told Frank to bring her over for dinner. She ain't a bad kid, after all.'

'Thank you for everything.'

'You're me daughter-in-law. I don't need no thanks. It did

me and Bill the world of good to see Frank and Danny shake hands. Do you think Danny's got the measure of this Vella?'

'I hope so, Gertie.'

'I don't want to see Frank give up the pub. Not now things are square between him and Polly.'

'It won't come to that.'

'You're right,' Gertie admitted reluctantly. 'But I thought our freedom was won in 1919. Didn't expect to have to fight for it again with roughnecks from our own turf.' Gertie clutched Lizzie's arm. 'Danny ain't mentioned this April. But Tom did. And I don't like what I heard.'

'What do you mean?'

'The cow has got Danny to send my grandson to one of them posh boarding schools.'

'Danny wouldn't do that,' Lizzie insisted. 'Tom must have got it wrong.'

'She's taken the kid to be measured for the uniform. Tom said there's this woman that April's pally with. All airs and graces. The son of this cow took Tom aside and told him he's in for a bashing when he goes to this school. And I tell you for nothing, love, it worries me stiff.'

'Has Tom told Danny?'

'No, the boy's kept schtum.'

Lizzie couldn't believe that Danny would give his consent to this. But why would Tom lie?

'If Danny loves April there's nothing I can do.'

'Yes yer can. Fight for him like you're fighting for the pub.'

'But how?'

'You'll find a way.'

Just then, Danny joined them. 'Thanks, Gertie, for the welcome.'

'You've always got that, son.'

'Can we go back to Auntie Lizzie's, Dad?' Tom asked. His collar was dirty and undone and his shirt tails flapped over his trousers. Lizzie smiled affectionately. It was the Tom she knew of old.

Danny shook his head. 'Aunt April will have cooked dinner.'

'I wanted Tom to come with us,' Polly protested as Danny and Tom walked across the street to the big car. 'Why can't he?'

'Enough of that, young lady,' Gertie intervened. 'Give us a kiss goodbye.'

But as Bert drove them home, Polly demanded, 'You ain't gonna send me to a boarding school, are you?'

Lizzie looked at her in alarm. 'Of course not.'

' 'Cos if you did, I'd run away to Australia.'

'How you gonna get there?' Bert boomed over his shoulder.

'On a ship of course, like Tom,' Polly huffed indignantly. 'There ain't no other way, Uncle Bert.'

'That'll teach me to ask daft questions,' Bert mumbled, but Lizzie said nothing.

Tom must be very unhappy to consider making such an escape, she thought.

CHAPTER 54

DANNY POURED HIMSELF A STIFF WHISKY. He sat down with the newspaper and studied the front page but didn't see a word. He was listening for voices upstairs; April had gone to say goodnight to Tom, but the boy was unsettled after the freedom he'd enjoyed at Gertie's.

April had been against Danny going to the funeral from the off. But his conscience had pricked him. He hadn't seen his dad or Gertie since last October and he couldn't rest. Added to which, was the threat of Salvo Vella. And that was one threat he wasn't taking lightly.

April came lightly down the stairs to join him.

'He was asleep before I could say good night,' April said as she closed the door. Her brown hair was elegantly drawn back. She wore a cream dress with a white striped jacket that Danny noted was not dissimilar to the fashions worn by Edith Murdoch. Lately April's wardrobe had 'improved' or so he had been told, for April had dressed very simply once. Her natural appearance had been a quality he had admired. Now, her appearance had changed. April often asked him if this would do, or was the other better? He answered appropriately, fearing to say the wrong thing. April was sensitive on the subject of dress.

His thoughts, flew back to Lizzie standing in the church grounds. She was neither fussy about her looks, nor did she need to be complimented. Her choice was her own; always had been back in the days when she wore working clothes for the shop and a leather apron. Back even further to the markets where he first met her, she'd been fifteen then, and to him, a beauty. With her Raven black hair and green eyes, the look of her always left him speechless. Though, he supposed he'd done quite well with his cockney banter and coarse humour. He'd hardly been able to keep his mind on the barrow as she'd walked past, pushing Tom Allen in his bath chair. His heart had turned over at the sight of her, even muffled up with scarves and gloves on those foggy, freezing winter days. Ah yes, he remembered every one of them. And when he'd watched her today, so composed and sure of herself, he had to remind himself of the years that had intervened. Hard years. Long years. Wondering why he'd ever left for Aussie without her ...

'Daniel?' April's voice broke into his thoughts.

'What is it?'

'I've asked you twice. Did you go to the funeral?'

Danny hesitated for this morning they'd had cross words on the subject. 'Not exactly,' he answered, folding the paper in two and placing it aside. 'We were too late.'

'Then what was the point in going at all? You didn't know the dead woman. If I didn't know better I would think you went only to see Lizzie Flowers,' April suggested as she took the seat beside his, sitting stiff-backed against the cushions.

'It was as good a place as any to – to warn her.'

'Daniel, you know I disapprove. I thought you'd left all that behind you. Why get involved again?'

'I had no choice, April.'

'Of course you did!' April's face tightened as she folded her hands in her lap. 'Since that dreadful man attacked you, you've changed.'

'Salvo Vella is not going to disappear, April.'

'He will if you go to the police.'

'We've talked that over endless times.'

'But not enough, it seems. Daniel, that man took you off against your will. He violated you and threatened you. Of course you must bring charges!'

'Against who, April? A criminal I couldn't even identify? A man and his gang who operate far beyond the reaches of the law? What evidence do I have? None – yet!'

'What do you mean – *yet*?'

'He means to take me over, April. The Mill Wall, too. I have to retaliate, to protect myself with any means I have.'

'Like every other common scoundrel,' April cried fiercely. 'Taking the law into your own hands and landing us in danger. What would our friends and acquaintances say if you were to be arrested?'

'I don't intend to be collared,' Danny said sharply. 'And to be honest, I don't care what your friends say, because in truth, April, they are *not* my friends. And once they weren't yours. When we first met, those circles were far above us. Folk like the Murdochs live in another world and I'm not about to try to fit into it when I'm quite happy in my own.'

April stared at him with disdain. 'Then you've learned nothing from the past. From the suffering you experienced at the hands of Leonard Savage. Indeed, for all the years you've been acquainted with Lizzie Flowers, you've known nothing but violence. And you've dragged Tom through the dangers with you. For the first time in his life that boy is being given the chances you never had. And it's thanks to me, Daniel, for the effort and time I've put in to achieve what you so readily dismiss.' She stood up and straightened her shoulders. 'I've given over my life for you and Tom. Made something of our future. And it has not been easy. Yes, I've changed. But for yours and Tom's sakes. For the sake of a family – our family. And I'm desperate to think why you would throw it all away when we have come so far.'

Danny reached out to grasp her hands. 'April, don't take on so,' he said, drawing her close. 'I'm grateful for all you've done for Tom and me. Really I am.'

'Then please listen. You must forget Lizzie Flowers. She must act as she sees fit.' She placed her lips on his and whispered, 'While we do what we know is right.'

Danny felt her eager body pressed against his. There was no better time than now to give her the box in his pocket.

CHAPTER 55

FRANK MADE his way down from the upper rooms and peered into the noisy bar. Every night for the past two weeks as he had locked up, he'd imagined Salvo Vella jumping out from the dark and thrusting a knife into his belly. But so far, he was still breathing. However, he was likely to die of over-work at the rate he was pulling pints for the peasants.

He narrowed his eyes at the young girl behind the bar which had just opened. He had to admit, he'd been wrong about Elsie Booth. When Gertie had suggested she took Lenny's place, he suspected he'd been lumbered. But, with the help of Whippet, somehow the three of them had faced the scum of the earth who had fetched up here since word had got round that Lizzie Flowers's tavern had returned to a dosshouse.

The women were cats, bitching at each other in the snug, as lairy and foul-mouthed as any dock dolly. And he'd had to play his part, smile at their curses and laugh as they mocked him. But he'd managed to look pie-eyed and do his fair share of complaining about Lizzie. He'd stumble over his words while seemingly drunk drawing the beer. But as July had melted into August, he'd not had a glimpse of Vella. Syd and Doug had called in, but he'd not been able to give them the nod, as was the plan.

It was like waiting for bloody Doomsday!

Now it was a Saturday night and the men were traipsing over the sawdust spewing up their vomit and spittle. The tarts were happy to encourage and lighten their pockets at the same time. The regulars had enjoyed the colour at first. But the novelty had soon worn off. There wasn't a familiar face here now. The regulars were afraid to look the rabble in the eye for fear of being molested.

Frank moved cautiously behind the bar, wiping down the ale-soaked wood. His nerves were like pin pricks in his skin, infesting his gut and bringing him out in a fever. He swayed and snorted, coughed and heaved with no trouble at all. His mouth was dry with fear and not for the first time he deliberated on quenching his thirst.

The alcohol being swilled in front of his eyes was tantalising. The licking of lips. The boozy breath. And the stink of stout. He was often dizzy with desire. But to swallow one drop would be his undoing.

'We got the bully boy fixers in the snug tonight,' Whippet complained as he deposited an armful of dirties on the counter. 'They stand by and watch as them dirty whores gets on with it.'

'Stay clear,' Frank advised. 'Clear the muck after them as best you can. Keep behind the bar with Elsie.'

'The law would nab me if they came in. I'm fifteen going on fifty.'

'Never mind about that.'

Where you off to?'

'Down to the cellar to see if we've got a new barrel. The brewery left us short this week. Make do for now with bottles of mild.'

Frank left the bar and hurried along the passage. He took the wooden stairs carefully. A misplaced step would send him sprawling.

He paused at the bottom, took out his matches and lit the wick of the oil lamp. A flickering light filled the cellar. The musty odour of the casks and the mould on the walls made his eyes water. If he was on the razzle-dazzle, this would be his heaven. He'd be down here, relieving the barrels of their contents and going after a chaser as soon as he got to the bar. But those days were gone. At least he hoped so. The thirst was back, a monkey on his shoulder.

Rubbing his jaw which hadn't seen the razor in over a week, he moved to the curve of the arches. Bowing his head, he flicked away the sticky cobwebs. The first barrel was light and a scurry of mice darted out from their nest. These were followed by the swarms of flies that infested the corpses of rodents squashed or trodden on by the draymen. The brewery could at least, serve them a regular supply, without him having to check every five minutes. Muttering to himself, he bent towards the next barrel and froze.

A noise, too heavy for mice, too light for Whippet caused him to turn slowly. He stared wildly into the corners. There was no one there; just the darkness and the cold, clammy walls curving around themselves. The lamp still burned by the flight of wooden steps.

He listened, watching the shadows dance and jump. Nothing, just a trick of his imagination. Returning his attention to the barrels, he at last found one that was full. There would be enough for the thirsty buggers upstairs until the draymen arrived on Monday.

Heaving a relieved sigh, he turned on his heel and stared straight into a pasty grey face. The eyes were lost in deep sockets behind a china doll skin. In the light of the lamp, the red painted blush of its cheeks were garish, as if coloured in paint. The lips were clown-like and crimson and moved only to say his name.

Frank felt his insides fall away.

His legs buckled at the knees.

His heart hammered as the blade's tip flashed in the light of the lamp as it pressed into his Adam's apple.

CHAPTER 56

'THEM BUGGERS in the snug are cutting up rough,' Elsie complained to Whippet as she scrubbed the dirty glasses. 'Go and find Frank.'

Whippet agreed, not liking the sound of the commotion himself.

'Don't 'ang about,' Elsie commanded. 'I ain't gonna hang around if that lot gets nasty.'

'Just pull the pints,' the boy advised. 'The blokes are only interested in their bitches.'

'Yeah, but I still don't like it.'

Whippet drew his filthy hands down the back of his baggy bottomed trousers and made off down the passage. At the end of it he could see a faint light. Frank must've lit the Tilley, he decided and was about to hurry down the cellar steps when he heard voices.

He'd always had keen hearing, and his instincts were second to none. A childhood of thieving and nicking and listening out for the rozzers had developed his sixth sense.

He flattened his back against the wall. The silence, eventually, was broken by a cry. Then a groan. Whippet eased himself closer to the cellar door. There was a lower tone. A sinister one, taunting, whispering.

The boy steadied himself, bent down, unlaced his heavy boots and removed them. Stuffing them under his arms, he tiptoed in his holed socks along the passage to the yard, quietly letting himself out. Moving into the dark alley, he stopped, taking a breath.

The summer's evening was filled with familiar noises. A horse-drawn wagon. Women caterwauling in the distance. Dogs barking. Nothing closer stirred.

He replaced his boots and listened. Five minutes later he was pedalling furiously along the East India Dock Road towards Ebondale Street.

CHAPTER 57

'It's six o'clock. I'll cash up the till while you bring in the veg,' Lizzie told her brother.

Bert nodded. 'Do you want me to drive over to Lil's first and fetch Polly?'

'No. Ethel's taken her down the park with the boys. I'll go when we've packed up and stop at the pie and mash shop on the way back to buy supper.'

'Don't get none for me,' Bert replied. 'I'm off to see Jenny. The doctors said it's likely she'll be transferred to the burns unit.'

'I thought she was coming home.'

'There's this operation they did on the blokes who came home from war to cover their scars. I told her she don't need it. But she's gonna ask if they can do it on her scalp and hair.'

'Does she feel up to it?'

'She don't say much. That's why I want her home. I don't want her to get her hopes up if they can't help her.'

'Yes, but a woman's hair is … '

'I know, I know,' interrupted Bert impatiently. 'If I had a bob for every time I'd heard that I'd be a rich man.' Bert trudged out to the pavement where he hoisted a sack of potatoes onto his shoulders as though they were a bag of feathers.

Lizzie knew he missed Jenny. The hospital routine was very strict. They insisted that he left after an hour. It was still frowned on to have more than one visitor. The ward was small and became congested if everyone's relations and friends turned up.

Just as Lizzie was wondering if it was really possible that Jenny could be helped, a small figure on a bicycle came racing up. Whippet leaped off the saddle, let the bike fall and sprinted towards Bert.

Bert dropped the sack as Whippet spoke rapidly. They came hurrying into the shop.

'Lizzie, gel, leave the cashing up. It's Frank.'

'What's happened?' Lizzie asked closing the till.

Whippet gulped breathlessly. 'You gotta come. We had all these geezers pour in as soon as the doors opened. They got to it with the women like rabbits and just about drank us dry.'

'What did Frank do?'

'He went down to find another barrel. The brewery left us short last week.'

'Is that all?' demanded Bert.

' 'Ang on a minute,' Whippet retorted, catching his breath. 'I ain't finished.' He looked at Lizzie and lowered his voice as though someone was listening. 'When he didn't come back from the cellar, I thought to meself, that's odd. So, I left Elsie in the bar and went to look for him. Thought he'd need me to help him lug up a keg. But it was then I heard voices. Frank was one of 'em but he weren't having a laugh. No, he was like – well, gaspin'.'

'Gasping?' Lizzie said. 'Did you go down there?'

'No, 'cos it was then I heard this 'orrible whisper. I tell

you, it made me blood run cold.'

'Was it Salvo Vella?'

'Could be.'

'What did you do?'

'I took off me boots and crept out. There wasn't no one in the yard, thank Gawd. I come over to you as quick as I could.'

Bert grabbed him by the shoulder. 'You wasn't spotted was you?'

'Course not. I reckon I've done me lungs in, pedalling so fast.'

'What're we going to do?' Bert asked Lizzie. His face was white as he added, 'We've got no back-up. I knew we should have kept Ron and Maurice, not sent them back to Murphy.'

'It had to look genuine, as though we'd given up the fight,' replied Lizzie. She felt a moment's panic but then her mind cleared. 'Whippet, if your lungs will let you, go and alert Murphy. Tell him what you know and that I'll meet him outside the pub.'

'Got yer,' agreed Whippet, 'but I'll have to use the tunnel to cross the river. Then it's a stiff ride to Deptford.'

Lizzie opened the till and took out a ten-shilling note. 'Here, this will help your lungs, I'm sure.'

Whippet grabbed the money and jumped on his bicycle.

'Bert, take the van and pick up Syd and Doug,' Lizzie said hurriedly. 'Ask Ethel to keep Polly a bit longer. I'll drive to Danny's and we'll meet you at the Mill Wall. Don't do anything till we get there.'

Bert went to the storeroom. 'I ain't being caught short-handed this time,' he vowed as he reappeared with Fowler's wooden club.

But as big and strong as her brother was, Lizzie wished, like Bert, that she had kept on Ron and Maurice, and Elmo and Fowler at the pub. Their absence could prove a costly mistake.

CHAPTER 58

THE ECHO of Lizzie's rap on the knocker echoed in the quiet Poplar street. Lizzie thought how April's house stood out from the rest. Fitted blinds were lowered at each window and the window ledges were painted white. Lizzie had been here once before but it had been dark then. Now it was daylight, and every pane of glass seemed to sparkle in the late sunshine.

It was April Williams who opened the door. Lizzie stared at this fashionable woman. Gone was the homely, retiring widow. Instead a smart and elegant woman stood before her. April wore a fashionable evening gown and a stole around her shoulders. Her brown hair was set in a bobbed style and pearls adorned her neck.

'I'm Lizzie ... Lizzie Flowers,' Lizzie said hesitantly. 'We've only met in passing but -'

'I know who you are,' April interrupted. 'What do you want?'

'Is Danny here?' Lizzie asked. 'It's important I speak to him.'

'We're just going out,' April replied coldly, about to close the door when Tom appeared.

'Auntie Lizzie, Auntie Lizzie!' he cried excitedly. But April caught hold of him.

'Tom, go upstairs and put on your uniform. We'll be late if you dawdle.'

'I don't want to go,' Tom answered, shrugging himself free.

'Do as you're told,' April retorted, her pale cheeks flushing angrily. She turned to Lizzie. 'Why can't you leave us alone?'

Danny, dressed in a smart grey suit, white shirt and dark silk tie came running down the stairs.

'Dad, I don't want to go to the school tonight,' Tom cried.

'Now then, Tom,' Danny murmured and looking at Lizzie he smiled.

'It's Frank,' Lizzie said. 'He's in trouble.'

'Just as I thought!' April exclaimed. 'Daniel, are we to be hounded by your family for the rest of our days?' She glared at Lizzie then went into the house.

Danny placed a hand on Tom's shoulder. 'Tom, I'm going with Lizzie. I'd like you to stay here and keep your Aunt April company.'

'But I want to go with you, Dad.'

'Do this for me son.'

A few minutes later, Danny was sitting beside Lizzie in the Wolseley. He made no mention of April, or the outing to the school, but instead asked briskly, 'Tell me what's happened at the pub.'

She repeated everything that Whippet had said.

Danny nodded thoughtfully. 'Have you alerted Murphy?'

'Whippet will tell him to meet us at the Mill Wall. Bert's gone for Doug and Syd.'

'Vella must have decided to make his move tonight. But

when Murphy arrives, we'll have enough men to confront him.'

Lizzie hoped that was so. But she couldn't imagine the man who called himself *The Prince* giving up his kingdom quite so easily.

CHAPTER 59

FRANK PURSED his lips together as tight as he could. After being dragged up from the cellar at knife-point, he'd been thrown to the wolves. They were baying around him as he sat, forced into the snug chair, with a filthy whore on his lap.

This was the first time in his life that he had ever dreaded a sniff of the booze. An hour ago, he had been yearning for it, his throat as dry as a desert. Now he was in a state of acute fear that the frothy ale poised in the glass she held would be forced down his throat.

'Come on ducks, drink up,' she roared to a gale of laughter from Vella's men. 'What's wrong with you?' screeched the blowsy woman who wriggled on his knee. She placed the glass to her own lips and swallowed.

Frank could smell her sweat and cheap perfume. She laughed, swaying backwards and forwards. She bent her head and placed her lips on his. The sickly, sweet taste of the stout rolled onto his tongue and he twisted his head away. But she pinched his ear and dragged his head round again. 'What, I ain't good enough for you, is that it?' cried the tart angrily. 'I suppose you're bedding that stuck up bitch over there.' She drunkenly pointed to Elsie who Frank saw was cowering behind the bar. That bloody, good-for-nothing Whippet had done a bunk by the looks of it and left Elsie to her fate.

Frank tried to move, but he was pushed down by the many onlookers. 'Make him drink wiv' yer, Queenie,' one bellowed, 'then get your drawers down and give us all a laugh.'

'They want a to see a bit of how's-yer-farver,' spluttered Queenie as she leaned the glass against his cheek. 'Let's give 'em a show, shall we?'

'Get off me!' Frank protested and tried to stand, but she had her hand inside his trousers. He closed his eyes in distress as the alcohol spilt over his face, into his mouth and down his clothes. The taunts were so loud he thought he'd be deafened.

'Drink up, you bugger,' said a voice suddenly. And before he knew it, what seemed like a gallon of ale was forced down his throat. He choked and spat. He tried to vomit. But as much as he brought up, they thrust more into his mouth. His head began to throb. Since he had not eaten, the alcohol soon took effect. After being dry for so long, he felt his insides resemble a sponge.

The bitch grabbed his hair. His mouth gaped open. The jeers grew louder as he gulped, unable to defend himself.

As the first wave of drunkenness came over him, he saw the painted face. The cruel eyes, the ash grey skin and a clown's leering mouth.

'You're a fool,' hissed Vella, the man in the mask. 'My women laugh at you. The man under Lizzie Flowers's thumb. A beaten dog.'

'Bollocks,' slurred Frank. 'Get your bitch off me.'

'With pleasure. Enjoy the favours of one of your own kind.'

Suddenly Queenie was gone and Elsie was sitting on his lap. She stared at him from under her long, straggly hair with terrified dark eyes. Hands were going over her, pulling at her blouse as she tried to resist.

'Help!' she cried.

Frank thought he must be in a nightmare. He tried to beat off her attackers, but his attempts were ridiculed.

Elsie's screams drove into his brain. He wanted to protect her. But they made him drink again. This time the ale was chased down with whisky.

'Take your time, Frankie,' urged Queenie. 'See what a nice girl you've got there. Go on, feel her tits.' She pushed his head towards Elsie, who shrieked so loud, he felt his blood turn to water.

The sting of spirit was on his lips. His stomach churned in protest. He choked as the tumbler was forced against his mouth.

'Drink,' whispered Vella, 'drink heartily. We are all friends here. Your complaints against Lizzie Flowers have been heard. Now it is time for you to talk.'

Frank stared into the abominable face. And he knew in that moment that Vella hadn't been fooled. This man knew everything.

Everything there was to know about the Mill Wall – and Lizzie.

CHAPTER 60

THE THREE MEN looked down at the cellar doors. They were impenetrable. 'Frank fitted new locks after the last schemozzle,' said Syd, scratching his head.

'They didn't get in this way,' agreed Doug.

'Let's go round to the front,' Syd suggested.

'Lizzie said to wait,' Bert reminded his brother-in-law.

'We won't go in,' Syd assured him. 'We'll just open the front doors a crack. See what's going down in the snug.'

They all prowled round to the pub's entrance where Syd gave the doors a push. 'They're locked too,' he said in surprise.

'Why would Frank do that?'

'Dunno. Perhaps it wasn't him who locked them.' Doug looked up and down the deserted street.

Syd pointed to the high window above their heads. 'Bert, put your hands together and give me a lift.'

Bert did what was asked of him and soon Syd was in position.

'This stained glass is like a bloody kaleidoscope' he

complained as Bert supported his weight. 'Just a minute, I can see something.'

'What?' Bert and Doug cried together.

'Dunno,' muttered Syd, flattening his nose against the window. 'Could be Vella and his tarts in the snug. They're making a hell of a to-do.' Syd wiped the glass with his cuff, but years of neglect had made it opaque.

'Any sign of Frank or Elsie?' called Doug.

'No one's serving behind the bar.'

'Better leave it at that,' decided Doug. 'Let's wait for Lizzie.'

Back in the van, Syd sat in the windowless rear trying to see over Bert's shoulder. Suddenly his foot collided with a hard object.

'What's this?' Syd demanded. 'Christ, it's a bloody club!'

'A little insurance,' muttered Bert.

'Did you bring one for me?' Syd was alarmed that in the rush to get here he had neglected to bring something with which to defend himself.

'No,' Bert admitted, 'but there's tools for changing a tyre, back there.'

Syd searched around and found a lumpy coarse cloth amongst a pile of cabbage leaves. He unwrapped it carefully. 'What's your poison, Doug?' he called. 'A wrench, a crowbar or a hammer?'

'Blimey, do I have to choose? I don't know how handy I'll be at my age,' Doug spluttered.

'You ain't expected to get physical,' Bert insisted. 'Like I said, though, no harm in a little insurance.'

'All right, the wrench will do.'

After passing the heavy tool to Doug, Syd pushed the hammer in the belt of his trousers. 'That feels better.' Removing his jacket, he rolled up his shirt sleeves and undid his collar ready for the fray.

They all sat very still watching and listening. 'Look, who's that?' Doug asked after a while and pointed to a figure creeping along the pavement.

'Don't look like a regular,' Syd observed. 'He's gone round the back to the cellar.'

'Well, he won't have no joy round there,' huffed Bert.

'Reckon it's Vella's man,' Syd agreed.

'Yeah, he's a lookout, I'll bet,' nodded Doug.

When the Wolseley drew up. Lizzie and Danny climbed out. They all stood together on the quiet street.

'There's trouble brewing,' Bert warned after Syd had described what he'd seen through the window. 'Wish we knew what the score is.'

Just then there was an almighty crash from inside. A window splintered. 'I'm sure I heard a woman's scream,' Lizzie cried.

'Where the bloody hell are Murphy's men?' demanded Syd beginning to panic. 'What the hell's going on?'

'There's only one way to find out,' Danny decided. 'We'll go in.'

'I'm with you there,' Bert snarled, flexing his biceps.

'Me too,' Syd said fiercely. 'Those buggers mean business. But so do I.'

Danny looked at Lizzie. 'Wait in the car. If it's not us you see coming out, drive straight to the cops.'

'Murphy might be here soon,' Lizzie protested.

'Or not at all,' replied Danny. 'Whippet may never have got to Deptford. Or, Murphy might have his own troubles.' He put his hand on her shoulder. 'It's our fight, Lizzie. This time, it's a win for the firm.'

Syd felt the adrenaline rush through his body. It was the old firm facing up to the villains again. Back to the bad old days, he reflected proudly, when Mik Ferreter and his cronies had ruled the roost. It had been Danny and Lizzie and Flo and him who had faced the bastards. There had been no bloody help from the coppers then and if he had a say in it tonight, there would be no blue uniforms today. It was a long time since his last bundle. But he had grown up with scrappers and kickers – he could thank his brothers for that.

'On a count of three, right?' said Danny as the trio crossed the road.

Bert nodded, his huge hands brandishing the club.

Syd pulled the hammer from his trousers.

'One,' Danny shouted as they stood at the pub doors. 'Two …' He gave the nod. '*Three*!'

CHAPTER 61

FRANK KNEW he was three sheets to the wind, but the sight of Bert's towering figure bursting through the pub doors, shook even him from his lethargy. Bert swatted his opponents like flies, roaring so loud that Vella's men fell over themselves in an effort to beat a retreat. Frank narrowed his blurred eyes as Syd manhandled a brute twice his own size; the hammer he held soon settled the argument. His brother was throwing punches and the ugly mug who had tipped half of the brewery's beer down Frank's throat, went sprawling.

Frank found himself smiling. When Elsie screamed again, he put his arms around her, holding on as tight as he could. But the hand on her wrist was pulling her. She looked pleadingly into Frank's eyes as she was torn away.

He tried to follow but found himself on his knees instead. His head swam violently, his stomach revolted. Somehow, he managed to stagger to his feet. Elsie was within reach, but he misjudged his direction. Tumbling onto a table, once again he tried to steady himself.

It was then an uncanny silence descended in the room.

He looked drunkenly around. A slight figure stood at the

pub's broken doors. A stranger with a curled lip and eyes that blazed wildly stood with a pistol in his hand.

'No!' Elsie screamed. 'Please, don't do it!'

Frank was confused. Who was this man who nobody seemed to know? The first bullet ricocheted into the pub's mirror. The second splintered the oak beam above it. The whores ran out from the snug and fled into the street. When the man took aim again, Vella's men followed.

Frank stared at the wavering pistol now trained on him. He found the irony amusing. Just when he was getting his life together, this bastard, who he didn't know from Adam, was about to bring down the curtain.

At least he was drunk. The bullet wouldn't hurt.

'No!' Elsie cried again.

The last thing Frank saw was the fouled rim of the table as he sunk into oblivion beneath it.

Lizzie watched as a few minutes after the men had stormed into the pub, a man appeared from the backyard. He paused outside the pub's broken doors.

'Do you recognize him?' Doug asked.

'No.'

'We thought he was a lookout.'

Lizzie gasped. 'Doug, he's got a gun.'

'What?'

She pushed open the car door but Doug pulled her back.

'No, Lizzie, stay here.'

But Lizzie was stung into action. 'This is *my* fight, too, Doug.'

'Then I'm coming with you.'

They crept together towards the pub; Lizzie could see the man standing with his back to them. A few feet in front of him stood Danny, Bert and Syd, with their hands raised as the gun swung violently from side to side.

'This bloke's a nutter,' Doug breathed. 'Christ, look over there! A man in a mask has got a knife at Elsie's throat!'

A shot rang out and the women fled past them, screaming and hollering. When the gun fired next, Lizzie and Doug were almost sent flying as Vella's rabble charged by.

'They're doing a runner!' exclaimed Doug. 'Bloody cowards!' But before he could say more, the gun fired for a third time.

Lizzie saw Danny, Bert and Syd jump back, but it was Elsie who broke free from Vella as his mask splintered in two. He stood, swaying a little, as though surprised by the hole the bullet had made in his forehead.

Dropping to the ground, he lay unmoving on the floor. It was then the stranger turned to face Lizzie, the revolver slipping from his hand as he looked down at the knife in his chest.

Lizzie felt a chill go over her as a short while later, she looked into the lifeless face of the man once known as *The Prince*. His black hair was spattered with sawdust. There was very little blood, for the bullet had passed cleanly through his head. Beside him lay Ted Booth, whose gun had fired a few seconds after Salvo Vella's knife had found its mark. Both corpses now lay behind the bar and out of sight, where Danny and Bert had dragged them.

As Lizzie comforted Elsie, she tried to study with detachment the unremarkable features that had been revealed as Vella's mask had crumbled. Eyes too close in a narrow, sly face. A nose that was slightly hooked and a weak chin, all of which had been disguised by a dramatic flamboyance that Vella must have cultivated to dominate his women.

No longer a prince, Lizzie thought, but as the coroner had remarked, a pauper. Death had finally claimed this indiscriminate villain and murderer. She could barely find it in her heart to wish him salvation, for all the harm he had done.

Tearfully Elsie gazed down at the body of her late husband. 'Ted must have been watching the pub,' she sobbed. 'I knew he would find me one day and bump me off like he did Madge.' She gulped a breath. 'Who would've guessed that it would end like this? One minute I saw the knife flying through the air. The next it stuck in Ted's chest. He just stood there, gawping, as if he'd been stung by a bee. Then his gun went off - '

'Doing us all the final favour,' supplied Danny.

Elsie shivered again. 'I hope Madge can rest in peace now. She got justice. Still, Ted was her son even though he did her in.' She peered at Danny through the strands of her lanky hair, her eyes wide in their dark sockets. 'Is yer brother all right?'

Danny nodded. 'He collapsed with the drink. Me and Bert took him to the yard and stuck his head under the pump. He's going to need a square meal to sober up.'

'I'll see to that.' Elsie wiped her eyes with a rag. 'You know, yer brother ain't a bad bloke, Danny. But they kept pouring the booze down his throat. Still, as drunk as he was, he told 'em to take a running jump.'

'You're free now, Elsie.' Lizzie smiled. 'Ted won't bother you again.'

'But what will the cops do when they see them dead bodies?' Elsie worried. 'They might think I done Ted in!'

'No chance of that,' Danny assured her. 'The cavalry's arrived at last.' He nodded to the battered doors of the pub where Syd, Bert and Doug stood with Murphy. 'There will be nothing to see by the time the Irishman has cleaned up.'

'In that case,' Elsie grinned, 'I'll go and stick something on the stove for Frank.'

'It's over,' Danny assured Lizzie when they were alone. 'Truly over. We can start afresh, without ever having to look over our shoulders again.'

'I hope so,' Lizzie replied. 'But this is the East End after all.'

'The mistake I made was leaving it … ' he drew her into his arms, ' … and you. There is only one way to say I'm sorry, and I'm saying it now, with all my heart.'

Lizzie gazed into his remorseful blue eyes. 'Danny, please don't break my heart again.'

'Will you give me another chance?'

'I won't give up the pub, Danny. Or the shop. There's more that I want to do, as well. It's the way I've led my life; the family comes first. And, it will stay that way until I take me last breath.'

'I know,' he answered, 'I know.'

Lizzie hoped he did. For now, if they were to be together, he would likely break another woman's heart instead of hers – an affliction that Lizzie would not wish on any soul, not even April Williams.

PART III

CHAPTER 62

September 1935

'CHILDREN, please sit on the grass in front of the bride and groom – and behave!' cried the flustered photographer as he bent to take another photograph. 'If you stick out your tongues, the images will be spoiled.'

With smothered laughter and a clip round the ear for Nelson from his mother, the photographer finally took his picture.

Lizzie, as matron of honour, folded Jenny's lace train over her arm, so that Jenny could sit comfortably in the shiny black limousine that was to take her and Bert to the heart of London's West End. The reception, Lizzie's wedding gift to her brother and his new wife, was to be held in the spectacular rooms of the Art Deco Strand Palace Hotel, currently so fashionable with Londoners.

Jenny, small and dainty in her ankle-length, white satin-silk dress, clung to Bert's arm as they stood in the arched doorway of Poplar's Christ Church. Jenny's head was covered in a fragile lace cap decorated with tiny pink rosebuds. Her hair was beginning to grow again, although she had told Lizzie it would be some time before she could entirely disguise her burns. The operation on her legs had been a success. She had proudly worn Lizzie's gift of a garter and blue ribbon above her knee. Now, two months on from her discharge from hospital, she was a beautiful and blushing bride.

Lizzie thought how her big and brawny brother looked somewhat out of place in his deep grey morning suit, the tails of which had been especially sewn to accommodate his height. He was tender and caring as he looked after his bride, the devotion quite clear in his brown eyes.

As the cheering and shouting began, Lizzie, wearing a fitted cream dress and bolero jacket, with her long dark hair flowing around her shoulders, glanced at Ethel who stood beside her, tall and slim, in a discreet pale green crepe-de-chine dress that Lizzie had taken her to buy at Selfridges.

Ethel's gaze was centred on her daughter, Rosie. Now turned seventeen, she wore a pale pink gown with a slim white belt and high heels to match. She stood with Lil and Doug as they threw confetti at the happy couple.

'Rosie takes after you,' Lizzie said, threading her arm through Ethel's. 'All that blonde hair and fair complexion. She's the spit.'

'Give or take two decades,' Ethel replied with a smile. 'She is very lovely, though.' She turned to Lizzie. 'I never thought she would accept your invitation to the wedding.'

'Have you spoken to her yet?'

'Not really. But Mum and Dad have. I thought we'd have time together at the reception. Perhaps she has a message from Timothy.'

'Perhaps,' agreed Lizzie. 'It can't be easy to live with Cora Ryde.'

'No, but Timothy seems not to mind, or else he'd have come today.'

Lizzie knew at least Rosie's presence must be giving Ethel hope for the future. 'Be patient, Ethel.'

Ethel nodded thoughtfully. 'I love my kids, Lizzie. But what can I offer them? It ain't easy finding a place to live. I've looked everywhere. They're either dumps or the landlords demand a lot of money for very little.'

'Ethel, Ebondale Street is too cramped for the four of us. Tom is sleeping in the small box room and Polly is growing out of hers. I'd like a back yard or small garden for the kids to play in.'

'You're not leaving the island, are you?'

Lizzie hesitated. 'No, but we'd like a place nearer the factory we leased last week on Chandlers Wharf. It was an old engineering firm once. Your dad says he remembers it as a going concern from before it closed in the Depression. With Danny's engineering experience and Syd and Bert's manpower, well, it could be made into something special.' She glanced over at Rosie and added, 'my point is, I'm not sure what to do with the shop.'

'But it's been a greengrocer's for years,' protested Ethel. 'You can't close it!'

'I'm looking for the right tenant,' Lizzie said slowly, hoping the penny would drop. 'It's a good business with only a peppercorn rent. Whoever ran it could continue the fruit and veg or turn it into something else. The rooms above are nice and cosy and I'd leave it fully furnished.' Lizzie looked at Ethel steadily and repeated, 'That is, if I could get the right tenant.'

Ethel frowned. Suddenly her eyes widened. 'You mean…?'

'Would you be interested?'

Ethel gasped. 'But Lizzie, I couldn't run the shop by meself!'

'You wouldn't have to. Jenny will want a job soon. She ran the bakery very well. I don't see why you couldn't make a go of it together.'

Ethel stared at her. 'Do you really think so?'

Lizzie nodded slowly. 'Ron and Maurice could come in to do the lugging. Bert will be on hand after he comes home from the factory.' She nodded to Rosie who was chasing Callum and Nelson as they ran around on the green. 'You never know, Rosie might be interested in joining you.'

'Oh, Lizzie, that would be my dream!' Ethel dabbed a tear from under her eye. 'I don't know what to say.'

'Say yes,' Lizzie chuckled.

Ethel sniffed back her tears and nodded. 'Yes …. yes!'

Lizzie squeezed Ethel's hand as they watched Rosie bend down to straighten Callum's shirt. He looked shyly into her eyes and they laughed.

Ethel heaved a sigh. 'Oh, Lizzie, I think she's taken to him.'

'He certainly has to her.'

'Do you think she'll want to leave Lewisham and all her friends?'

'You could offer her a Saturday job at first. It would be a start.'

Ethel let out a long sob. She blew her nose and pulled back her shoulders. 'I'm so happy I want to cry. But I mustn't spoil me make-up!' They laughed together as they had done so many times in the past.

Then it was time to wave off the happy couple. Bobbing about in front of them were hats with feathers and hats with bows and hats with delicate lace veils. Lil wore the most outrageous of all, a flame-coloured cloche to match her scarlet two-piece suit. Flo had managed an eye-catcher in her floral elasticated high-waisted maternity dress, blooming once again as she walked with her handsome husband. All the men wore morning suits of grey jackets and pin-striped trousers, as was the high fashion. Bill and Doug laughed as Gertie, sporting a taffeta beret and assisted by Tom dressed in his Ebondale Street school uniform, attempted to tie one of Bert's old boots to the car's rear bumper.

After Ethel had gone to wave the bride and groom off, Danny came to stand beside Lizzie. The smile he gave her was more than enough reward for all the hard work she had put into the carefully planned wedding day. Tall and handsome in his deep grey morning suit, cream silk waistcoat and cravat, she felt her heart lift wildly. Was his presence in her life really assured? Lizzie wondered anxiously. Did he still think about April Williams?

But as Danny took her hand in his, Lizzie knew that the love that bound them was stronger by far than any other. Fate had brought them together and deep in her heart she knew they would never be separated.

'You look beautiful,' Danny whispered. 'And one day you will be the bride stepping into that car.'

Lizzie thought of the long nights and passionate embraces they now shared together. Of the joy of waking up each morning to see the man beside her that she so dearly cherished. Of the way they had become a true family with Tom and Polly; milestones in her life that were far more meaningful than a wedding ring or marriage certificate.

'I'm happy we have each other,' she replied and smiled when she saw Frank and Elsie walk hand-in-hand from the church. They were dressed to the nines in their wedding attire and beside them skipped Polly in her pretty blue frock.

'My brother is a lucky man,' Danny observed ruefully, narrowing his eyes at the couple.

'Whoever would have put Frank and Elsie together?' Lizzie murmured gratefully. 'It takes all kinds to make up this world, doesn't it?'

'Come here, Mrs Flowers.' Danny's strong hands slipped around her waist. 'As long as you are in my world then I'm happy. I have the most wonderful woman for my life's companion; Tom and Polly to care for; and peace at last between my brother and me. What more could I want from life?'

Lizzie pressed her lips on his. 'That's all I wanted to know.'

'I've said it before, but this time is different, Lizzie,' Danny whispered. 'One day you'll have my ring on your finger to prove it, I promise.'

What need have I of a ring, my darling? Lizzie thought to herself as she gazed steadily into his eyes. *Fight for him as hard as you fought for the pub,* Gertie once advised. And Lizzie smiled at the memory, for Gertie's advice had been sound.

Through the good times and the bad, Lizzie had never lost hope that Danny would return. Or that Frank would love his daughter as much as Polly loved him. Or that Babs and Vinnie might feel the need of family again. If her brother or sister were ever to return to the place they were born, then they would know where to find her. She would welcome them with open arms, just as Ma and Pa would wish.

It was love that brought people together. Hope and faith that gave people the strength to continue. Though there were rumours of war and the world was far from united, her roots – and her family's – were planted firmly in the East End.

This was her manor; the Isle of Dogs, a curved horseshoe of land jutting out into the River Thames, that, God willing, would remain her turf until the day she died.

THE END

I do hope you enjoyed Lizzie's third story. I would be most grateful for a short review on amazon.co.uk - if you have a spare few minutes. Thank you so much. Carol x

Just to let you know, I've left some freebie short stories for you on my website; there's no subscription - they are there for you to enjoy. (Hopefully.) But if you want to receive my Newsletter I would love to include you. Leave your email address at www.carolrivers.com

ACKNOWLEDGMENTS

My thanks go to all those who helped with the creation of *Lizzie Flowers and the Family Firm*.

Carol Waterkeyn for her painless editing and proof-reading.

Beverley Ann Hopper for being the best Book Lover ever.

Susanna Bavin and Julie Boon for always being there.

Jane Crabb for her awesome Fantastic Fiction alerts.

Mark Dawson, James Blatch and Joanna Penn for their independent publishing mentoring.

Paul Teague for including us in his journey.

Twitterers and Facebookers everywhere who have generously shared their posts and pages with *Lizzie*.

For Him Indoors who threw in his lot with *Lizzie*.

DEDICATION

In the past, I've dedicated several of my books to Readers and I'm delighted to do so again. For Readers have learned a great secret. They know that the whole world lies in the palm of their hands when they read a book. It's as simple as that.

ALSO BY CAROL RIVERS

Bestselling Lizzie Flowers series

BOOK ONE LIZZIE OF LANGLEY STREET
BOOK TWO THE FIGHT FOR LIZZIE FLOWERS
BOOK THREE LIZZIE FLOWERS AND THE FAMILY FIRM

Seasonal Christmas themed books
TOGETHER FOR CHRISTMAS
A WARTIME CHRISTMAS
IN THE BLEAK MIDWINTER
CHRISTMAS TO COME (Excerpt at the back of this book)
MOLLY'S CHRISTMAS ORPHANS
LILY'S CHRISTMAS WORKHOUSE BABY (Short story)

ABOUT THE AUTHOR

Carol is a Sunday Times bestselling author whose family comes from the Isle of Dogs, East London. Her writing life began with short stories for women's magazines, then novellas for Mills & Boon and eventually, sagas written for Simon & Schuster. Recently she's published more short stories as well as her sagas; *Lily's Christmas Workhouse Baby* is a Victorian short, with a strong romantic theme and *Kate of The King's Arms, available free from her website,* is set in 1930 and tells the story of lost first love. Her books, in all forms including audio, can be found on Amazon. Now living in Dorset, she and her husband, who has a background in art and technology, are enjoying the exciting new venture of independent publishing. She would especially like to thank all her readers who have supported her over the years.

f 𝕏 ⓟ

PROLOGUE

Christmas Day 1940
Isle of Dogs
East London

'TERRY'S COLD, BELLA.' Five-year-old Terry Doyle squatted next to his sister in the dank, rubbish-strewn alley opposite the row of derelict cottages. Bella Doyle, only eight-years-old herself, slid her arm protectively around her brother's bony shoulders, painfully aware his thin white shirt was no protection against the winter's bite.

Terry was starving and today was no exception. They'd been scavenging on the debris all day and found little to satisfy their appetite. If only their mother and that pig of a man she'd picked up at the Rose hadn't decided to come home early! They must have had a skinful, then run out of booze or money or both.

Bella was weighing up this problem carefully; a problem she had been faced with more times than she had eaten hot dinners. In fact, to Mary Doyle's children, a hot dinner was something they could only dream about, and often had.

Bella knew that to enter their home now, a rundown dockside cottage dripping water from its mouldy walls, would be a risky business. After the week-long binge that their mother and her boyfriend Jack Router had enjoyed, even setting eyes on her children would be aggravation to Mary Doyle.

Bella understood the evils of alcohol even at her young age. If asked, she couldn't put it into words. But she knew through bitter experience how it could corrupt a person's nature. Their mother hadn't always been the drunkard she had turned into and Bella somehow understood this. She sensed the sinful nature of Mary's work and the crucifying poverty of their life-style, though she suspected that once upon a time her mother had been a child too. Perhaps with a brother or sister or both, and part of a real family. Mary Doyle had been innocent once. Before she had turned into a wild animal and lay with men to earn her living. And the blame for this degradation, Mary had daily informed Bella, lay squarely on her children's heads. They were bastards, appearing unbidden in her life. At the best of times, the sight of them was almost more than she could bear. At the worst, she left them alone with Jack Router.

'What we going to do?' Terry mumbled, trembling with the cold, his hand frozen inside Bella's.

'We'll wait a bit, right? Till they go out again.'

'But the planes might come over.'

Bella shook her tousled and filthy copper curls. 'They won't come over tonight. It's Christmas. Even the Germans know that.'

'Do Germans have kids as well?'

'Course they do.'

'Do they give 'em presents?'

'Dunno. Might do.'

Terry leaned his slight weight against her and Bella sighed heavily. All the buildings in Bow Street were condemned. She knew that because she'd read the notice nailed to their door. "This dwelling is considered unfit to live in and is condemned by the council."

But this had been in the summer before the Blitz started. Since then, the paper had worn away and life had gone on much the same, Blitz or no Blitz. Bella had been thankful that at least, she and Terry still had a roof over their heads. More so, when Mary and Jack were not sleeping or fighting underneath it.

Now snow was drifting across the street and Bella's stomach churned emptily. She had stowed a crust of bread between the floor and the bug-ridden mattress they slept on in a corner of the cottage. Bella had planned to share it with Terry as soon as they'd got home from the debris where they'd been looking for anything of value left over from the raids. But today they had come home empty-handed. And they'd been waiting an eternity in the hopes that the cottage would soon be vacated.

'They must be asleep,' Bella decided, taking off her coat and folding it around Terry's shoulders. It wasn't much protection; threadbare and darned, it was the only comfort she could give him. If only Terry could remember to dress himself properly. He didn't seem to know what kept him warm and what didn't. He had a habit of forgetting and Bella was always looking out for him.

'I don't like it here,' Terry complained, his bare knees knocking under his short, raggedy trousers. 'I'm cold. I wanna go in.'

'So do I,' Bella agreed impatiently. 'But not for a bashing. And we'll get one, as they won't be in no mood to see us.'

'Where we going, then?' Terry asked forlornly, swiping the running snot from his nose. 'To Micky's?'

'Don't reckon Micky would like that, either,' Bella said, shivering in her thin dress that was more tears and holes than fabric. 'It's Christmas Day. His mum will be dishing up the dinner.'

Micky Bryant was their benefactor. The one light in Bella's dark life. He was twice as old as her, but he didn't seem like it. He seemed like her other half. He looked out for them. And all the other street kids. He paid them for what they found. And sometimes gave them grub. He told them to keep shtum, as if his mum knew he was knocking off stuff, she wouldn't be best pleased.

Micky had two brothers too. Sean was all right. But Bella didn't care for the oldest one. She'd seen him at a distance and he looked - well, she didn't know how he looked. But she suspected he wouldn't encourage Micky's friendship with kids from the slums. Micky would laugh at that if she told him. He'd give her a wink and roll his lovely eyes. Micky didn't have airs and graces. Not like his brother, Ronnie.

'I'd like an 'ot dinner,' Terry said hopefully, his thin face and hollowed dark eyes under his thin black hair looking to Bella, like the face of an angel. A dirty, grubby, smelly little angel, but an angel none the less. She loved Terry with all her heart. She'd cared for her baby brother since the day he was born. Mary had brought him into this world with language so foul that even the old girl - who was always in at the deliveries - had turned away in disgust.

Bella remembered the violence of her mother's labour. As though she cursed nature and everything in it for her unwanted condition. But to Bella the miracle of birth had opened her young eyes to the first sensation of love. The blood soaked newspaper on the floor where Terry had suddenly appeared from between Mary's legs had seemed like a royal blanket of welcome. The old girl had slapped his silent body, all mauve and sticky with blood, and Bella had held her breath as she listened for Terry's first cry.

When it came, it was as if her own lonely heart had called back. And because there was no where else to put him, Bella had reached out and there he was! In her arms. This speck of life, staring up at her, with eyes like jewels in an old man's wrinkled face. She'd loved him from the off. And instinct had told her to keep him safe. So she'd kept him away from Mary until his pathetic screams had to be silenced by her huge, milk-swollen breasts. Mostly Mary had fallen asleep and Bella had held him there, snuggled up to the round fullness, his tiny fingers pleated around Bella's as he learned to suck.

Bella looked at her brother now. He didn't have a bad bone in his body. At least, what bones were left after the bashings he got from Jack Router. And that was what hurt her the most. What made her angry. What made her feel so powerless. She could take the man groping her. She made herself take it, so he wouldn't touch Terry. And the one thing in her favour was Mary's jealousy, her need for men as much as their money. She was still young and beautiful in her own eyes. Her daughter's youth was an anathema to her. She resented it. Jack knew that too and he played on it.

Another hour passed and dusk began to fall. The pretty snow flakes stuck to Bella's dark lashes and surrounded her brown eyes like tiny stars. They couldn't stay here much longer. Bella knew they would freeze to death. Terry's lips were blue and his face a ghostly white.

'Come on, we're leaving,' she told him, shaking him awake from the frozen doze he was falling into.

'Where to?' Terry whimpered as she hauled him to his feet.

'Back to the debris.'

Terry's big eyes filled with tears. 'I want to go home, Bells.'

In a grown up fashion far beyond her eight years, Bella took hold of her brother's shoulders. 'Listen Terry, might as well face it. We've got no home. Not when *he's* with her. Not when he thumps you like he does. And certainly not when they're both pissed. We'd be dead meat if we went back now and you know it.'

The tears trickled down Terry's cheeks. He said nothing, just stared at Bella and sniffed back the mucous streaming from his nose. She took his hand and squeezed it. 'I promise I'll find us a place to kip. And something to eat. All right?'

He nodded slowly and Bella took one last glance at the cottage. No sign of them coming out yet. She could only guess they'd drunk themselves daft. There would be hell to pay when they woke; in the absence of alcohol, the fighting and screaming would start. Bella had hoped that her mother would tire of the man, but for better or worse, she kept with him. And as far as her children were concerned, it was mostly the worst.

Shivering uncontrollably herself now, Bella hugged Terry to her. 'About a mile down the road is the pie and mash shop. In the blackout, no one will see us turn over the bins.'

Terry sobbed softly. 'I was sick last time we did that.'

'Listen,' Bella consoled him with her innocent logic, 'if pigs can eat that muck, so can we.'

He hung his head and she pulled him along the alley. It was dusk and the blackout was strictly enforced. There was no light showing, not even a full moon. But she knew every step of the way. When they'd eaten, they'd walk to the debris. She'd seen the remains of a burned-out house today. Some of its blackened rafters hung loosely inside. She'd take Terry there. It was better than sleeping in the open. And if the rest of the roof didn't fall in on them, that would be a bonus.

They could even make-believe they were in a posh house and were having a proper Christmas. They could pretend to open presents from under a Christmas tree. And sit round an imaginary fire opening them. She liked pretending. As they stuffed themselves with plum pudding, she would tell Terry the story about Joseph and Mary riding on the donkey and following a star. Mary and Joseph didn't have no home at Christmas either. In the end, the star led them to a stable where Mary had her baby in the straw. There was cows and sheep and the donkey, too. It was a pity there wasn't no animals on the island, only rats. Thousands of 'em, all over the place. Just as hungry as she and Terry were.

Bella hurried on, dragging Terry beside her. She was eager to investigate the bins at the back of the pie and mash shop and find shelter before it was too dark. And she might be wrong about the Germans. Their planes could be on their way over this minute. P'raps they hadn't even heard of Christmas.

Well, nor had she and Terry, really. Not until last year, when Micky had bunged them both a tanner along with two of his mum's apple pies.

～

CHAPTER 1

PART ONE

The London Blitz
March 1941

'YOU BUGGER, don't you hit our Terry again!' Eight-year-old Bella Doyle stared defiantly up at the big man whose fist was clenched in readiness to strike.

Jack Router turned his bloodshot gaze slowly from the small boy huddled in the corner to scrutinize the parcel of rags and lice infested hair gazing up at him.

'What did you say, girl?'

Bella moved cautiously backwards, out of reach of the man who had just knocked seven bells out of her little brother. Drunk and swaying Jack Router might be, but when the occasion warranted it, she knew he could turn on a sixpence.

'I said leave him alone. You're a bastard bully for clobbering our Terry. And I'm telling me Mum when she comes home.'

'Oh you will, will you?'

Instantly regretting her quick tongue, Bella knew there was no escape. Above her, the gaping hole in the ceiling where the rafters of the roof hung down and to her right, the closed door and blacked-out window. Not that she'd try running anyway. Not without Terry.

Jack Router curled a thick, grubby finger in her direction. 'Come here now, Bella. We should be friends you and me. Give your Uncle Jack a little cuddle. That's all he wants. And you like it, you know you do, girl.'

With her back pressed hard against the wall of the derelict cottage, Bella inched her way towards Terry. The man watched in amusement, his belly quivering above his belt as he enjoyed the child's terror.

'What's it to be then, eh? You or him?' He reached out his hand and Bella froze as a look of satisfaction crept over his face. Tilting his head, he shrugged lightly. 'You know, it was just a tap I give him, that's all. No more than he deserved for spinning your mother a pack of lies.'

'It wasn't our Terry's fault,' Bella protested in a whisper. 'It was Rita Moult from number nine. I heard her myself. She told everyone.'

'Rita?'

'She's all smiles and winks to you,' Bella burst out, 'but behind your back she told our Mum that you've had more dock dollies than hot dinners.'

'You lying little cow! She wouldn't dare, the bitch!'

Bella began to panic. 'I'm not lying, honest.' She watched furtively as the man thrust hesitant fingers across his sagging jaw his eyes moving slyly in their sockets. After his midday session at the Rose and Crown, he was breathing fumes. Even from where she was standing, Bella could smell him. Her stomach turned as he belched and rubbed his gut.

'Well now, you've got me all confused,' he grunted as his gaze travelled back to the boy. 'Let's see what your brother has to say for himself, shall we?'

Bella knew this was a trap. In a second or two he would swing round and catch her. But she couldn't let him clobber Terry again. Whatever he did to her, was nothing in comparison to what he'd done to Terry.

But this time he surprised her and with a powerful lunge he aimed his boot into the boy's hip. For all the ale in his belly, he delivered a blow that swept the human bag of bones along the filthy floor like a duster.

Without hesitating Bella threw herself forward and sank her teeth into the outstretched hand. Even as he screamed and pulled her up by her hair, she clamped her teeth tight, hanging on like a terrier. He shook her violently but Bella bit deeper, tasting his salty blood on her tongue. She imagined him dying the worst death possible like burning in one of the bombed buildings or boiling in oil. And the wanting of it was so strong it wasn't until all the air was punched from her stomach that her teeth finally parted.

'Look what you've done to me!' the man yelled in pain.

His eyes gleamed as he brought her against him. 'Fight me would you, Bella Doyle? I'll teach you, girl. See this?' He tapped her nose with his knuckles as he held her aloft with one meaty hand. His tongue rolled out to lick the dried beer coating his lips. 'This is for girls like you that need to be taught a lesson.' He pushed hard, sliding his fist over her cheek and finally downwards to her chest.

'Whisper to me, Bella. Say the nice things Uncle Jack likes to hear and it'll soon be over.'

All the struggle was gone from her now. Her legs and arms were suddenly weak as if she'd run up to the top of a hill and down again. It was a familiar pattern and she recognized it, knowing that no power on earth could now save her. Closing her eyes she tried to pretend she was up in the sky above the planes. Her mind began to draw pictures, taking her aloft on the clouds, flying in the blue ocean over the earth where there was release and freedom.

But just as he brought her against him, his fingers peeling away the layers of her clothing, the door flew open. Mary Doyle's faded green eyes flashed as she took in the scene before her. Fully attired in her working clothes, her chipped red nails dug into the worn black skirt that crinkled tightly over her stomach. Above her belted waist, a thin white blouse trembled on her drooping breasts. Slowly, a patch of angry crimson spread over her throat, creeping up into the lifeless red hair that fell on her neck. 'What in the name of Jesus is going on here?'

Jack Router stared innocently at the woman as he dropped Bella to the floor. 'She's an animal, Mary. She bloody bit me. Look! See them marks? All because I was trying to treat her decent.'

Laying still, Bella knew her luck could go either way now. Their mother was as likely to land him a punch as she was to believe him and blame her children instead.

'She was cursing me, Mary, love. I swear on me old mother's life. All I did was walk in that door and they gave me a mouthful before I'd even taken me coat off.'

Mary Doyle's gaze narrowed suspiciously. 'If you've lifted one finger against my kids – '

The man laughed suddenly. 'What'll you do? Chuck me out?'

'As sure as hell I would and you know it.'

'Ah, you drunken slut.' He pushed his face into hers. 'You'd do me a favour if you did. If I found myself a pigsty to kip in, it would be an improvement on this shit hole. I'm sick to death of you and your brats. I must've been mad to take the bastards on.'

'You were willing enough at the time,' she reminded him sourly, returning the crude gesture. 'You had nothing, *were* nothing! And if it wasn't for me you'd be six feet under and still scratching the coffin lid. You're a curse to women, you bag of shite.'

Bella gulped down her fear. Her wary brown eyes looked out from under the tangled curtain of auburn hair; she was waiting for the inevitable, a verbal and physical assault that had begun from the moment Rita, alias *Mouth Almighty*, had set her poisonous tongue free.

The first blow cracked aloud in the air. Jack Router stumbled, the heel of his boot landing heavily on Bella's leg. With a stifled cry she scrambled aside, dragging Terry with her into the only other habitable room of the dwelling. Here they crouched on a filthy mattress covering themselves with a threadbare blanket.

Bella buried her head against Terry's. He stank where he'd peed himself but the room smelled like the bog anyway. She prayed the planes would soon fly over and when the siren went, Mary Doyle and her man would be off, screaming at one another still, but thirst would drive them to search for liquor.

Terry's snuffling grew loud. His mouth fell open as the blood congealed in his nose.

'Tomorrow we'll tell Micky,' she whispered as a plan formed in her mind. Micky would know what to do. He always did.

Bella comforted herself with the picture of Micky's gun, not aimed at the wriggling sewer rats but pointed lightly against the brow of the man's head.

BELLA RUBBED her bruised cheek as she sat up.

A pale morning light seeped under the blackout. She stretched her stiff limbs as Terry stirred beside her, his long brown lashes laying softly on his swollen face. He'd rubbed the scabs from his nose in the night and was snuggled down in his coat. Both children were frozen, the temperature in the room at an all time low.

'Terry, wake up.'

His almond shaped eyes flickered. He groaned at he sat up. 'Terry hurts.'

'He gave you another bashing, that's why.' Bella took his hand and pushed the blanket away from his tight grasp. 'We're leaving before they come back.'

His eyes filled with tears. He lay down and pulled the blanket back over him. 'Terry don't want to.'

Bella wondered why God couldn't have left just a few brains in his head. Enough to tell him when he was safe and when he wasn't. Enough to make him understand that the man would kill them both after last night. Why had God forgotten Terry?

She ruffled his thin brown hair. 'Be a good boy, now. And do as Bella tells you.'

In the clothes they had worn day and night for more than a month they stole into the street. The cold March wind whipped around them and rain spattered down. Bella gazed up and down the rows of cottages. Only the rats, bugs and fleas that infested them moved in the early light. She looked up at the rotting pile of bricks that comprised number three, at the sunken roof and shattered windows lost in the drifting smoke of last night's raid. She shivered. It was the only home they knew and they were leaving it.

'Terry wants to stay.'

'We've got to find Micky.' She pulled his gas mask tighter across his shoulder. Jack would be home first, looking for trouble. And resisting the tears herself, she urged him forward.

'Is the bombs coming?'

'Tonight they will.'

'Terry don't wanna run away.'

Bella didn't want to either. But if only God had given him half a mind he'd know they didn't have a choice. The man said one day he would put them in a pot and cook them. And after last night, Bella believed him.

CHAPTER 2

RONNIE BRYANT STOOD in the big kitchen of the rambling three-storey building and frowned out on the cold March morning. He pushed back his hair and stretched his aching arms. From the kitchen window he could see the piles of junk that filled the yards of Piper Street, and spilled around the Anderson like a shark-infested sea. No one would ever guess what was hidden under the floorboards of the air raid shelter. That's good planning, Ronnie my lad, he congratulated himself. The dugout had its uses after all. If the law came sniffing round, they were welcome to sort through all Dad's rubbish piled high on the stones. But it would take a shrewd copper to suspect the neat interior of the Anderson where all the booze and fags him and Micky and Sean had nicked from the docks were stashed safely away.

A gentle dew sparkled on the legs and arms of the ancient furniture and junk going back to the year dot. Their Dad's treasure trove, his legacy to his sons as he was always telling them.

Ronnie smiled, the quirk of his full, sensual mouth giving his young face a touch of maturity beyond his sixteen years.

His cool grey eyes gleamed penetratingly, missing nothing under the heavy shock of raven black hair.

He glanced across the kitchen to his brother dozing in Dad's old armchair by the range. Micky's curly dark hair flopped over his thin face and his size ten boots were filthy from the mud that had congealed on their soles. The lino in the hall needed cleaning before Mum arrived back from Auntie Gwen's. Another bonus that, Auntie Gwen asking her to stay the night. Luckily it was a good bus ride to Poplar from Cubitt Town. The two widowed sisters liked to chinwag and they wouldn't stir once the fire was made up.

Ronnie sighed heavily as thoughts tumbled in his brain. Him and Micky hadn't had a wink all night and hadn't expected to what with dodging the raids and bringing the haul up from the docks in the old van Dad parked under the railway arches. It was a real rust bucket and on its last legs but it had done the job. What a night it had been! They'd worked like stink digging up the Anderson floor and battening down the boards again. When they sold this lot off he was going to give her and Auntie Gwen a good holiday. Send them to the seaside. That's what Dad would have wanted ...

Ronnie felt a moment's deep miss of the father he'd worshipped and the gap in their lives that had never been filled since his death three years ago. His loss hadn't been easy for Mum or indeed for any of them. But Sean had only been eleven when Dad went and taken it the worst. Odd that, as him and Dad had been opposites. Dad was a real man's man, and Sean all curls and a mummy's boy. Still was, in fact. Yet Dad's death had knocked him sideways. Micky on the other hand, had been down the market the very next week, trading junk up the Caledonian or Cox Street. Where there was a gap in the market it was up to a Bryant to fill it, Dad said. Mum didn't know the half of his escapades and never would. And when the Blitz had started last September, well, who wouldn't have made the most of what was on offer? The black market had come into its own and you were an idiot to ignore it.

Ronnie was well aware that 1940 had seen the island at its best and worst. Not a night passing without catastrophe, destruction and death in some poor sod's case. But out of the turmoil came the best living they had ever made. Dad would have been in his element. And whichever way the war went, opportunities like last night were priceless.

There was a loud knock and Ronnie started. But quickly he pulled himself together and went to the front door.

There were two children on the doorstep. The girl, taller than the boy, had hair full of knots and the colour of brass, with eyes as round as pennies. Her coat had more holes in it than his mum's crocheting. The boy's hung down to his ankles. At first he had them down as beggars, but then she asked for Micky by name.

'Who wants to know?'

'Bella Doyle.'

'Well, Bella Doyle, you're out of luck. Micky's not home. Come back some other time, kid.' He was about to close the door, when she stuck her foot inside.

'I'm not a kid. I'm eight.'

Ronnie was impressed. She had a mouth on her all right. 'Yeah, well, the answer's still the same. Micky's out.'

The girl pointed behind him. 'What's he doing there then, if he's not home?'

Ronnie swung round to find his brother propped against the wall. Micky Bryant yawned and narrowed his bright blue gaze. 'What's up then, Bells?'

'Got something to tell you.'

'Yeah? Such as?'

Her eyes darted back to Ronnie. 'Can't say standing 'ere, can I?'

Ronnie looked hard at his brother. 'Not now, bruv. Get rid of them.' He was about to walk away when Micky grabbed his arm.

'Hang on a bit, Ron. These two turn up a few tasty bits now and then. They're as regular as clockwork on the debris come rain or shine. Don't look a gift horse, as they say.'

Ronnie frowned. 'It's not a good time, Micky. And anyway Mum'll be back soon.'

'Well why don't we let 'em stay till she gets back?' His thick, dark eyebrows lifted persuasively. 'She loves kids, probably call them dirty faced angels, feed 'em up and sort 'em out. Take her mind off what we've been up to whilst she's been away.'

Micky had a point, Ronnie decided as he gave the suggestion due consideration. Anything to divert the numerous questions that would come flying at them the minute she walked in. And, with Sean kipping upstairs like Sleeping Beauty, she wouldn't have time to wonder why he was so dead to the world.

He nodded grudgingly. 'Have it your way, but I don't like it.'

'All right, you two can stay for a bit,' Micky said, grinning. 'But no nicking and no pissing on the floor, pal. OK?'

'What's up with the boy?' Ronnie frowned as the children stepped in.

Micky shrugged. 'Got bashed in the head once too often I reckon. You gotta wind him up and push him in the right direction. Their mum's one of them dock dollies that works the Rose. Don't suppose she ever gave it a thought as to why he's a screw loose.'

Ronnie noticed the boy did look a bit vacant under all the

dirt. He went down on his haunches. 'Here kid, what's your name?'

'Terry,' his sister said.

'Can't he speak for himself?'

'Depends what you ask him.'

Ronnie smiled. She was a card all right. 'Where'd he get all them bruises?'

'It's the joker they live with,' Micky offered with a dismissive shrug. 'A big geezer who kips at their mum's gaff over Bow Street. If he's not on a bender he's knocking off any old skirt. Gives the kids a belting every day if they don't make themselves scarce.'

'Thought no one was living over them places any more,' Ronnie said thoughtfully. 'Condemned by the council years ago, weren't they? '

'Yeah, but who takes any notice of a bit of paper slapped on a wall?' Micky yawned once more. 'Funny thing is, Jerry's never landed a bomb on Bow Street. Makes you laugh really, when it'd only take a breath to knock it over.'

Ronnie cursed lightly under his breath. This was the last thing he needed. Two kids and a bastard drunk wasn't his problem today. He had enough of his own to be going on with. But he also knew it was way too late to stop the anger that was already building inside him. If it was one thing he couldn't stand it was a bully. Granted, there were blokes who walloped their women and kids and got away with it. Bullying the weak and infirm was a way of life for some on the island, but not for his own kith and kin. Mum and Dad had brought them up to observe family values. The old ding-dong now and then was only natural. His folks had gone at it hammer and tongs sometimes like all cockneys did. But only a row to clear the air. When an injustice like this got shoved right in your mug, it was hard to ignore it.

'How did they know where you live?' he enquired suspiciously.

'Must've told them, mustn't I?'

Ronnie studied the girl again. Now that he looked she was blue with bruises. The clothes they wore were no more than rags hanging on bones. His Mum would have a fit when she saw them like that.

'You two hungry?' he asked.

The girl's eyes widened. They were troubling eyes, Ronnie noted a little uncomfortably; there was so much hidden in the depths of them.

Micky laughed scathingly. 'Don't mention grub. These two are like bloody gannets. You want to see them demolish the rubbish they find in the bricks. Thick with dust it is and tastes like shit. But it goes down their gobs like dripping.'

Ronnie stared incredulously at his brother. That he could talk so lightly of what in effect was starvation. He was seriously worried about Micky's state of mind. Nothing seemed to bother him these days. It was as if all he cared about was number one. Though if he was really honest, that had always been so, even before Dad died.

'Come on then,' Ronnie said over his shoulder as he led the way to the kitchen. 'But after you've got to clear off.' Now he'd taken a closer look at them he knew he couldn't let them stay. His Mum wouldn't like those bruises any more than he did, a fact that Micky seemed to have overlooked.

In the kitchen he took the loaf from the larder. Carving off four thick slices, he lay them on the oilcloth. There was butter under the china dish, but it was still rationed and if it was one thing his mum loved it was a good helping of her old cough and splutter. The jam though, not that she knew it, was well and truly off the back of a lorry and more where it had come from any day of the week.

The girl wolfed it down and swiped her mouth with the back of her hand.

'See what I mean?' Micky chuckled. 'They'd eat horse dung if you served it up hot.'

'And so would you,' Ronnie answered him shortly, 'if Mum didn't put food in your belly.'

'That's why I help 'em out,' Micky stated quickly. 'If it wasn't for me they'd be brown bread.'

Ronnie sneered. 'Yeah, I can believe that an' all.'

'No kidding, bruv. Nicking from the debris is what keeps 'em alive. If it wasn't for me giving them a good whack for what they find, they wouldn't be standing here today. As half dead as they look it's me what keeps them breathing. Their mum don't give a toss what happens to her kids and sure as hell the ugly bastard that belts 'em don't.'

Ronnie knew the only reason Micky had half of London's back street kids working for him was for his own gain. He worked them like stink, returning the poor sods a pittance. Ronnie had turned a blind eye so far but now he was thinking twice. As for the nutter who used two little kids for a punch bag...

'What is this bloke to them?' Ronnie asked heavily. 'He not family or nothing?'

Micky laughed as he stuffed his mouth with bread. 'He's Mary Doyle's pimp and that's a fact.'

Ronnie cut another slice and halved it. 'Here, put this away, you two.'

They were at it like vultures when someone knocked on the front door. 'Keep quiet,' Ronnie warned them all. 'Not a whisper.' He went to open it. A warden was standing there and his uniform was covered in dust.

'Yeah?' Ronnie asked irritably.

'Is this the home of Winifred Bryant?'

Ronnie nodded. 'She's out.'

'You'd better let me in, son.'

Ronnie put up his hand to stop him from entering. 'Why should I do that?'

He looked into Ronnie's eyes. 'The Luftwaffe hit Poplar bad last night ... and your mum ...'

Ronnie stared into the warden's face. He must have got it wrong. Somewhere along the line, there was a mix-up.

'We dug this out, well, what was left of it.' He lifted an identity card and his mum's black purse with a metal clasp. Ronnie saw a stain, a dark red one smeared across the felt. Then he knew she was never coming home again.

~

CHAPTER 3

Nine days later

RONNIE PUSHED his hand under his open shirt collar and squeezed the tense muscles of his neck. Mum would have made him wear a tie, but he hadn't worn one since he was at school and never a suit. Removing his jacket he placed it carefully over the back of his chair as Sean and Micky walked in the room.

Mum would have approved, Ronnie thought as he studied his two brothers who were dressed in identical dark suits. They were wearing what her idea of real class looked like. But now she was gone and her sons being done up like a dog's dinner for the funeral was a sting in the tail if ever there was one. For years she had meticulously ironed their shirts and pressed their trousers, nagging them to smarten themselves up. Now she wasn't here to see the result of her efforts.

'How long is this going to take?' Micky peeled off his jacket. 'I've got things to do.'

'Such as?'

'Dunno, just stuff.'

Ronnie narrowed his eyes, the sense of foreboding that had beset him after Mum's death, growing inside him. 'Whatever it is Micky, forget it. There's family business to be taken care of this afternoon. Now shut up and sit down.' Ronnie nodded to the seat on his right. He had swallowed his irritation all week as Micky's attitude had gone from bad to worse. He accepted his brother was grieving, but he was well out of order today and Ronnie's patience was growing thin.

Micky dragged out a chair and slumped down on it. Sean was already seated; his elbows resting on the big oval dining table polished each day by their Mum for as long as Ronnie could remember. A pang of sadness went through him as he met Sean's red-rimmed eyes. He had wept openly, unafraid to show his sorrow. Of the three of them, Sean had been their mother's favourite and it wasn't surprising to Ronnie that he'd taken her loss as badly as he had Dad's.

When he'd returned home that day after identifying his mother and aunt in the makeshift mortuary, he'd gazed into his brothers' faces, unable to speak. He had felt as if all the life had drained out of him from that moment. Mum and Auntie Gwen had looked as if they were asleep, their faces unmarked by the hand of death.

'You're certain it's them?' the warden had pressed as he'd identified the two corpses lying side by side.

Of course he was certain. The dead women were his family, the only family that he, Micky and Sean had.

'We found her bag straight away,' the man had told him gently. 'I know it's no consolation, but she wouldn't have known a thing.'

No, it's no consolation at all, he had thought bitterly as he stared at the marble white face of his mother that had, twenty four hours ago, been full of life and energy. They loved their father, but all three of them worshipped their mother. Perhaps she had been asleep when it happened? Ronnie hoped to God that it was quick.

He could still hear the rustle of the utility tarpaulins as they were replaced over the two still forms. See in his mind's eye the uniformed man who had taken his arm, intending to lead him away. Felt the frustration in his gut as he'd tried to decide whether it was all some sick joke.

All he could think of then was the fact he wouldn't be looking into Mum's eyes again, their expression alert to whatever catastrophe had befallen her sons in her absence. She wouldn't be conjuring up a fried breakfast. Or chewing them off about they way they refused to get up in the mornings. Life as they had once known it had now come to an end.

Ronnie looked hard at his brothers. 'Sean, I know there's no way we can bring back Mum. But if she was here she would tell us to pull ourselves together and sort ourselves out. So that's what we've got to do, right?'

Sean shrugged helplessly. 'Why did it have to happen to her, Ron? I just don't understand.'

'There's no answer to that question, Seany. I wish I could give you one.'

'She never hurt no one. She'd give the coat off her back to anyone who asked. It was us that's done all the nicking. Why didn't that bomb fall on us?'

'I wish it had,' Ronnie muttered darkly. 'But what's done is done and we're still alive and kicking.'

'But that's just it, Ron, I don't feel right about what we did – you know – just before she went. It's as if it was us who made the bomb fall on her.'

Ronnie jerked his head round. 'That's rubbish Sean, and

you know it. Get it out of your head. We loved her, treasured her. And what we did was all for her, to give her a comfortable life as Dad would have wanted.'

Sean swept the tears from his cheeks with a grubby hand. 'I don't know anything any more, only that Mum turned a blind eye to what we did and we took full advantage. She didn't have a clue as to what was happening half the time. If we'd told her we knocked off a load of stuff and wanted to bury it in the Anderson she would have given us all a slap for even thinking it.'

Ronnie's face tightened. 'Point taken, Sean, but the fact is what the eye don't see, the heart don't grieve over. After Dad died it was too late to change what he'd started and I for one wouldn't have wanted to, anyway. The old man didn't spend his life teaching us the tricks of the trade for nothing. We was Robin Hood and his Merry Men. Give anyone a helping hand if they asked and bugger the sheriff. He kept telling us them stories over and over again. They came out of him like verbal diarrhoea and we believed every word. Still do.'

Sean blinked his long lashes. 'I know Ron. But the country's at war and the punters we deal with are all in this lark for a profit, not to give to the poor and needy.'

Ronnie couldn't argue with that. But his priority was family. If he didn't hold them together now, they'd fall apart. 'Look if it makes you feel any better, I'll agree that expanding the business into black market after Dad died was my decision, and I take full responsibility. I'm not saying I was right to do so, mind. That is a matter of opinion and you are entitled to yours. But I know in my heart it was the road Dad would have gone down. In my book, there was no doubt whatsoever as to continuing the business.' He paused as for a second saw his mother gazing back at him in the form of Sean's honest blue gaze. God only knew how the old man had worked the flankers he'd done and kept the old girl in such blissful ignorance. But he had and Ronnie commended him for it. Now it was history repeating itself and with Mum gone, it was Sean who had taken up her mantle. But Sean was the new generation of Bryants and as such, had either to support the business or get out of it completely.

'Seany, let me put you straight on one thing. Mum never died because of what we did. It was nothing to do with us, so get that through your Uncle Ned. She died because a maniac in another country decided to start a war. And that's a fact you're going to have to accept.'

There was silence in the room. Ronnie glanced at Micky who was sporting a face as long as a fiddle. 'Right, Micky, now it's your turn.' He braced his shoulders back and added firmly, 'I'm not sitting here all day looking at your moody gobs, so speak your mind or forever hold your peace.'

Micky kicked the table leg idly. 'Since you're asking, Ron, what I don't fancy is Old Bill sniffing round. I've been shitting bricks lately, every time the door goes. Stands to reason they know Mum's gone and she won't be here to tell them to sling their hook. So where does that leave us, I ask? And the answer is, we're sitting here like three orphaned ducks.'

'So what is the alternative?'

'I reckon we get shot of this last little bundle. Take a dip on our profits if we have to, but just get clear of it.'

Ronnie nodded slowly. 'Fair point. Any suggestions what we do with it?'

'It's too hot for the markets and it would take too long to flog it round the pubs. What about shoving it Luffman's way? He'll rook us something chronic, but we'll have to swallow on that.'

Ronnie begrudged giving Goldy Luffman the contents of his nose, let alone a generous deal, as he was the meanest sod this side of the river. However, Goldy took anything and everything and asked no questions. 'All right. Suits us this time, but from here on in we'll find somewhere legit to stash our Georgie Woods.' He turned slowly to Sean. 'So, are you up for a clean sweep, Seany?'

'What choice have I got?' Sean replied moodily.

'You've always got a choice in life.' Ronnie stared hard at his kid brother who up until this moment had always been just that, a kid. But with Mum gone he was going to have to step into the real world. 'You don't have to come with us on this one, bruv. Me and Micky will do the business. We'll sort out the Anderson and see Goldy.'

'You *what?*' Micky objected, for the first time sitting up and paying attention.

'I said Seany can sit this one out.'

'But it took all three of us to move it,' Micky protested. 'A whole lorry load it was, buried six-foot down under a bloody shelter. We was at it like navvies and only finished just before the All Clear went.'

'We'll manage.' Ronnie's tone was final. 'Sean's staying put.'

'So what if I decide to sit on me arse all night, too?' Micky sulked.

Ronnie sighed heavily. There was something in both his brothers' attitudes that worried him. Sean was frightened of his own shadow and Micky was in love with himself. They both needed to realize they had to give a lot and take a little between themselves. They were family. And if family couldn't hack it, who could?

Micky continued to stare at him resentfully. There were rings round his blue eyes and a hollow look to his face. With his curly brown hair he was like their Dad, a charmer. Sean had the same intense blue gaze but with his light brown hair and soft, smooth features he was their mother all over. Now Ronnie looked at his two brothers and knew they would never be kids again, at liberty to fight amongst themselves and be stopped by a cuff round the ear. Now there could only be one leader. And as the oldest, he was it.

'Right then,' Ronnie said decisively. 'I'll dig out the van and bring it round as soon as the first raid starts. There'll be no lights on anywhere and plenty of noise to distract any nosy parkers. I'll reverse up to the back wall and Sean, you can help us load the stuff, but then you'll come back in here and lie low. Me and Micky will drive over to Goldy's and be back before first light.'

'It'll be a bloody miracle if we are,' Micky grunted.

'We did it before. We can do it again.'

'That is if Jerry don't drop one on our heads.'

Ronnie smiled. 'He'll have to catch us first.'

Ronnie expected further protest and was prepared for it. But Sean hung his head, trying to disguise his wet cheeks and Micky was busy still kicking the table leg. He had always had a laugh at anything remotely serious. After Mum, he didn't know how to act.

'And just to refresh our memories,' Ronnie continued, his gaze not leaving his brothers' faces. 'We'll keep this gaff ship shape, then. I don't want to find so much as a fag end under your beds – or anything else come to that. In other words, if the law was to shove its nose inside this house, all they'd find is a layer of dust and even that would be sweet smelling. Are you hearing me, you two?'

'Yeah, yeah.' Micky rolled his eyes.

Sean nodded in silence.

'And no outside jobs,' Ronnie added firmly. 'No creeping, no spotting, no fitting. Not even a touch at the market. No nicking wallets, bags or goods. Nothing goes down unless I say so. The Bryants think, act, even shit as one.'

Micky turned to face him and Ronnie was relieved to see a glimmer of humour return to his brother's eyes.

'What about them kids outside?' Sean asked suddenly. 'They've been kipping right on top of the stock.'

Ronnie had almost forgotten he'd allowed them to sleep in the shelter. After Mum's death he hadn't had the heart to send them back to Bow Street.

'They'll have to go,' Ronnie nodded.

'Lambs to the slaughter, I reckon,' Micky murmured, a glint in his eye.

'But they're not our problem,' Sean said anxiously. 'Are they?'

Micky shrugged. 'I reckon sending them back to Bow Street is like feeding mice to a cat. I'd like to see how handy the bastard is with someone his own size.'

It wasn't often Micky made sense, Ronnie thought, but this time he was in full agreement. He felt a grudging admiration towards Micky. More than that, he knew his brother was no coward and had taken his punishment on the streets as well as dolling it out. Inside him there was a vicious streak that was pure hate for authority of any kind. Ronnie knew that if this trait could be harnessed for the good of the family, they would have a valuable asset in Micky.

'You want to sort it out?' Ronnie asked.

Micky's dark eyes lit up. 'Now you're talking, bruv.'

But Sean was shaking his head. 'I don't like it. Those kids are bad news.'

Ronnie was under no illusions as far as Sean went. He was never cut out for the physical. Mum had spoiled him rotten, and him and Micky had understood why. Sean was the total opposite to Micky who, given the chance, would happily take a swing at a bull with a match up its arse.

'We'll start as we mean to go on,' Ronnie said without hesitation. 'Ask yourself this question, Sean. What would Dad have done if we had a sister and some lairy sod lifted a hand against her?' His face was set hard, its handsome proportions chiselled out in the broad daylight. 'This is our patch and we need the respect.' He paused, assessing his brothers' reactions. When no argument was forthcoming he continued. 'Now, are we all done?'

Ronnie looked at them again. Then he stood up and felt the smooth material of his trousers fall over his long legs. He liked that feeling. He liked the fact that he now had his brothers' undivided attention and made a vow to keep it that way.

Before leaving the room he picked up the newspaper. The polish of the table sparkled. He could remember his mum polishing it and the joy she took in doing so. It was a big, solid table, like the family he intended to cultivate. This was the first meeting he had called, but it wouldn't be the last. There would be many more to come.

Now he instructed Sean to change his clothes and put on his working clobber. Ronnie had already convinced himself that the action he was about to take to remedy a bad situation, would achieve a result that his Dad, if not his Mum, would sanction.

∼

To buy *Christmas to Come* for your ebook click HERE

To buy *Christmas to Come* in paperback go to Amazon.co.uk and check out Carol Rivers

Thank you so much, dear Readers, for visiting my world of sagas!

Leabharlanna Poiblí Chathair Baile Átha Cliath
Dublin City Public Libraries

Printed in Great Britain
by Amazon